ABOVE T[

Rosemary Cohen

THE AUTHOR

Since she first climbed on Harrison's Rocks in 1974, Rosemary Cohen has travelled in the Himalaya, and climbed in Europe and America. A medical doctor, she is married with two sons, and continues to combine climbing with a family, a career and the many other hazards of life.

ABOVE THE HORIZON

ROSEMARY COHEN

a&b

First published in Great Britain in 1997 by
Allison & Busby Ltd
114 New Cavendish Street
London W1M 7FD

Copyright © Rosemary Cohen 1997

The moral right of the author is asserted

This book is sold subject to the condition that it shall not, by way of trade or otherwise, be lent, resold, hired out or otherwise circulated without the publisher's prior written consent in any form of binding or cover other than that in which it is published and without a similar condition including this condition being imposed upon the subsequent purchaser.

A catalogue record for this book is available from the British Library

ISBN 0 74900 376 6

Designed and typeset by N-J Design Associates
Romsey, Hampshire
Printed and bound in Great Britain by
Redwood Books
Trowbridge, Wiltshire

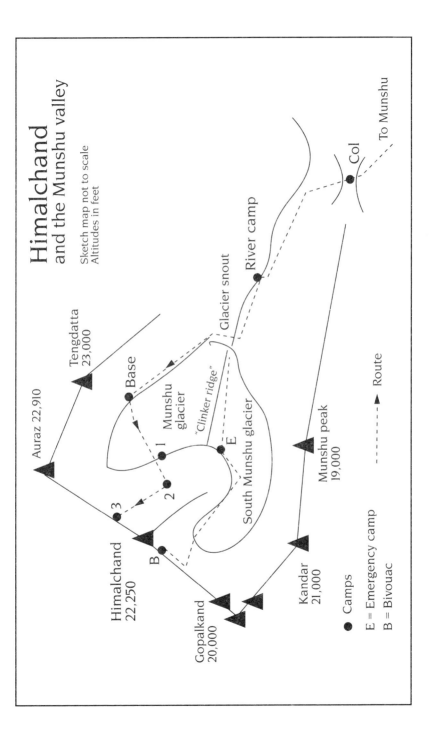

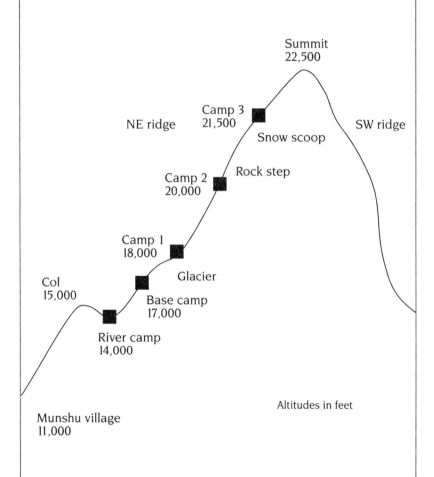

CHAPTER 1

A great mass of snow landed with a soft thump in the gully, as if someone further up the crag was playing snowballs. The three climbers halted, and remained for several seconds without breathing or moving.

'Where did that come from?'

They all looked upwards. The black Scottish mountainside was oozing moisture from every crack. The westerly wind had raised the temperature above zero, and all the accumulated snowfall of winter was dissolving away, like an unlicked ice cream.

The leader shoved the haft of her ice-axe into the snow. It went in easily, right up to the hilt.

'This stuff's like butter.'

The other two were still gazing upwards, as if looking for a practical joker on the ridge above. They were both young men, one tall and broad, the other shorter and even broader.

'If that's one of the others playing silly buggers, I'll slaughter them,' said the tall one.

'Don't be an idiot, Rowley,' replied his friend.

'Then it's going to avalanche, isn't it?'

The three of them were strung out on the easy approaches to the climb, following the right-hand bank of the gully into which the snow had fallen. They had not yet roped up, because the ground was still easy. If the snow in the gully chose this moment to avalanche, they would be right in its path.

'Let's keep to the rocks,' announced the leader. She stumped on upwards, ice-axe in hand, to the place where the rocks met the snow.

The others followed reluctantly. When they caught up with

her she was rootling around in a crack in the rock, trying to find somewhere to attach the rope. The black rock glistened. Over part of its surface the patina was due to an old layer of ice; in others, it was simply wet rock. Beneath the ice, small rivulets of water made ever-changing patterns of light and dark. Everything dripped.

'This is stupid,' declared Rowley. 'We wanted an easy route, but this one is too easy to be worth dying for.' He glanced up again, watching for new missiles from above.

'We'll be all right if we stick to the rock,' insisted the girl. She did not look upwards.

'Christ, we've got all week. Let's go back to the hut and have a brew.'

As if in answer, another solid mass of snow slid down into the gully; it had come from one of the pinnacles on the left-hand bank.

'See?' Rowley's voice was a mixture of panic and triumph.

His friend looked as if he were considering the problem. 'I agree. It's unjustifiable – an 007 route.'

The girl turned on him: 'It was you who insisted on us all coming up here. Nothing's changed since this morning. Or was it all just for show, Rat?'

'Anything you like, Petra. Let's just get out of this.' He hit the rock with the blade of his axe. A circular sheet of ice broke away, and shattered on the ground. 'See, it's dinner-plating.'

He turned around to face the valley. A lingering mist hung around in the corrie below, hiding from sight the climbing hut to which they must return. He began an awkward, high-stepping descent, trying to place his feet in the footprints which he had marked out on the way up.

With one more glance at the teetering, fragile mountainside, Rowley turned and followed. Petra had begun to uncoil a rope. She had to recoil it, tightening the knot with her teeth. Her gloved hands were sodden, and by now they were too cold to feel anything properly. She muttered curses under her breath, but she too started to descend.

For 200 feet or so, the trail of footprints followed the trajectory of any avalanche that might come out of the gully. It was hard work keeping from looking behind every half-minute. When, once, Petra did look behind, her feet gave way on the slippery surface, and she fell over in the snow. This was old tired snow, as soggy as wet cotton wool. It stuck to everything and promptly turned to water, soaking all her clothes.

She had not been afraid on the ascent; the retreat was another matter. Having admitted the possibility of fear, the potential dangers became enormously magnified. She remembered every story she had ever heard about climbers being swept out of Scottish gullies by avalanches. This was not a danger limited to high mountains; it was here and now in Scotland. She remembered the perverse sense of competition that had sent her and her friends out to try to climb during a thaw.

She increased her pace. The other two were well ahead by now, and they had begun to laugh and chat together. She made one great stride and fell down in the snow again. She thought that the jolt should have sent the whole slope sliding. Then she made herself look back. The mountain looked the same as it had when she had climbed up to it an hour before. Strings of mist hung about the icy pinnacles, and the sky was blank. Even now, she wished she were still up there, climbing.

The bottom of the gully opened out into a shallow snow-slope, which swept down gently to the floor of the corrie; Allin's Hut was now in sight, and the two lads were almost at its door.

The first sound was a crack, then a low rumble, which broke into a rushing sound, like the wind. Petra floundered sideways out of the direct path of the fall. It was a pathetic effort, achieving no more than a couple of yards' gain. She put her gloved hands over her face.

The gale of wind hit her, knocking her flat, but the avalanche rushed past, in a storm of noise and terror. She had been spared.

In the hut, three days later, tempers were getting short. There were five of them: two girls and three young men, all in their early twenties and all impatient to climb. The first day's failure had not helped matters, but after so many days of bad weather the near-disaster no longer had the power to frighten. They had planned a week's worth of climbs; they could only watch and wait while warm snow slid off the ridges and down the mountain gullies. A day or two more and there would be no snow left to climb.

The snow outside the hut was slashed by yellow streaks, which became dark holes as the dirty snow melted in the westerly weather. No one wanted to have to empty the Elsan toilet before the end of the week.

Each had their own method of survival. Petra was the youngest, with the least tolerance of this kind of frustration. She only wanted to climb. She knew, given any less lethal snow conditions, that she could tackle any one of a dozen routes. She had one free week, and the weather, however characteristic of the west coast in winter, seemed to have timed its arrival with deliberate and malevolent intent.

She and her friend Diane, a little older and not quite so keen on climbing, were lying on one of the sleeping platforms, reading from the hut's dismal collection of books. There were bound editions of old climbing journals, a few paperbacks and the inevitable *Ascent of Everest* and *Scrambles in the Alps*.

'This character's always stopping to smoke a peaceful pipe. No wonder he gets puffed. What's your book like, Pet?'

'A lot of manful striving. And complaining about the food and the sarky porters. I don't think I'm into expedition books.'

'No.' Diane shut her book and began to chew idly at a lock of her hair, which was auburn, and slightly the worse for a lack of washing. 'To think I could be sludging around at home, doing nothing. I could watch telly or wash my hair.'

At that point there was an upheaval on the other half of the sleeping platform, as Daz turned over in his sleeping-bag. He had the useful skill of being able to sleep all day when the weather was bad. 'You could make tea, love,' he suggested laconically.

'It's not time yet. We had the last cup at two. There are only seventeen teabags.'

'So who planned the food?'

Diane threw her book at him. He merely burrowed deeper into the bag.

Seated at the deal table in the centre of the hut, Rowley prodded at a spluttering candle with a pair of small scissors, while moaning about the weather.

'When do you think we should start eating up the food?' said Rowley, not for the first time. 'You don't want to have to carry any of it back down.'

'Daz put marmalade on his porridge at breakfast,' said the Rat, who was seated opposite, sewing up a hole in his Dachstein mitten. 'We don't need to worry about using up the food if Daz puts marmalade on his porridge.'

They paused, waiting for the hoped-for reaction. Daz kept the sleeping-bag over his head, with only a few strands of dark greasy hair visible to show that the occupant was human.

Rowley shrugged his shoulders. 'Saving his strength.'

'Pass me those scissors, Rowley.' The Rat cut the thread and carefully darned the needle back into the lining of his sewing kit. This was not merely housewifely obsession: in winter climbing conditions a hole in a glove meant very cold fingers, if not frostbite. But it was characteristic of the Rat that he was the one with the mending kit to hand. He began to examine carefully the state of his other glove.

Rowley, deprived of the scissors, took a comb out of his pocket and combed his hair again. He had a wild thatch of blond hair, and a fair face which was already slightly weather-beaten from exposure to the sun and wind. He would never have kept a glove long enough to grow a hole in it – he always went for the latest new product in outdoor gear. The current ensemble was a symphony in contrasting colours, with bright green climbing salopettes and a purple fibre-pile jacket. His socks were yellow.

For a while there was silence, apart from the sound of the eaves dripping. There was nothing to talk about. The silent rapport which was so necessary a part of being a climbing team still retained some control over the frustrated climbers, and so far had prevented arguments about anything really serious.

Then Petra got off the bunk and began to pace about the hut. After she had brushed past Rowley's chair a few times, he leant over backwards and enquired solicitously, 'Can't you mellow a bit, Pet?'

'I'm just so sick of being stuck in here. This place is so totally sordid. I want to go out there and climb.'

Rowley grinned, and deliberately began a falsetto chorus of 'Climb Every Mountain'. At the end of the verse he shouted, 'Look out! Avalanche!' He dived for the floor, knocking his chair over, and making a noise like the Dambusters.

Petra realised the uselessness of being angry, and the obvious need on her friend's part to tease her, but she could not help feeling annoyed. She was so much better a target than the impervious Daz. She and Rowley were probably too alike in temperament to get on together smoothly. The Rat was the opposite: he could keep Rowley in line when he became impossible, and the combination of the obsessiveness of one and the anarchic streak in the other made for a friendship that was as powerful as it was understated. They climbed together almost without the need for verbal communication. But in the hut, the Rat tended to withdraw into his own occupations, and Rowley was left at a loose end. He knew all Petra's weaknesses, and if left alone might continue to tease her until she flew off the handle. Allin's Hut was too small a place to walk away from an argument.

There were bunks for twelve, which took up a large part of the one room of the hut. The remaining floor space was perhaps fourteen feet square, and had to accommodate a shelf for gas rings and some food lockers, as well as the table, benches and chairs. More of the space was taken up by rucksacks, from which climbing gear emerged in untidy heaps. There were two small windows, and no other means of ventilation, so the condensation from cooking and breathing simply congealed on the walls and ran down the whitewash in sooty streaks. The floor was always wet, and had begun to fray into splinters where it had rotted at the edges.

The door led into an outer passage, where climbing boots were stacked, and wet clothes and waterproofs were hung up. Nothing ever dried out completely, but this arrangement kept the wet stuff segregated. If anyone wanted to dry out their clothes they had to put them on and get into a sleeping bag. There was no source of heating apart from human bodies.

For Petra, bored by the human squalor, the only escape was to go out into the bad weather. She opened the door and Rowley at once shouted: 'Shut the bleeding door!'

She went out, shutting the door loudly, and stooped to find her boots in the dim corridor. The leather was still wet from the melting snow, but then so were her socks. She pulled on the cold boots and found her red neoprene cagoule. Though waterproof, the cagoule had collected condensation on the inside and stuck to the sleeves of her jersey as she pulled it on.

Outside, the drizzle had abated, though the eaves were still dripping merrily. A little way from the hut the snow was clean and white, with a few odd-shaped rocks protruding. The rock was black and greasy. The cloud, which had been sitting firmly at the altitude of the hut, had risen slightly, giving a funnel-like view down to the brown snowless forest in the valley.

There were two figures creeping up the beaten track through the snow. When Petra first caught sight of them they were at least half a mile distant, and only intermittently visible as the cloud level rose and fell. She wondered who else could be optimist enough to come up to Allin's Hut in such weather.

The wind, which had howled about the hut for three days, seemed to have fallen calm. For the first time, the lower section of the mountain crags could be seen, and there was still snow on the face. Optimism, always hard to suppress, crept back into Petra's thoughts.

She went into the hut, introducing a blast of cold air into the still damp room. Rowley was warming one of his socks over the candleflame.

'Visitors,' said Petra. 'And the weather's clearing.'

The five friends had climbed together for several years; a loose association of friendly acquaintances, not quite a club, but united by a common desire to climb. Petra had been at school in south London with Rowley and the Rat, in days when they were called Ben Rowley and Tim Radinsky, before either of them had acquired a *nom de crag*. When they were fifteen or sixteen, Petra had discovered that climbing was a way of escaping from the atmosphere at home: a mother with ideas about ladylike behaviour and a father with no ideas at all. The three of them used to set out on Sundays with a cheap day return from Waterloo, and go climbing on the sandstone outcrops in Kent. The rocks were in the woods, damp boulders covered in slippery lichen and so soft that the holds were wearing away year by year. Rowley had forty feet of hawser-laid half-inch rope which he had stolen from the Scouts.

They had climbed together for a year or so, in a spirit of perpetual competition. This had an edge to it because Petra was the only girl, and they were all vigorous teenagers. The Rat had suffered an attack of studiousness around 'O' level time, partly reinforced by financial incentives from his father, and had disappeared from the scene for several weeks. At that time, Petra was spending as much time as possible away from home, because her parents were going through one of their non-speaking periods. Rowley was temporarily without a girlfriend. The resulting affair was almost inevitable. Like most adolescent lovers, they were preoccupied with finding opportunities, mainly in the corners of woods or in tents, which made for a rather chilly and uncomfortable sex life. It was no romance.

The Rat stood by while all this was going on, with an impatience which did not seem to be tainted with envy. He was required to cast about for other expedients if he wished to continue actively climbing, and it was thus that he recruited Daz at the café at Harrison's Rocks. Daz had a proper rope and boots, and several pieces of other gear. He was a lad from Oldham, a couple of years older than the others, who had come down to college in London, and who was only just realising that London was a desert for climbers. He was self-sufficient, and mildly sardonic, and never volunteered for anything. It was several months before Petra and her friends discovered that his real name was Derek.

In the autumn, Petra's love affair exploded, when she publicly accused Rowley of attempting to own her. His reply was, 'Whatever for?' For a while they did not speak to one another, and did not climb together either. But love, in this context, was an experiment. The overwhelming necessity was to keep on climbing. The group did not fall apart. As the Rat remarked cynically, 'Rock's great stuff for working out your urges on.' The main fall-out from that summer of incautious passion was that neither Petra nor Rowley ever referred to the matter thereafter; it was more of an embarrassment than something to treasure. It left them knowing rather too much about each other's weak spots, and there was mutual benefit in avoiding such areas of danger.

That winter, Daz produced his own girlfriend, Diane. She was a pretty girl with a private education and a rich stepfather, but there was no doubt that she wanted to be part of the scene too. Petra took her climbing. That experience was as profitable to Petra as to Diane. She found for the first time that she had control over the climbing, rather than going second to one of the boys. Petra's climbing technique improved no end. Diane climbed well enough to enjoy herself and hang on to Daz, who would never stay long with a girl he could not drag around the crags.

In the following summer, when Petra was seventeen, their horizons expanded abruptly. Diane had a job at a car-hire firm, and could get one of the cars at weekends. The five of them drove to north Wales, taking seven hours over the journey and stopping for chips at a transport café on the way. Petra found that Welsh rock was easier to climb than sandstone, and these were real mountains. That was the point of no return.

Petra took Diane up the grooved arête on Tryfan, in Nant Ffrancon, while the boys did something harder as a rope of three. They arrived at the summit at the same time. There was a group photograph, with everyone precariously balanced on top of the twin columns of Adam and Eve. Daz, with his dark greasy hair half across his face, looked woodenly at the camera, having run round to beat the self-timer. He was a tall youth, his extreme thinness disguised by baggy tracksuit trousers and a Pink Floyd T-shirt, and his face obscured by strands of long dark hair. Rowley, fair and still slightly chubby, had exposed his ultra-white skin in a lemon-yellow vest and satin rugby shorts; there were scabs on his knees. The Rat, half a head shorter and twice as wide, had stuffed his black curly hair under a baseball cap turned backwards, and was showing his broken front tooth in a vampirish grin. Diane wore her hair long and loose, the cascade of glossy auburn rather rumpled by the mountain wind; she had been one of the first people to take to climbing in ballet tights. Petra had imitated the tights, worn under an equally tight T-shirt; she was smaller and slimmer and wore her pale brown hair at shoulder length.

In the six years since then, they had all found the means to get the proper gear, and everyone except Daz and Diane had cut their hair short. They were well on the way to becoming hard climbers.

They had left London one by one. Daz went back to Manchester to a job in engineering. Diane followed. Rowley and the Rat hitched up to Sheffield one summer's day, and discovered a subculture of climbers who lived a cheap communal life on dole giros and occasional bartending jobs. Petra was left alone in London, hitching up the M1 at weekends, but becoming rapidly separated from the only life she found tolerable. Her parents were ever more uncommunicative – her mother immersed in coffee-morning culture and her father dividing his time between the television and the saloon bar. Staying at school seemed a waste of time. Her teachers muttered about retaking exams, but there seemed nothing much on offer beyond that – certainly nothing suitable for a female rock-rat ('Have you ever considered nursery nursing?'). She left at Easter and took a hotel job in the Lake District. She moved on to various seasonal jobs on the fringes of the outdoor pursuits industry, and eventually acquired the necessary certificates to work as a climbing instructor at an outdoor centre in north Wales. Once or twice when the money ran out she had gone home to Denmark Hill, but never for long. By the age of twenty-three she had climbed all over England, Wales and Scotland, and had been out to the French Alps three times, but there was always something new to be climbed. Even during her own short career, the new climbs had become harder, and the climbing gear more sophisticated. She always remained a step or two behind the leading edge of the sport.

The trip up to Allin's Hut was part of a search for new territory. Ben Nevis and Glencoe were crowded with climbers on every route. Further north, away from the great mass of Lochaber, the mountains were smaller and the weather was even less reliable. But, given luck, the climbing was of high quality, and those willing to trust their luck would get the mountains to themselves.

'I hope the bastards aren't after our route,' said Rowley. He stood up and stretched. He looked like a dormouse coming out of hibernation, with his round rosy face fringed by blond hair. The Rat did not speak but skidded his chair back and made for the door. He was five foot six of solid muscle, and, unlike his friend, he showed three good days' growth of chin-stubble. He was still dressed in the long underwear in which he had been sleeping, but he put on a shapeless grey jersey as token protection against the cold.

The door banged open and shut again behind the three of them. Petra and the two boys stood huddled under the eaves, surveying the opposition. The approaching figures were nearer now, dark dots against the snow.

'Maybe if I chew my toenails that'll get rid of them,' remarked the Rat.

'Get Daz to light his farts,' replied Rowley.

Petra kicked at the dirty snow. The hut, which had seemed such a trap, had suddenly become territory to be defended. 'Just so long as they don't snore.'

The three of them waited, shivering, as if their watching would somehow delay the arrival of strangers. The wind, which had fallen, started again in abrupt gusts. There was a perceptible change in its direction.

'North-east,' said Rowley. 'Maybe it'll freeze.'

The Rat peered into the grey distance. 'They're big blokes. Twice my size. One of them's got a beard.'

Within a few minutes, the pair came up to the hut. They had been moving very quickly through the soft snow, despite being laden with enormous rucksacks. The sacks were neatly packed, with no ropes or dead men or snow shovels tied on the outside. Both men wore old green Ventile anoraks, woollen breeches and balaclava helmets. One was young, the other grizzle-haired and bearded; they had an indefinably old-fashioned air, like a black and white photograph, but they were undoubtedly competent.

They arrived at Allin's Hut with no breath left for talking. They had come at a very quick pace up the valley. When they saw Petra and her friends they stopped and grunted a breathless version of 'How do?'

Petra stamped her feet to bring the warmth back to her toes. The snow was seeping moisture into the already damp leather of her boots.

Rowley said straight out: 'Have you heard a weather forecast?'

'Don't believe in them.' The older man swung his rucksack

off his shoulder and dumped it under the lee of the hut. He stretched his back, as if he were stiff from the load-carrying. 'It ought to get better, though. You can see Ben Ewe.'

The remark was directed more to his companion than to Rowley. The younger man had also got rid of his sack, and was automatically stretching with relief at having shed the load.

'Is that a good sign, Tom?'

'Believe me,' his friend replied. Then, to the three damp inhabitants of the hut: 'Well, lads, is there room for us in the hut?'

'Plenty,' replied Rowley.

'If you can put up with Rowley's feet,' added the Rat.

Petra ought to have been accustomed to being included in a general greeting of 'Well, lads'. She had spent her career actively discouraging the idea that she was merely a good climber 'for a girl'. She did not aspire to Diane's standards of feminine glamour. And indeed it would have taken an observant eye to see anything feminine at all in her present appearance: she was covered up in a shapeless cagoule, hood up and hands in pockets, and there were about eight inches of visible leg between the hem of the cagoule and the tops of her boots. Nonetheless, she recognised the characteristic assumption on the part of a traditionalist climber that lasses were not to be found in Allin's Hut in February.

'Where are you from?' Rowley asked.

'We're up from Lancaster. Are you going to let us in the hut for a brew?' The old-timer picked up his rucksack and went inside. Petra and her friends exchanged glances.

'Chummy, eh?' muttered Rowley.

The younger of the newcomers had got his breath back and taken off his balaclava. He could not fail to hear Rowley's words, but his response was to smile.

Petra found herself smiling too; she had not realised the extent to which incarceration in the hut had destroyed her sense of humour. 'Who are you?' she asked the newcomer.

'I'm Tom's mascot, I think. I put his arm in plaster when he broke it last year. Ieuan Price.'

'Ian?'

'Ieuan. Welsh, not Scots.' He did not sound very Welsh; his accent was nondescript – what Petra's mother would call 'educated'. Ieuan was probably a little younger than Daz, but he had none of Daz's air of a young man in a hurry.

Petra found herself making introductions, as if she were at one of her mother's coffee mornings. In the past, she had spent days together in mountain huts without learning the names of all the other climbers. But Ieuan seemed to expect it. She also found herself saying her friends' real names.

'This is Tim Radinsky, the Rat for short. Ben Rowley. And I'm Petra Merriman. Petra, not Peter.'

'Ah.' Still the smile. 'You think Tom mistook you for a lad? You'll have to put him right.'

'I wouldn't dream of it.'

The four of them went into the hut, out of the cold. In the dim, evil-smelling interior, Tom was sitting at the table while Diane, a startling figure in striped blue and yellow combinations, was busy making tea. She asked him how he took his tea.

'Sugar?' She sounded as if she was offering to help him across the road; Diane was, after all, a receptionist by trade, and was used to dealing with feeble elders.

'I'm Diane Ponder, and this is my fiancé Daz.'

Petra crawled into her sleeping bag to get warm again. The hut was still wet and chilly. But even before she had stopped shivering, she was aware of how the human atmosphere was changing.

Diane had asked the old-timer his name. The rest of them should probably have recognised him from photographs in mountain journals and books, but those had been taken a long time ago, and no one was expecting to encounter Tom Ormerod himself in an obscure Scottish hut.

'Ormerod?' The Rat was almost excited. *'The New Moon of the Snows?'*

'That's right,' Tom Ormerod replied. 'I shan't live that

down, ever. What've you managed to climb this week, Tim?'

'Oh.' Even the self-confident Rat was brought up short by this entirely negative reaction. Tom Ormerod did not want to talk about the past. He covered his tracks quickly. 'People generally call me the Rat.'

'Is that so?'

Petra knew that Tom Ormerod was something rare. The name was an excuse for anything. But his reaction prevented any of them from asking him further questions, the usual questions that a stranger gets asked in a group of climbers: 'What routes have you done?' or: 'Where do you usually climb?'

'We got avalanched out of Main Gully on Sunday,' volunteered Rowley. 'It's been foul weather. I hope you've brought some better weather with you.'

'It'll clear,' asserted Tom.

'We had an ace season at Chamonix this year, though. The conditions were perfect. Daz and I did the Walker, and Petra and the Rat had an epic on the Dru. They had to rescue some Japanese who got lost. The Alps are getting really full of wallies.' Rowley sounded like some veteran of twenty Alpine seasons, recalling the good old days.

It was all a deliberate if not entirely conscious pose, in line with Diane's continuing to parade about in her long underwear. A hero Tom Ormerod might be, but somehow they all had to show that they did not rate heroes.

At that moment, Petra realised where she had seen him before. It was the air of something old-fashioned about both Tom and Ieuan that reminded her. The sense of familiarity was due not just to recollections of faded expedition photos. She had seen him climb only a few months before, on a wet Sunday at Shepherd's Crag in the Lake District.

The crag was part of a miniature, picturesque landscape between the Lodore falls and upper Borrowdale, the subject of watercolour paintings and poetry. But Shepherd's Crag itself was not part of Wordsworth's Lake District. The cliff, of rough grey slaty rock, stained black and green in places by the damp, was enclosed in a wood, so that only the upper pitch showed above the treetops.

On that Sunday the trees were the dull yellowish colour of early September, before the true change of autumn had come. The crag was crowded with climbers of all sorts, because a night and morning of rain had left the higher Lakeland crags unpleasantly cold and wet.

The place was full of people snatching a quick route before returning home after the weekend. There were a hundred or so individuals who could see nothing but the rock, and who saw its intricate facets and grooves as a series of parallel routes of ascent.

Every route had its name and grade, set out in a plastic-backed guidebook of a size to fit into a trouser pocket. The book, with its distinctive orange cover, was conspicuous in the hands of those who were standing about at the bottom, trying to decide on a route. Other books lay abandoned on heaps of gear and rucksacks at the base of the crag. Coloured ropes festooned the rock wall, punctuated by the round helmeted heads and coloured clothing of those already climbing.

At the far left-hand end, a party of novices, all in bright orange hard hats, were attempting routes on the Brown Slabs. These routes were graded 'Very Difficult', and thus were easy enough to be climbed by any novice, however reluctant, given a good tight rope and plenty of shouted advice.

The instructors were two men with military haircuts, and with more than a touch of the sergeant-major. They were explaining the principles of rope work.

'This is a rope. It is 150 feet long and half an inch thick. It will hold an elephant, so it should hold most of you.'

Pause for laughter. One or two of the boys and girls obliged.

'Now you will be tied on tight to one end of the rope by means of a bowline. That is a type of knot. Your instructor will be tied to the other end. He will also be attached firmly to the rock by means of a belay. A belay is something which ties you firmly to the rock.'

Another pause for obligatory laughter.

'For example, a rope tied around a tree is a belay. So is one of these chocks, which are also called wedges, nuts or runners. A great lump of metal on a wire. This I place in a handy crack and attach to myself by way of a karabiner, otherwise known as a snap-link or a krab. Right?'

The other instructor had been at the top of the cliff, uncoiling a frayed, pinkish-coloured rope. He shouted 'Below!' far too loudly, and threw the coils to his friend.

'Right. Here we're using a top-rope. The rope runs straight up from the climber, through a krab attached to the tree at the top, like a pulley, then back down to the instructor. This is an example of a running belay, or runner, as we call them.'

The audience maintained an awed silence.

'Right. Now you all know about climbing calls?'

'Um,' said one of the novices.

Petra had been an unwilling witness to this scene; this was a stage of mountain training which she had been fortunate to miss. She still could not see how this kind of bullying could be character-building. As a part-time climbing instructor herself, she tended to use gentler means of persuasion.

She went past the novices, looking for a route. Conditions were lethal, the rock wet and slippery after rain. She was climbing with the Rat, who was in a disaffected mood after the wet weekend, and was inclined to find fault with most suggestions. The sergeant-majors did not aid concentration.

'Climb!' one shouted.

'Tight rope!' squealed a novice.

'Stand up on your feet!' bawled the instructor.

The novice clung silently to the gently sloping holds, the rock worn smooth by more than fifty years of ascents. He was evidently too scared to move.

'Stand up – don't hang on like an ape. It's easy when you try!'

The rope ran taut around the instructor's shoulders, then upwards at sixty degrees to the tape loop around the tree, then back at forty degrees to the novice. There was no slack. When the novice fell he bounced upwards slightly and swung sideways into a deep groove. He was clutching the rope, as if he did not trust the knot around his middle. He did not even cry out.

'Get back on the rock. I can't hold you for ever!'

Into the middle of this drama had walked two more climbers, the same pair who later turned up at Allin's Hut. The tall, spare, weatherbeaten man, with grizzled brown hair, whom Petra was later to discover to be Tom Ormerod, was wearing corduroy shorts like the mountaineering instructors, but there the resemblance ended. He was entirely quiet and efficient, and he did not consult the orange guidebook before pointing out a suitable line. He said a word or two to his companion, then went forward to a place just around the corner from the novices, and began to uncoil a rope.

His friend Ieuan was probably twenty-five years younger, taller and broader but with a long thin face and wispy blond hair. It was the kind of face that would look much the same in twenty years' time, all bones and angles like the crag. He was wearing a brown jersey with shoulder patches, like a bird-watcher.

He began to uncoil another rope, a new clean red kernmantel. Petra found herself thinking that here were two ramblers who had decided to take up rock-climbing and had gone out and bought a new rope and lots of up-to-date gear out of a catalogue.

'God, more wallies,' muttered the Rat. They were not quite out of earshot, sitting on tumbled rocks among the trees.

'Well, they've made up their minds what to do. What shall we do?'

'I've climbed every route on the crag. This is ridiculous. We should've stayed in the café with Rowley and Daz.' The Rat stood up and stretched himself. He reached up to an overhanging branch and began to do pull-ups, to an accompaniment of grunts. The branch was worn smooth of bark, and had evidently been used for this purpose before.

Petra continued to sort out rock gear, but gave voice to her ideas on this type of athletic training.

'You'll pull a muscle and have to stop climbing, Rat. Balance and technique is what matters. Look at those instructor wallies. All muscle and no brain.'

'Oh-ho,' said the Rat, pausing in between grunts and dropping to the ground. 'Look at that for technique.'

Tom, despite the corduroy shorts, had started climbing up an apparently blank wall. The route was not described in the guidebook. The line it followed threaded its way between lesser climbs, but the easier routes were well out of reach once the climber was applied to the central wall. And the old-fashioned climber used only two running belays, at about twenty and thirty feet respectively.

'It's a decker,' muttered the Rat, 'and it looks hard.'

They stopped to watch, considering the notion of forming a queue for the route. Petra's thought was 'Who is he?', because the really good climbers who might choose to climb on 'Extreme' grades on damp rock without significant protection were numbered in a handful.

When Ieuan followed, he put a bit more effort into it. His greater size was not an advantage, since he carried greater weight. He climbed in a way that showed what he was thinking, and so he proceeded jerkily. He had none of the fluid, apparently effortless grace of his older partner, but he still got up the climb.

This was slightly encouraging. The Rat said, 'Maybe it's possible.'

He and Petra sorted out gear. The possibility of protecting the leader was limited to placing very small wedges in awkward cracks, so the larger runners were left behind in the rucksack. They also used a double rope, so that the rope would be less likely to cause friction as it went through the running belays. In this sort of climb, a tiny increase in downward pull might be enough to put the leader out of balance on a delicate move.

The Rat was eager to lead. Petra did not make an issue of it. They both knew that the route might be out of their class. It had been invented since the last edition of the guide, so they had no clue to its actual grade. But there was a mutually agreed feeling that the younger generation was not to be bested by an old-timer who climbed in corduroy shorts.

They succeeded, after a fashion. The Rat put in a few more points of protection, but took a fall from several feet above the top runner as he lunged for a hold. He let himself be lowered to the ground, amid a blistering monologue of expletives.

The Rat handed the lead over to Petra. They swapped ends of the rope, and what remained of the small wedges. Then Petra repeated the lower part of the route, safely supported by the top runner. The rock was completely vertical, which put considerable strain on the arms. The Rat's plunge had been a result of his running out of strength, after hanging around on very small holds, slightly out of balance, trying to wedge a tiny nut into a crack.

In a way, Petra had the easier job. The top runner was manifestly secure, having been tested to destruction. The move just beyond it was technically hard and required concentration. But thereafter the rock was slightly less than vertical, and the holds, though tiny, were not impossibly widely spaced. There was a place for one more runner; a fine crack which tapered to a point and clasped a tiny brass wedge as if designed for it. The old-timer had ignored that placement and had carried straight on to the top.

'Is there some gear there?' called out the Rat.

'A micronut!' Petra clipped the rope in thankfully. This was the situation that the Rat had classed as a 'decker'. The new runner meant that Petra would not hit the ground if she fell off near the top of the route.

But then the last few moves were easier, and Petra crawled over the top with aching arms and tingling fingers. The accepted term for this kind of assault on a route is 'dogging'. Petra was quite glad that their performance had not been viewed by Tom or his friend; they had already left the crag.

Five months later, at the cold end of February, in Allin's Hut, the pair were no longer strangers. Damp climbers sat about on chairs and bunks, drinking their strong tea, and everyone, including the newcomers, began to talk about the prospects for climbing. Suddenly it no longer seemed impossible that the weather would clear and everyone would get to do a route. The worst of the posing ceased, as the lads got down to a really interesting subject about which no one had to pretend.

The Rat started to pick at the scabs on his hands where he had grazed them on the rock. Daz emerged from his bunk, scratching himself in the places where his clothes had stuck to him.

'You reckon the routes will be in condition tomorrow, then?' asked Daz.

Everyone had their own ideas for routes, and almost immediately Tom Ormerod became drawn into the discussion. 'It'll clear tonight – it's already clearing. We'll get a freeze which will set the gullies solid.'

Petra did not want to hear any of this. She wanted to hear from Tom's own lips the stories which he was said to be so good at telling: stories which were part of the mythology of post-war climbing. Ormerod was a name that cropped up in accounts of ascents in distant places, from Alaska to Patagonia; it featured in guidebooks to Welsh and Scottish crags, where it was synonymous with a particular style of route. It carried a reputation which seemed strangely at odds with this plain-spoken man.

Tom sat at the table, drawing diagrams in the pools of spilt tea. He spoke concisely, and always to the point. His voice was definably Yorkshire, but he used no flamboyant dialect expressions. He was tall, lanky, greying and fiftyish, and face to face he seemed nothing remarkable.

Petra looked up and caught Ieuan watching her watching Tom. Ieuan winked. He had his mug of tea, and was seated at the table, but it seemed that he too was sitting and watching, rather than taking part. Petra got the impression, which was later to be confirmed, that however well he could climb, Ieuan was not one of the climbers. He was not in awe of Ormerod's reputation. Perhaps it was that quality, rather than any skill at setting broken limbs, that had made Tom Ormerod take him out climbing.

Petra spoke up: 'What were you saying about you mending Tom's arm after he'd broken it? Are you a doctor?'

'I'm afraid so.'

Tom had heard the exchange. 'Don't belittle yourself, Ieuan.' He had still barely glanced at Petra since their initial meeting. She realised that he was talking to an audience, as if he did not want to become engaged with the individuals with whom he had been forced to share a hut. That was why he began to tell a story. It kept them all at a distance.

'It was a prime bit of amateur cack-handedness. Young Price will bear me out. It's what happens when you try to gallop down the scree to catch the pub before it shuts. At my time in life I ought to know there's always another opening time.'

He took a sip of tea. 'Haven't you got something more you could put in this?'

A flask was produced from the recesses of Daz's sleeping bag. No one else had known of its existence. Ormerod sniffed the neck of the flask. 'What is this stuff?'

'Austrian rum. 100 per cent proof. It carries light.'

Tom added a dose to his tea, where lumps of powdered milk were already floating in the greyish fluid. He drank. 'That's better.'

'Where were you?' enquired Daz.

"White Ghyll. I knew that gully when the grass grew green all over it. I say that to make you jealous.'

'I am,' said Daz.

'It's the privilege of us pioneers – telling young folk they'll never have climbing days like we did. Rubbish, of course. Luckily for me that day young Dr Price here was passing by on a ramble. He gave me a piece of his mind – didn't you, Ieuan?'

The younger man nodded. His hair, sleeked down over his head by the sleet, was beginning to dry and spring up in fine tufts around his head, like a halo.

'You called me a damned old fool.'

'I did not,' said Ieuan unheatedly.

'You thought it, though. Me, scree-running in gymshoes. You said it was people like me, wandering out of the car park in their Sunday suits, who caused trouble for the mountain rescue.'

'I overreached myself,' said Ieuan. 'I wasn't aware then that you had been climbing solo on the crag. That would have been quite safe, of course.'

Daz interrupted at this point. 'What were you climbing?'

'One of the Nots. I don't remember which. It was the one that didn't have the rope of three climbing it. I thought I'd just get the one route in before the pub shut after lunch. Instead I got dragged out of the stream bed, all over peat and moss, and got lectured by the Ambleside Rescue's spare medico.' He took another drink of tea and rum. 'I wasn't to know that he had got his exams about a week before, and I was giving him something to practise on.'

That remark raised a laugh, rather for the way it was told than through any intrinsic humour. Petra, huddled in her sleeping bag, began to feel warm again.

'Daz, can I have some of that stuff in my tea?'

'It's for emergencies.' Nonetheless he leant over and topped up her mug. 'If we get rain tomorrow we'll be going home, and we'll have to carry everything out with us. So we might as well finish it.'

Diane said brightly: 'More tea, everyone?'

The day was beginning to fade into the afternoon twilight of a northern winter. The wind, increasing steadily, had begun to howl around the corners of the hut. The outer door, sucked one way and another by the changes in air pressure, slammed open and then abruptly shut again.

'Ah. Allin's ghost,' remarked Tom.

'You made that up,' accused his friend.

'It's well known, the tale of Allin's ghost. Isn't it, lads? And lasses.' The afterthought was for the benefit of Diane, who was leaning across the table to pour out tea. 'Listen, lass. You'll hear the old gentleman's footsteps stamping up the hallway. Then he'll stop by the door and wait. He'll wait so long you'll think he stopped and died there. Then suddenly this door flies open and you'll see a horrible black Nothing.'

At that, the door did fly open. Diane gasped. The candle blew out, and the room was suddenly all shadows. Something was clattering and rolling about in the outer corridor.

It was a moment before anyone moved. Then Rowley jumped up, saying: 'My helmet fell off its hook.' He went out and retrieved his helmet and shut the door again. 'Light the candle, Rat.'

The whole period of darkness was no longer than a minute. The smell of the extinguished candle hovered over the odours of unwashed bodies and overproof rum. The window of the hut was a blue-grey square which admitted no actual light. Petra clutched her warm mug, now empty. For that moment, a small irrational part of her admitted the possibility of ghosts.

It was as if she had been in this place before, a long time ago, as some other person. Taken sceptically, the feeling was one of *déjà vu*, a trick played on the mind by a familiar scent. But it was nonetheless a powerful sensation.

When the light flickered to life again, no one but Rowley had moved. The interior of the hut was familiar in its squalor. It was no place to be imagining things. Petra had made a success as a climber by not allowing imagination too much free rein, because out of imagination came fear, and risks were better taken with a clear head.

She blamed the rum. That was the easiest solution. She pulled the sleeping bag over her head, to shut out the sound and light. She felt the bunk slide away from beneath her, whirling into a void. Then she was asleep.

CHAPTER 2

The new day was all they could have wished for. The snowy ridge was clear-cut blue against the light-blue sky. The spurs of the craggy hillside outlined deep snow-gullies. The air was completely still.

The wind had fallen, and the regular drip of water had ceased altogether. During the night, everything had frozen solid. The wild north-easterly wind had veered to the north and then died. The cold heart of the northern winter had crept just far enough south to engulf the whole of Scotland.

It was a day for haste, because conditions like these might be found once or twice in a winter. The freezing solid of the melting snow had formed a perfect surface for climbing. The soft snow had frozen to the glutinous texture of ice cream. The fine crystal structure was elastic rather than brittle, making it possible for the point of an ice-axe to sink in a couple of inches and then be gripped tight. There was no possible risk of avalanche.

Petra stayed hunched in her sleeping bag, having slept too long. Daz was almost ready to go, and even Diane was completely dressed for the mountain. Rowley and the Rat already had their rucksacks packed, and were strapping their crampons to the outside of their sacks. The Rat was eating a Mars bar by way of breakfast. Rowley glanced towards Petra's apparently sleeping form.

'Let's go.' He kept his voice low. 'She's dead to the world.'

Not for the first time, Petra considered how five was a poor number for a climbing team. Everyone climbed in pairs. It was the safest and best arrangement. But she had never developed a permanent climbing partner. She had always relied on being part of a crowd. At times like these, the ambition to succeed as a climber tended to take precedence over anything else. In this instance it appeared that Rowley was trying to make sure his team did not end up with a third on the rope. In his place, Petra might have done just the same, given the fiasco with the avalanche on their first day at the hut.

The two strangers were taking a little longer over breakfast, having gone to the lengths of making porridge out of Quaker oats. They were sitting in solid silence at the table, chewing through large greyish bowlfuls. Sugar and milk were not in evidence. The two men were dressed for climbing, and their neat rucksacks were leaning against the bunkpost.

Petra stretched herself and scratched at her untidy head. She was not feeling entirely well. She knew that she must not miss such a prime opportunity to climb, but she lacked the energy that would have to be exerted to stop her friends from leaving her behind.

'You all right?' asked Rowley.

'Yeh. OK.' She scratched at her head again. 'What are you going to do?'

'Ransom's Gully. With the waterfall pitch, if it'll go.'

It was a fearsome route. Hard, vertical and only recently put up, it was certainly not for a rope of three.

Daz had taken the opposite tack. 'I'll take Diane up Main Gully. Do you fancy Main Gully, Pet?'

It was a question expecting a negative answer. That was the gully out of which Petra had been chased by the avalanche. Though she suspected that Daz might actually change his mind on the way to the climb, she did not voice the thought. After all those days spent stewing in the hut, the conventions of friendship were under considerable strain. She could either keep quiet or start an argument. She kept quiet.

'I need breakfast,' she said.

After the four climbers had gone, and Petra was still searching the food locker for something edible, Ieuan Price spoke up: 'There's more porridge in the pot. It's still warm.'

'Thank you,' she said. 'I've got a muesli and dried milk mixture here somewhere. It'll only be something to carry down if I don't eat it.'

Tom Ormerod was scraping his bowl. 'You won't climb far on that rabbit-food. The Doc makes quite passable porridge, for a Welshman.'

The porridge in the pan was solid, bearing craters formed by the removal of previous helpings. It was still a little warm, and at least it was not burnt. Ieuan dumped a large spoonful into a bowl. He grinned. 'It's the antidote to Austrian rum.'

Then, as Petra took a tentative mouthful, and washed it down with strong tea, Ieuan asked the question, 'What route were you after?'

She replied without thinking, 'Cave Wall, of course. It's the classic.'

'Ah.'

She looked up, but Ieuan had already turned his attention to his friend. 'That's our route, isn't it, Tom?'

Tom nodded.

'Didn't someone call it a nice outing for a lady, Tom?'

'Harry Lennard did, when he put the route up in the fifties.'

Petra unglued her tongue from her porridge. 'Patronising idiot.'

'Is that me or Harry Lennard?' enquired Tom. 'Did you want to come along with us, lass?'

'My name's Petra.'

He scraped his stool back and stood up, then stretched himself. 'You don't want to come?'

'Yes I do.' Petra realised that she was about to explain why her friends had abandoned her. She stopped the impulse. The whole thing must have been perfectly apparent to anyone listening, and Tom had chosen to offer the remedy without requiring explanation. In another reversion to south-London coffee morning manners, she added: 'Thank you. Thank you very much.'

'Then bustle, girl. You've got five minutes. I'm not wasting a day like this.'

Tom stumped out and could be heard putting on his boots and jacket in the corridor. Petra swallowed several mouthfuls of porridge without chewing and then emptied her mug.

'Does he mean it?' she asked Ieuan.

'All of it. If you aren't ready you get left behind. Ormerod's rules. Leave the washing-up for the mice.'

Outside the hut the landscape was like the first day on earth. The snow was a pure white reflecting surface. The crust was so hard-frozen that the feet of the earlier party had hardly left an imprint on the surface.

Petra set out with the other two, and inevitably fell behind. Tom had the slow, economical stride of a lifelong mountaineer, and Ieuan's advantage of height was mostly long leg. Petra had packed her kit hastily, and her rucksack was poorly balanced; the porridge was a clumsy lump in the pit of her stomach. But compensation for all that was the easy going over the snow, and the prospect of Lennard's Cave route ahead. Her anticipation of the climb to come was heightened by anxiety that the route would somehow not be possible.

Half an hour's walk brought them to the start of the steep snow. They put on crampons. The twelve steel spikes, strapped on to their boots with hasty, clumsy fingers, turned the half-vertical ice rink of the mountain into secure ground. At every pace, the spikes bit into the snow with a satisfying crunch, like the first bite of an apple.

The snow grew steep quickly, and the sides of the gully narrowed inwards, until the distance between the side walls was no more than ten yards. A ribbon of white snow ran upwards, straight ahead, steepening to vertical before it met the overhanging snow-ice at the rim of the cliff; the snow, blown on the wind, had built up by tiny accretions to form a magnificent sculpted cornice which protruded fifteen feet beyond the true crest of the summit ridge. The walls to either side were black, with each crack in the surface of the rock outlined in white. Where the rock met the snow to the left of the gully, the wall was vertical, almost overhanging. Ten or twenty feet up, the angle eased, and this easier-angled rock allowed access to the subsidiary ridge of the mountain, which could be tackled as a mixed rock-and-ice climb.

Access to the ridge was hindered by the steepness of the rock at the base. But to the left of the gully, thirty feet or so from the place where the climbers had put on their crampons, a line of weakness in the rock gave rise to a diagonal crack of the type known as a chimney. In winter conditions, the crack itself was full of snow, and it formed the first pitch of the route.

They halted below the chimney. Tom went and had a close look at it while the other two stamped about in the snow, making a stepped platform for the belay. They uncoiled both ropes.

'There's a placement for a peg here,' Tom called out. He was scraping at the rock with the pick of his ice-axe.

'How shall we rope up?' asked Ieuan.

'You second. Petra third.'

That was the usual arrangement. No leader would choose to have an unknown quantity second on the rope. The second had the essential task of belaying the leader, paying out the rope evenly and steadily, and being ready to catch the leader should he fall. It seemed an unduly cautious arrangement for Tom Ormerod, who would have no difficulty whatever with this style of climbing, and who was of an age to have started climbing at a time when there was no protection for a leader fall. The code had been simple, then: 'The leader does not fall.'

'That peg'll keep you both from sliding back down. Lend me your ice-hammer, Price.'

The ice-hammer had a hammerhead, with an ice-axe pick in place of the claw. Ieuan carried it in a holster on his climbing harness. He handed it over.

'Where's yours, lass?'

Petra held up a hammer which was distinctly rustier and more battered than Ieuan's, as was her ice-axe. They were modern, steel-handled ice-tools which had cost her a fortune before her first trip to the Alps. Tom looked at the hammer and then at Petra. 'Did you buy that lot new?'

'Yes, of course.'

Tom began hammering his peg into the crack in the rock. The sound of each blow, initially low and cracked, became higher and purer as the peg became more firmly embedded. The echo of each blow came back from the far wall of the gully, jangling against the one before.

Petra, busy though she was uncoiling the rope, had time to realise what Tom had meant by his last question. The experience of a climber could be gauged to some effect by the state of their climbing hardware. And Tom had not thought Petra could be quite as seasoned as her ice gear. She could not resent the implication; she had made just the same kind of mistake about Tom and Ieuan, with all their new rock gear at Shepherd's Crag last year; everyone had to replace worn gear from time to time.

'Climbing,' said Tom. He set off up the chimney, which only had just enough snow in it after the days of thaw. He had to jam himself and his axe into the crack from time to time, and there was a continuous pelter of falling ice fragments as the crampon-points and ice pick scraped away at the frozen rock. But he got to the top of the pitch in record time. There was more hammering as a peg went in above. Then Ieuan's rope went tight.

There was no shouting. Ieuan just unclipped from the peg and set off up the climb. Petra, waiting at the bottom, began to feel cold. That was the problem with ropes of three on winter routes. You had to rely on keeping moving to keep warm under these conditions, and a three-man rope always took disproportionately longer than two. There were more ropes to tangle, more time was spent in sorting out belays and there was a constant problem of communication.

Petra stamped her feet to warm her toes. She did not feel very tigerish. The Cave Wall had been put up by Harry Lennard in l952, seconded by Hannah Kemp. It had been an unusual feat in its time, and the route had the reputation of being one that was dependent on the condition of the snow. It was probably not a route to try after a long thaw, even in the company of Tom Ormerod.

Petra was jerked out of her thoughts by a sudden tug on the rope. The rope went taut and stayed taut, and she had no choice but to get on and climb. Once she was firmly engaged in the task of inching her way up the ice-filled chimney, she had no time for any other thoughts, past or present.

It was an ugly, strenuous little pitch, with no good places to rest, and no opportunities for the use of sophisticated technique. Petra heaved her way upwards, finding a purchase for her ironmongery wherever she could, and making a good deal of use of the friction between the rock and her clothes. She was soon very hot indeed from the sheer exertion, although the ambient temperature was still well below freezing.

She emerged, breathing hard, on to the easier rock above. Ieuan and Tom were standing on the ridge, their breath forming clouds in the still air. The sky above the ridge had become slightly yellow, as if the sun were trying to rise above it. The north-facing slope, in deep shadow, was in clear contrast to the country on the far side of the valley. The forested slopes of Ben Ewe were already luminous with winter sunshine.

'One more pitch to the cave,' said Tom. Then, even as Petra fought for the breath to speak, he was off again. She was left perched on a pinnacle of rock beside Ieuan.

'Have you been out much in winter?' she asked him.

'Not this sort of thing. You have to be in such a hurry the whole time. But Tom makes it easy. I've been spoilt, I expect. You couldn't get a view like this any other way.' He smiled. 'Maybe you enjoy being scared?'

'I do.' It was impossible not to smile back. 'Being afraid is part of the fun of it all.'

'Good. I'm glad. You climbers all seem so desperately serious to me.'

Petra thought of Rowley and the Rat, whose line in humour

was deep – once they had done their route and got back to the pub. 'We're only serious about climbing. It's an addiction, really. You can't stop.'

'Like the Chinese proverb. He who rides the tiger can never dismount.'

'I wouldn't want to stop. I can't think of anything else I'd rather be doing.'

'In spite of that sordid hut and the vile weather?'

'It's such a contrast. You must feel it.'

'I believe I do. Maybe I'm getting the same bug.'

They fell silent. The view in all directions was very fine. But that was nothing to the simple fact of being there, in that almost inaccessible position. With steep rock on three sides, and the narrow ridge above, they were as separated from the earth as was possible without actually taking off and flying.

The sound that broke the silence was a hollow shout from Tom; then came three good tugs on the rope. Ieuan fumbled to undo the belay device with his mittened hands.

'Stupid gadget.'

'That's a good way to lose your sticht-plate,' said Petra. 'Clip it into a krab first.'

'Ah, that's better. I couldn't understand why Tom insists on my using one of these sticht-plates.'

'Have you ever tried to catch a leader on an old-fashioned body-belay?'

'No, but I've seen it done. The Scouts at school had to do climbing and abseiling. It was dire. Most of us were scared silly. I swore I'd never turn into one of those idiots who stands on top of a cliff and shouts orders. That's what put me off when I was a kid.'

The rope gave another flurry of tugs. Ieuan clipped the sticht-plate on to his harness, and settled his ice-axe in his right hand. A wrist-loop of tape kept the axe firmly in place.

'Climbing!' he shouted. The echo sent the word back. 'See you,' he said to Petra.

He climbed the narrow ridge carefully, as if thinking about

every place where he put his foot or his axe. It was as if he were still painting by numbers, whereas Tom was an artist.

Not for the first time, Petra wondered what she herself looked like when she was climbing. Grace and balance were what kept you safely in contact with the rock, but those were things only an outside observer could judge. You could not practise moves in front of a mirror, like a ballet dancer.

Before long, it was Petra's turn to climb. The sun finally appeared over the main ridge as she came up to the third belay. She had to duck to get the sunlight out of her eyes. The belay-ledge was tiny, and was already occupied by the two men, both firmly tied on.

'Your lead,' said Tom. It was a moment before Petra realised that he was not joking.

This one was not in the rule book. The pitch ahead was the famous cave itself. A traversing ledge led back in towards the gully, teetering out above a smooth vertical wall. To regain the ridge, it was necessary to pick one's way up an icy, slanting ramp which led into the mouth of the cave. The ramp was possible only if the ice on it was well frozen. In milder conditions, it became shiny, green and lethal, as all the drainage from the upper ridge seeped out through the cave. In wet conditions, in spring or autumn, it was a waterfall.

It was not a long pitch, or a very steep one, and there was said to be a running belay inside the cave. All that was needed was faith. The ice had been known to come away as a complete sheet, with ice-axe and crampons firmly embedded in it, and the climber swinging across the rock face in a vicious pendulum. No one had actually died on the route. Not yet.

'You'll cause less disturbance,' said Tom. 'It's a route for the elegant and delicate. There's an old peg at the end of the traverse.'

Petra was standing on two small footholds. She was keeping herself in balance, but the position was not one that could be sustained indefinitely. The problem of changing over the belay to let someone else lead would be time-consuming and dangerous. The sensible, rational thing was to let her take the lead.

'Give me the gear,' she said.

As Tom handed over the sling with the pegs and ice-screws attached to it, Petra felt that sudden thump of the heart which precedes a racing pulse. Then followed a sudden rush of fear and courage combined: that readiness to fight or run, which is the primeval protection against danger.

'Don't hold your breath,' said Ieuan. 'The belay's bombproof.'

Petra calmed her shaking knees and took a deliberate deep breath. Her success would depend not on being bold but on being technically accurate. This was the kind of climbing at which she excelled. It was not the brutish thuggery of the chimney pitch, for which all that was needed were good strong muscles. This needed a different kind of strength, based on confidence in the pure art of climbing.

She said the word 'Climbing', and her mouth was dry.

The traverse at the start of the pitch was a series of ledges covered in crisply frozen snow. The ledges were wide enough to take the front six points of the crampons. For balance, the ice picks could be tapped into ice-filled cracks, or else a mittened hand could grasp at a knob of rock. Petra moved across carefully, in a crab-wise walk, face to the rock.

Then she came to the waterfall. The ice was crisp and blue, the surface perfectly smooth after the thaw. In places it was transparent enough to see the rock beneath, with its coating of frozen moss and lichen. Beneath one transparent icicle was the old peg. Petra could see it, like a fly embalmed in amber. She struck the icicle away with several blows from the triangular adze-head of her axe.

The peg was rusty. It looked as if it might have been in place for the thirty-odd years since the first ascent. But the alternative protection would have been an ice-screw in the frail shell of the waterfall. Petra clipped a karabiner into the peg and attached a long sling of bright blue tape. Her trust that the peg would serve to protect her was as much a matter of faith as calculation. A leader fall in this place would turn a pleasant day's outing into a long-drawn-out exercise in self-rescue, and no one would be off the mountain before dark.

Away on the belay ledge, the murmur of voices showed that the rest of the party was relaxing and having a chat. Petra felt as if she was in a different country, isolated by danger. She was perhaps thirty feet away from the belay as the rope ran. She sank her axe, and then her ice-hammer, firmly into the waterfall ice. The deliberate blows embedded the tips of the picks perhaps half an inch into the ice. But the ice was solid. The ice tools held. Petra moved her right foot up and kicked the frontpoints of her crampons into the ice. Then, spider-like, she got into a regular rhythm. Left hand, right foot, right hand, left foot, always keeping three points of contact with the ice. It was unlikely that any one of those precariously embedded spikes of steel could have held her weight alone. The three points together provided balance and security, and with it an exhilarating sense of being on the edge of the world.

The challenge was over almost too soon. The ice gave way to steep frozen snow at the mouth of the cave. A natural spike of rock formed a ready-made traditional belay. Petra slung a sling round it and clipped in. She shouted 'Safe!'

But the exhilaration remained. The joy caught up with her as her heartbeat slowed down to its natural pace. The world around her seemed perfect, blue and black and white, with the distant pale gold of the larch trees on Ben Ewe. She had strayed for a moment to a place outside the natural boundaries of space. It was as if she were looking on the world from outside, from some distant planet or star.

'Climbing!' came Ieuan's voice, attenuated by distance. Petra took in the slack and let him climb.

A long time later, the weary party of three returned down the corrie. They had crept out onto a windblown, crisply sculptured ridge, a place of pure, lonely beauty which tempted them to linger. But the short day was already closing in, and they had to turn downhill immediately, retreating through a crumpled, precarious cornice into the concave, packed snow of Main Gully, and then reversing past the frozen, tumbled debris of the avalanche. Only when they came to the curving, lessening slope of the base of the hanging valley, with the white snow turning grey in the fading light, did the immediacy of the present adventure lose its grip. Physical relaxation brought weariness, and the loss of a need for continual vigilance allowed for wanderings of the mind. Petra, remembering more of what she had learned of Tom's life, at last asked him what was almost a direct question.

'Wasn't Lennard the same one who went with you to Himalchand?'

'He was,' replied Tom.

'What's Himalchand?' asked Ieuan.

'Ah.' Tom carried on, his booted feet scrunching the crystalline snow. The silence in the corrie was otherwise complete. 'It's my past, as young Petra knows. A pearl among the Himalaya. The 'New Moon of the Snows'. A mountain that has never had a second ascent.'

He went on for a few more paces in silence, then addressed Petra directly. 'You've read the book?'

'Yes.'

'And you've a mind to try for the mountain?'

'How did you guess?' Oddly, her heartbeat was suddenly going as fast as it had when she was toiling up the slope.

'You're not the first. Since the détente in Tibet, the mountains on the borders have become accessible again, for the first time since the sixties. The Indians are handing out permits for the mountains north of their 'Inner Line' and Himalchand is the one that people have heard of. I get handwritten pleas for information, written on pages torn out of exercise books. You could guess how I reply.'

Petra blushed. 'I wouldn't want ...'

'No. You've kept admirable silence so far.'

She did not know how to reply. The blood was hot about her ears. It was as if she had displaced one small stone and released a landslide. There was no mistaking the suppressed feeling behind Tom's words. It was a feeling strong enough to deter curiosity. She had not supposed that this self-contained man of the hills could be prey to any such emotion; still less that it could lie so near the surface after more than thirty years.

But Ieuan, the newcomer, failed to catch the echo of times past. 'Was that one of your expeditions, Tom? When did you go?'

'Fifty-three.'

'The Everest year?'

Tom nodded. 'But ours was a different kind of affair altogether. Petra can tell you. She's read the book.'

'We all have,' declared Petra bravely. She plunged on, her feet sinking deeply into the brittle snow. 'We've read it from cover to cover, even the Rat, who only reads magazines. It's just that it was so completely different from all the Everest books. No military-type logistics. No strings of Sherpas. No nationalism. Ieuan, did you ever read *The Ascent of Everest*?'

'Yes. Years ago. At school.'

'Do you remember the discussion as to whether Edmund Hillary or Sherpa Tenzing got to the top first?'

'Who did?' asked Ieuan.

'Hillary never said, and nor did Tenzing. But fancy having to keep quiet about a thing like that because someone is going to make political capital out of it.'

'Sounds bad, but what makes Tom's trip different?'

'It's an adventure. I mean, there were only eight of them, and no high-altitude porters. You'd call it an alpine-style ascent nowadays.'

She stopped. Tom had his shoulders hunched, more than the weight of the rucksack demanded. He had not attempted to interrupt.

'It's true, isn't it? It was a climb that was out of its class, for the time. And no one's been able to go back and do it again, because of the political restrictions. It's not just glamour. It was real.'

Tom glanced once at Petra, but kept his head low and his hands in his pockets. The snow underfoot was now tinged faintly with orange, as the setting sun crept down beneath a straight low cloud to the west. The place was empty of all but man-made sounds.

'It seems to me,' he said at last, 'that all that glamour fixes itself around the disaster, not the triumph. The mountain has been climbed before. There are still plenty of unclimbed peaks. Why settle for a second ascent?'

'Because of Hannah,' said Petra. 'She climbed the mountain, and no one else did. Because of what she wrote about it. You know:

> The mountain keeps his own peace, under the centuries of snow. He is not to be climbed and conquered by footprints. He can be discovered again and again, each year slightly different, but with new snow blown over the tracks, and new danger among the rocks and séracs, and from the weather. The discovery is not of the mountain, which is old, but of ourselves, who are always scrambling after new things.

'You've got it by heart?' Tom looked up now.

'Easily,' replied Petra. 'I know she wasn't just writing about Himalchand. It comes back to me from time to time. I don't have to try to remember.'

Ieuan's curiosity was now thoroughly roused. He looked over Petra's head, at Tom. 'Is that a summit quote? It sounds better than the thing from Hillary that turns up on the back of the Kendal Mint Cake packet.'

'Sure,' replied Tom, 'but a bit more than that. What the girl hasn't told you is that Hannah Kemp died on the mountain. It's an epitaph and a lure. If I'd known what kind of a lure, I would have done my best to stop them publishing the book of her diaries.'

'It's well known?' Ieuan sounded both subdued and surprised. 'What's it called?'

'*New Moon of the Snows*. There was one small edition. People keep finding it in second-hand bookshops and club huts. It's a peculiar kind of fame.'

'You don't like it?'

'I'd rather have got to the top of Himalchand myself.'

The hut was well in sight by now. There were busy black figures outside the door. The rest of the party had already returned. For an involuntary moment, Petra was glad to see them safe.

But she could not resist the last question: 'Did you ever want to go back yourself?'

'Of course. That's why I won't help every Tom, Dick and Harry to go chasing their dreams. That's my mountain.'

'Why don't you go back?'

'There hasn't been much chance, recently. None of us was going to go back very soon, and once we felt like it again, the border had closed. It's been more than thirty years. Harry Lennard is a bank manager in Somerset now.'

'But if someone asked you along, would you come?'

'I don't know. People don't ask.'

'Would you come with us?'

She knew, even as she asked it, that the question was impossible. For Tom, Himalchand had to do with times remembered, with the unattainable dreams of youth. It was not a subject for the present, for the end of a long day in the freezing air of twilight. All three climbers were still a little detached from reality by the exhilaration of the climbing and by tiredness at the end of the day.

Yet it was perhaps for that very reason that Tom replied as he did. Perhaps he too was suspended a little way above the earth, in that state of mind where the impossible becomes real.

'I might come,' he said. 'When were you thinking of going?'

They were at the hut now, with Daz banging his crampons against the hut wall to loosen the impacted snow. He looked up and pushed a draggle of hair out of his eyes with his elbow.

'What did you do?'

'The cave,' replied Petra.

'It's in condition?'

'Brilliant.'

Tom sat down on a rock to undo his crampons. The straps were encased in snow, requiring some fumbling and tugging. Petra, still in full climbing gear, axe in hand where she had pulled it out from between her rucksack straps, stood with her feet slightly apart, looking from one to the other.

'We were talking about Himalchand,' she said.

When Daz did not immediately reply, she went on, 'Mr Ormerod might want to come too. It could make the whole thing a lot easier.'

'We haven't got it that planned,' replied Daz, but his attention was thoroughly captured.

Tom bent down and picked up his crampons by their straps. They clashed together with a faint metallic clink. 'It was Petra's idea, but you wouldn't want the extra baggage?'

Daz shook his head. 'We could do with more climbers. Four's no number for that sort of jaunt. And none of us has gone high.'

'But you don't like the idea of me coming in and taking over? I wouldn't do that. I'd let you do the hard work. But I may be able to oil some wheels, with sponsorship, political permission and so forth.'

Tom's tone of voice was as diffident as would have been possible for a Yorkshireman. And Daz was being unnaturally polite. But negotiations had opened in earnest.

'We'll have to put it to the committee,' said Daz. 'Diane went to put the kettle on. Let's go inside. It's getting parky out here.'

Petra bent down to undo her own crampons. She was conscious of having initiated something that was already passing out of her control. Tom followed Daz into the hut.

'Are they serious?' Ieuan had remained a silent onlooker, but seemed to have been unfrozen by the departure of his friend.

'Of course,' replied Petra, although she could hear the misgivings in her own voice.

'He rather jumped at it. Doesn't sound like Tom.'

'I didn't expect that. I don't know why I dared ask. But it would be an incredible chance.'

'You mean you're serious about going to the Himalaya? You haven't climbed there before, have you? Just Scotland and those Dru things in Chamonix. Isn't this biting off a bit much?'

'Come on, you're not that much of a novice, Ieuan. You know that Scotland has things that are harder than anything on a classic Himalayan route. And there's nothing like the Walker or the Dru. It's not the climbing that's the problem.'

'No,' Ieuan replied drily. 'Just 22,000 feet of altitude, and the journey getting there, and the porters, and the dysentery bugs, and no bloody way out if you do fall off.'

'That's where Tom's knowledge will help, isn't it? He's been there.'

'Fine. Thirty years ago. Before we were even born.'

Ieuan moved away towards the hut, accompanied by the inevitable clangour of metal gear. By now the darkness was almost complete, and Petra could not catch a sight of his face. The door opened and he had his back to her, framed against the light. The interior of the hut was brightly lit and noisy with excitement. Ieuan scuffed his boots on the sill and went in.

CHAPTER 3

The sense of the incredible persisted. There really was going to be an expedition. In the van going home, the five young climbers divided up the different jobs that would need to be done for the organisation of a Himalayan expedition. This was something they had done before, in pretence, but now no one said 'What if?'. They believed that they were going to climb the mountain. It was as if all they had had to do was to decide to become an expedition, and all else would follow; as if infinite possibilities lay beyond the moment of choice.

'I'll do the food.' Diane was jumping before she was pushed. 'All those lovely freeze dried rations.'

'Who's the leader?' The Rat, rolled up in a sleeping bag in the back of the van, was assiduously picking the flaking skin off his bare feet.

'Das Daz,' volunteered Rowley. 'He's the eldest and he has Leadership Qualities.'

'What?'

'True. He put it on his c.v. for a job once. Climbing develops leadership qualities.'

'You get the job, Daz?'

'Nah,' replied the driver.

Petra was jammed in beside a lumpy rucksack in the rear seat. She elbowed the largest lump so that it was redistributed. 'We'll need completely new gear. I'll try and get it cheap through the Centre. I know of 800 feet of lime-green rope with a purple streak which isn't selling.'

'Tell you what.' Daz paused there for a particularly spectacular piece of overtaking, and the overloaded van swayed dangerously round the next few bends.

'What?' Petra felt thoroughly sick.

'You can be fundraising and paperwork too. Use the Centre notepaper. And the photocopier. You'll be good at that.'

'What about the riff-raff? What are Rowley and the Rat going to do?'

The Rat pulled a long strip of dead white skin off his foot and poked it out through the van window. 'We've thought of that. Rowley does the logistics bit, cheap airfares and rail timetables. I get mountain logistics, and porters and maps.'

'I've got this really good idea,' said Diane. 'I can practise making curry à la Himalchand, interesting dried pulses and things, to make use of local materials.'

'You're not practising on me,' declared her boyfriend.

By the time they got back home from Scotland, they had a plan which would run with or without Tom Ormerod. Tom had supplied the inspiration, but no one would have been surprised if he had decided not to get involved after all. A week or two back among the realities of his working life should have reminded him that his projected companions were young enough to be dangerously reckless, that they were nothing like a climbing team, and that his name and reputation would invest them with a respectability they did not deserve.

But ten days after Petra had got back home, she got a phone call from Tom. She was living in a shared house in Llanberis, where the owner of the house had put a padlock on the dial of the phone, so that the instrument would only take incoming calls. A previous tenant had run up an unpaid bill calling friends in Australia.

'Petra Merriman?'

For a moment Petra thought it must be her boss ringing up. The director of the Outdoor Centre, Mr Gobert-Jones, was the only person who used to call her by her surname. But the voice was wrong. This was not an ex-army officer from Guildford.

'Yes?'

'Ormerod here. I'll be up your way next week. Can you arrange a planning meeting?'

'Yes,' she replied, without thinking.

'I'll need a slide projector.'

'I'll borrow a room at the Outdoor Centre. What day?'

'Friday.'

'It'd have to be in the evening.'

'Of course. We'll get a route in beforehand. Keep an eye on what's in condition. I'll meet you at Pen-y-Pass at eight.'

A week later, Petra was hitching up the Llanberis pass on a cold winter's morning. She was reminded of the terms under which children and young people using the Outdoor Centre were enrolled on expedition projects. They were required to arrive at a rendezvous in the middle of nowhere, defined only by a map reference, and only those who arrived on time at the appointed place were allowed to go into the next stage of selection. She wondered if Tom had done it on purpose. She had spent the week feeding 10p coins into the call box in the canteen at the Outdoor Centre. Rowley and the Rat could be organised easily enough, since neither had current employment and they often spent whole days hitching across the country. Daz, however, would have to negotiate for yet another Friday afternoon off, so doing nothing for his standing in the engineering firm for which he was working. Diane proposed cheerfully to ring in sick on the Saturday. They were all going to have to sleep on the floor of Petra's sitting-room – another activity likely to annoy the landlord. And Petra herself had had to persuade a colleague to swap the Friday for an entire weekend in April, because she was meant to be teaching survival skills to a party of Scouts from Market Harborough.

But it was done, and the slide projector was signed for and working, and Petra had put a dozen bottles of beer in her locker at the Centre, in case the meeting should continue beyond closing time.

She met Tom in the grey morning at Pen-y-Pass. He had

parked his van at the youth hostel. The youth hostel warden, it appeared, was another old friend. When Petra arrived, dropped off by a sales rep on his way home to Birmingham, Tom was sitting on the tailgate of his van, lacing up his boots. There was a kind of freezing fog, which had formed into fine droplets on his beard, increasing the greyness of it. This was the time of day when optimism was at its lowest. For a moment, Petra doubted her own enthusiasm for involving Tom Ormerod in the project.

'Good to see you, lass,' remarked Tom. Petra wondered if he ever got excited about anything. She greeted him, and suggested a route. 'It's a short one. The weather's likely to change. We're better doing a short route.'

'Fine.' And with barely another word said, they were off along the Miner's Path towards Snowdon.

By the afternoon, Petra had forgotten all her doubts. She stalked into the kitchen of her house, stiff-legged from exertion, with her mind still high up on the eagle eyries of Yr Wyddfa. She had climbed the route before, but never in such style, and the weather, which had threatened in the morning, had retreated in the afternoon to give a cold white sky and a few perfectly-formed falling snowflakes.

'Anyone home?' she called. The other inhabitants of the house were usually out at work at this time, apart from an unemployed Welsh poet who lurked in bed all day and claimed to do his best work at night.

'Kettle's boiling.' Diane put her head around the scullery door. 'Daz and the lads are snatching a buttress on Crib Goch.'

'Don't you mind?' enquired Petra.

'I got some photographs of them as they were setting out. A real rope spaghetti. Blackmail material. Then I went round by Cyrn Las and back down the ridge. I met a nice man with a dog and 144 Scouts.'

Petra laughed, and finished peeling off all her damp outer gear. 'I'm going to put 20p in the meter and have a shower.'

'Where's Tom?' Diane's enquiry was just a little too offhand. She was swirling hot water around the teapot to keep it warm.

'He stopped at the Centre. Apparently he knows the director. Or the director knows him.'

'But you had a good day?'

'It was out of this world. I don't really believe Tom's real.'

Diane smiled. 'I know what you mean. Why us?'

Petra returned the smile and shrugged her shoulders. 'The tooth fairy, perhaps.'

She had her shower and changed into a jumper and jeans, and then went out to get chips. She and Diane had finished the chips and several cups of tea, and were lying around on sofas in the lounge, looking at the clock, when their friends finally turned up.

'It was magic,' remarked Daz as he flopped into the motheaten armchair and put his feet up on the wastepaper bin. Diane began to tickle him. Rowley and the Rat made rude noises and went to fetch beer from the kitchen.

'We've got to get up to the Centre,' said Petra. 'We're to meet Tom there at seven.'

'What is he, the Akela?' Rowley made an unofficial version of the Scout salute.

'That's rubbish. It's the Centre, not Tom, that's being a problem. They want to lock up the place at eleven.'

'You're real leadership material, you know. Ain't she, Daz?'

'You want my job?' Daz was ruffling Diane's hair.

'No thanks.' Petra knew that she was turning red. It was true that spending all day instructing unwilling children tended to exacerbate any tendency towards bossiness. Yet leadership qualities were something else. She could not say it of course, because they would laugh at her. She just had to continue with the intrinsically female job of steering from behind. Daz was meant to be the leader, because he was the oldest of them, and the best climber, but he was too relaxed to be interested in running things. It was just as well that the expedition was meant to be organised by consensus.

Having made his point, Rowley suggested that they all set off immediately for the Centre, via the fish-and-chip shop.

The Centre was about a quarter of a mile away, out beyond the upper end of the village, where the road narrowed between stone walls on a winding progress towards the Pass. The house had once belonged to a slate-quarry owner, and had briefly been a hotel. It had the dank slate walls and rotting white window-frames of Welsh Victorian architecture. Some prefabricated buildings had been added at the back, and the whole was lit by fluorescent tube lighting, for economy. Indoors, it smelt of rubber wellingtons and yesterday's gravy. There were notices everywhere: 'No boots in the dormitory'; 'Wash all saucepans before sitting down to eat'; 'Do not put kitchen refuse on the fire'. Someone had added 'No farting' in illiterate biro under a notice that read 'Quiet after 10 p.m.'.

The Scouts were just washing up after tea, with a lot of shouting and clashing of crockery. Rowley and the Rat ostentatiously wiped their trainers on the doormat. Petra led the way. 'We're in the briefing room at the back.'

It was in one of the prefabs, a damp cube of a room heated by a one-bar electric fire and a storage heater which was of course cold. A giant map of Snowdonia sprawled over one wall. Tom was there, sitting on the table, explaining something to the director.

'He's not coming too?' muttered the Rat under his breath.

Tom pressed ahead with introductions, and the director was seen to be smiling benignly. Petra had not seen him like this before. Mr Gobert-Jones (forename restricted to the single initial L.) had been in the Army. He was a large square man with very short hair and a moustache, and he always wore a tie, even on the hills.

'So this is your team. Well, well.'

Petra gawped slightly. She had not seen Gobert-Jones so genial. His attitude to women was unreconstructed. He was uncomfortable with the idea of females being climbing instructors, although he had to employ them. Petra herself had been reprimanded more than once for using bad language on a climb, a necessary aid on a difficult and strenuous move. She mistrusted his smile.

'Miss Merriman I know very well, of course. And your expedition leader?'

'Mr Stanton, known as Daz,' replied Tom. 'And this is Miss Ponder, Mr Radinsky, Mr Rowley.'

'Jolly good show,' declared Gobert-Jones, shaking a few hands. The three lads were almost rigid, the stiff upper lip in this case being supported by a mix of shock and amusement.

But Tom knew what he was about. Here he was demonstrating what he could do in the way of recruiting the interest of the Establishment in the expedition. That was one of the ways of raising money.

To Petra's relief, her friends managed to contain their laughter until after Gobert-Jones had left the room.

'Wizard prang, what.' Rowley imitated the director's stance. He was unable to maintain it for long, before collapsing into a heap. Daz patted him on the head, reminding him it was character-building. Tom was smiling too. Diane asked wonderingly, 'Were you in the Army with him?'

'No. Gobert-Jones was in the Regulars. I spent ten months in Aden, and that was quite enough.'

'Character-building?' enquired Daz.

'Just so. Are you going to convene the meeting?'

'Right.' Daz put his hands in his pockets. 'Settle down, everyone. Petra, take the minutes. Mr Radinsky, operate the projector. Mr Rowley, turn off the lights on the word of command. Miss Ponder, open the beers. Right?'

Rowley saluted him, Army-style. Tom went to sit down on the only comfortable chair in the room. 'I would like to begin at the beginning. Has everyone read the book?'

'Sure,' said Daz. 'The women can quote great chunks of it. Some sort of feminist kick. So we know what happened. But the book is sketchy about the route. The Rat has picked up all he can, and photocopied the maps and topos. He has a list of questions. Rowley has worked out what he thinks it ought to cost, but we need to find someone who has been in India during the last couple of seasons.'

'Rowley is your treasurer?'

The individual in question was sitting slouched at the back of the room, picking his scabs as usual. 'I'm on logistics and cheap deals. I didn't say I'd be treasurer.'

'I could do that,' volunteered Tom. 'I can add up. And you'd be best having a Yorkshireman for the job.'

'Right,' said Daz. 'Vote, everyone?'

'Aye.'

'Motion carried.'

All this time the Rat had been fiddling with the projector, that had a patent slide-cassette which tended to get stuck. At that point something gave way with a loud click. The Rat sucked his damaged finger and swore.

'I think that's the bugger working. First slide coming.'

The lights went out, and there was Himalchand, enormous in black and white, opening up the mildewed walls of the prefab to a vision of impossible distances.

Tom Ormerod described the topography in dry, unemphatic tones. The slide-projector clicked from view to view, illustrating the glacier approach, the lie of the rock strata, the snow slopes and ice formations, and the final glorious curve of the summit ridge. Many of the pictures had been used to illustrate Hannah Kemp's book, and so were familiar to the audience. But Tom brought the pictures alive; he supplied the third dimension to the mountain, which made it tangible for the first time.

Hannah's diary
3 July 1953

> Himalchand translates as 'snow moon'. It is not the tallest peak in the Munshu valley, but stands at its head, so that it dominates the scene, as the Matterhorn does at Zermatt.

The peak is triangular, with steep ridges to the south-west and the east, but the tip of the triangle is missing, as if a giant had gnawed at the peak and left a bite-mark. The south-east face is generally steep, and rises directly out of the Munshu glacier. But there is a scoop out of the centre of the face, corresponding to the giant's bite-mark, which runs diagonally across the face and holds snow at all seasons. It seems to link the east ridge with the shallower upper portion of the south ridge, thus suggesting a route by which the steepest parts of both ridges might be avoided. From the distance, the finely tapered curve of the snow-scoop is an identical match for a sickle moon. Lennard, who is something of a poet, has coined the arresting title 'New Moon of the Snows'. This is a bid to rival the romantical flights of the Everest climbers. But we are in the Western Himalaya and John Hunt and his New Elizabethan battalions are far away. The valley is steep and green, occupied by goats and little shepherd boys.

'Is there any access from the west?' The Rat had the photocopied sketchmap open on the table before him. 'There seems to be a subsidiary ridge on the far side of the South Munshu glacier.'

'We looked at it. Hayter and Amory camped on the South Munshu for two days. The weather was cloudy, and the upper slopes were out of sight. But the nearer part of the ridge was made of shale.'

'It was chossy?'

'As slippery as soap. It wouldn't take a belay. But maybe it runs out higher up. It might be worth a look.'

'It'd be a new route.'

'Yeah,' agreed Daz.

'We could say we're doing a new route,' insisted the Rat. 'Wouldn't that make sponsors happier?'

'It's a consideration,' said Tom drily.

'It may make all the difference. And if it goes, there's a new route.'

'And if not, will you have time to try both?'

'We'll have to think about that. It depends when we can get to Munshu.'

'The road may not be open.' said Tom, carefully. 'It may not even be there after the monsoon. If we go this year, we'll have to go for after the monsoon. It's too late to get permission for the pre-monsoon season.'

'You reckon?'

'I've checked.'

'I haven't had an answer yet. Who did you write to?'

'I phoned Gul Singh in the Indian High Commission. He used to be a climber.' Tom smiled, and glanced mischievously at Diane. 'He was in the Army with Donald Hayter, in the war.'

'And Hayter was on Himalchand,' countered Diane.

The Rat muttered 'Jesus!' *sotto voce.*

'What's that?' asked Daz.

'I can't get the High Commission to even answer the phone. If I do I get put through to someone who doesn't answer his extension and my 10p runs out. That reminds me. Can I make a claim on funds for expenses?'

'Ten pence for the Rat. I'll note it down,' replied Tom.

'Can I ask you something?' Rowley had picked all the scabs off his hands, and the beer had made him bold. 'Why do you want to come with us, Tom? You don't know us. OK, you know what we've climbed – you know we're not wallies, but I guess you could go back to Himalchand with anyone you please.'

Tom answered calmly, sitting there with his half-emptied beer glass in his hand. 'You could say that Petra did the persuading. She held her breath until I found myself agreeing. I had been thinking that I might not have many more chances to get at that mountain. The valley was closed to foreigners for years, for political reasons. You knew that, Rowley.'

'Yeah. Right. The Inner Line?'

'That's right.' There was to be no more explanation. 'Can you refill my glass, lad?'

The discussion moved from strategy to tactics, and the details of planning, money and equipment. The beer all went. Petra took notes of everything, and her handwriting got worse and worse. But by eleven o'clock, when all the lights went out and the visitors had to vacate the room, the expedition to Himalchand had made its first infant step towards existence. There was a rough outline of a timetable that should bring them to Munshu by the beginning of August. And there were jobs for everyone to ensure that the planning ran to time. From now on it would not be enough just to set one's sights on the mountain peak. The end was not to be accomplished without drudgery.

For the next few weeks, Petra found herself becoming wholly obsessed by the timetable. She had it set out on a board, with arrows in different colours of felt-tip marker. She was expedition secretary, in recognition of her efforts at organisation. She wrote hundreds of letters, or so it seemed, making use of Gobert-Jones's office typewriter. And when the job kept her up at night, and the daytime work of marshalling reluctant youths became particularly tedious, she had to try hard to envisage Himalchand as a desirable goal.

Another meeting took place a few weeks later, this time on Tom's home ground. It turned out that he worked for Lancaster University in some administrative capacity. His home was in a north Lancashire village, far enough south of the Lake District to be cheap, but near enough to allow him to visit Lakeland crags on a summer evening.

They met on a Saturday in the beginning of April, when the weather was making a pretence at spring, and there were early daffodils under the hedges. Petra came on a bus via Preston, with all the expedition paperwork in a cardboard box on her knee. The bus stopped at all the villages, but remained nearly empty. A few serious ramblers got on at Carnforth, and a party of children giggled together and smoked on the back seat.

Petra wondered if they would get any climbing that weekend. She had the feeling that this would encourage the expedition spirit more than all the hours spent chewing over paperwork. No, more than that, she was beginning to lose patience with the eternal 'jam tomorrow' of a climb that needed so much planning. She was not even as physically fit as she usually was at this time of year, because she had spent too much of her spare time at the desk or telephone.

The bus came to Tom's village, making heavy work of the incline up the wooded hill which led to the main street. A low outcrop of limestone, covered in tangles of ivy, was visible through the trees. Petra had one brief view of the rocks before the trees and buildings closed in about the road. The bus stopped by the grocery-store-cum-post-office and Petra alone descended.

She looked about her, trying to remember the directions to Tom's house. The street was a double row of stone cottages, with a chapel at the western end. Opposite the post office was a pub called the Rose and Crown, a free house with an ancient archway for carriages. On a bench in front of the pub sat Ieuan Price. He was reading a copy of the *Guardian*, and was dressed in full rambler's kit, from woolly balaclava to Cairngorm boots. All that was missing was a knobby walking stick.

'What are you doing here?' Petra forgot even to say 'Hello'.

'Meeting you.' Ieuan folded up the paper very neatly. He stood up and crossed the street. 'I pottered up to the top of Brant How in the morning. Tom said to meet the bus from Preston. Is anyone else with you?'

'They were hitching. No one here yet?'

'No.'

The feeble spring sunshine was already west of south. The greater part of the outdoor day had gone past. Ieuan stuffed the paper in his anorak pocket. 'Have you had lunch? The Rose does quite good pasties.'

'What are you doing here?' repeated Petra.

'I come up sometimes on free weekends. Gets me out of the hospital. Tom said the IMF won't give permission unless there's a doctor on the trip.'

'You?'

'I'm considering it.'

'Oh.'

'You think Tom should have put it to the committee first?'

'It's not that sort of expedition.'

'That's what I hoped.'

There was a pause. Petra shifted the weight of the cardboard box, which she had balanced on one hip.

'Would you like me to carry the paperwork for you?'

'No thanks.'

Ieuan answered the meaning rather than the words. 'Look, just because I haven't been dreaming of Himalchand for years doesn't mean I don't relish the idea of going to the Himalaya. If the thing is properly organised, it could be tremendous. You'd have to convince me of that, but I'm nearly convinced already.'

'You said it was biting off more than we could chew.'

'So it is. But I shan't be taking the risks that you do. I don't have ambitions for the summit.'

'Not yet.'

'No.' Ieuan was smiling again. 'Not yet. Give me that box. You'll find it's a long step to Tom's hermitage.'

Petra handed over the box which was certainly weighing heavy. She did not want to make a song and dance about it.

'So you've read Hannah's book?' she asked.

'It's funny – I found that it echoes my experience of being a climber, small though that is. She had something to say to everyone.'

'She just told the truth. God, I wish I could have met her. Does Tom say much about her?'

They were walking together up the uneven pavement of the high street. After fifty yards or so they turned into a narrow lane which ran steeply uphill. Hedgerows closed about them.

'You know Tom,' said Ieuan.

'I don't, that's just it.'

'Never talks outside the point. And almost never about himself. That was the first I'd heard about the '53 expedition, when we were with him up in Scotland. He holds on to things. Doesn't let anyone get near. And when he gets into a corner he starts telling a story. I'd guess his involvement in your expedition means letting go. But not all at once, and no more than necessary.'

'Because he's a Yorkshireman?'

'Because he's Tom Ormerod.'

Petra, who had nothing to carry, found that she was having to work to get her breath to keep up with Ieuan. The lane, winding uphill, had lost its macadam surface, and had developed deep water-worn ruts. Blackthorn flowers formed a white haze among the pale green of the hedge. Beyond the next turn, Petra caught the smell of woodsmoke.

The cottage was almost invisible among the trees: made of ancient stone, it was probably once the abode of charcoal-burners. Early daffodils formed a garden among the mossy stones in front of the house. Ieuan had referred to it as a 'hermitage'.

'It's Tom who interests you, not the mountain?' Petra asked.

'All these climbers interest me. But especially Tom and Hannah. Don't you think this is a sort of pilgrimage? Wouldn't you be fascinated to know what went on between the two of them? When you go into my line of business, you tend to be particularly curious about people.'

'Does that mean you're curious about all of us?'

'In different ways. Think of it as my handicap, like Tom's taciturnity.'

'What about me?'

'What about you?'

'What's my handicap?'

'Paranoia.'

It was not entirely a joke, but Petra chose to return Ieuan's smile. He had stopped to shift the weight of the box in his arms. 'And the box is bloody heavy. There's Tom at the door.'

Hannah Kemp had not wasted much time writing about the plans and organisation of the expedition. That sort of stuff had been put in an appendix by her friends when they prepared the diary for publication. It was a dryish list of costs incurred at various points in the year before the expedition, and then itemised costs in rupees, once they had got to India. In those days climbers had travelled out by ship to Bombay for fifty-seven pounds apiece. Their snow goggles had cost nine shillings. Porterage cost between one and four rupees a day. Even the price of cups of tea taken on the train had been itemised.

The Rat made his own calculations. The costs nowadays would be something near ten times that amount, given the superior equipment that they would have to buy. Travel was relatively cheaper than anything else, even taking into account the cost of shipping gear ahead in a container. The Rat had found a very cheap deal with a firm of brokers in an office near Leicester Square. He had found their advertisement in the back of *Crags*, a publication which usually represented the full extent of his reading.

At the time of the April meeting, there was a month's grace before all the air tickets would have to be paid for.

'Let's just talk about it again,' said the Rat. 'What about going overland to India?'

They had gathered in Tom's front room, where photographs and pictures of mountains covered the walls. Above the fireplace was a Heaton Cooper original. The furniture was covered in worn jacquard fabric, with tufted fringes along the seams. All the chairs sagged, and the floor was covered with a Persian-type carpet which did not quite reach the walls. The floorboards had been painted black and the walls were cream distemper. The window was tiny, and even in the afternoon they had to put on lights to read by. On the windowsill and mantelpiece were various mountain curios – pieces of rock, ancient snapshots, bits of outdated gear. A bookshelf held literature on a similar theme. All Tom's useful guidebooks and gear lived in a storeroom at the back. The sitting-room was neat, without a speck of dust, until the expedition members paraded in there. Petra reckoned that the room was for visitors, not for use. It was where Tom might have entertained the vicar, had he been in the habit of calling.

Daz had folded his long body into a small armchair by the fire. Petra and Diane got the sofa. Rowley and the Rat were sitting among the papers on the floor. Ieuan and Tom were in the other two chairs, either side of the window.

'We've gone over all that,' said Daz.

'Let's just be sure,' insisted the Rat.

'It depends if we want to climb, or have an exciting time dodging revolutions and dysentery bugs. Right?'

'I'd have liked to have seen Kabul,' put in Diane.

'No chance – you have to go through the desert now. Good fun if you break down. And you'll have to wear a veil.'

'Rubbish,' declared Petra.

'Ho ho.' Rowley leered horribly. 'We could exchange Diane for some camels.'

'Funny.' Diane folded her arms and aimed a kick at him.

'And it'll be no cheaper,' continued Daz, 'and anyway Tom reckons the paperwork would be dire.'

Tom had stayed out of the discussion until now. He was never one to argue for argument's sake. 'That's the long and the short of it. We can cope with the IMF and the Indian High Commission, but Turkish and Iranian border guards are another matter. We'd have to budget for bribes, and I'm not sure that even that would work these days.'

'It's odd, isn't it?' remarked Diane. 'All those years of the hippy trail. Girls I was at school with went in a double-decker bus which broke down in Bulgaria so they hitched the rest of the way to Kabul. I was jealous, I can tell you.'

Ieuan enquired: 'Really? What happened to them?'

'Their money was stolen so they had to be flown home by the British Consul. They never got to India.'

'Another reason why not,' declared Daz. Petra had the feeling that he and Diane had rehearsed this argument before. 'Anyway, you'd need an army with air support now. Rat can get us to Delhi by air for 300 pounds each. And there's a bus to Munshu.'

'Jawohl.' The Rat saluted him.

'Has anyone else got anything to say?'

Rowley put up his hand, classroom-style. 'If we're having theoretical arguments, I'd like to discuss why we need a medic. There's bugger all a medic can do up a glacier. If things go really wrong we'd need a helicopter anyway.'

'Why the objection?' Tom asked mildly.

Rowley did not look him in the eye. 'Another lead climber would make more sense.'

'Who, for instance?'

'There's lads who'd jump at the chance.'

'If offered on a plate like this, yes. Is that what you want?'

Rowley looked sheepish. 'I haven't done all this work to give some other bloke the summit.'

'Then your objection to Ieuan? His presence would cut a good deal of red tape.'

'Well.' Rowley glanced sideways at Ieuan. 'We'd have to rethink all the logistics, porterage, tents and so forth. It'll cost.'

Ieuan folded his arms. 'I'm chipping in, Ben. But no more and no less than the rest. I'm not after a trek for free. But I'm not a passenger. And you're not a holiday company.'

'Jesus, no. But if you don't mind me asking, Taff, do you have a notion of how hard it'll be?'

'And?'

'It'll be bloody boring, stuck at base camp, unless you like mountain lichens.'

'You won't put me off.' Ieuan kept his arms folded. 'And if it's myself you don't like, say so.'

'No.' Rowley suddenly looked much younger than his age. 'It's not that. You're a stranger. And we're a team.'

'Except Tom. But he's different of course. He's a proper climber. I've got seven years or so to make up. But you'll find

I'm easy enough to live with. I have to get on with people for a living. Like Tom, I want to come along. I think I'm needed. And I won't run the show or bag the mountain. Enough?'

Rowley reddened. 'Someone had to say it. And my name is Rowley. Only my mum calls me Ben.'

'Fine, Rowley. Will you climb tomorrow?'

'If the weather holds.'

'Then try and see if you can burn off the Taff. Let the Rat climb with Petra.'

'OK, Taff.'

Petra, looking from one to the other, recognised that there had been a kind of truce made, but that the true reason for Rowley's misgivings had not been declared. He had provided Ieuan with a *nom-de-crag* which Ieuan would have been quite within his rights to reject. But Ieuan had not, which was why there was a truce. And the reason? Petra guessed that it had something to do with an obscure masculine obsession with the pecking-order. Put crudely, Ieuan was a grammar-school boy and Ben Rowley had made a virtue of evading education.

28 July 1953

On a midday halt, halfway along our march, at a village teahouse among fields of drooping *Amaranthus*, I find myself wondering how this ill-assorted group has come together.

I have been thinking about Colonel E. F. Norton, and the splendid tales of the pre-war Everest climbers. In all those books there are whole chapters on the principles of choosing a team. He claimed to use logic, choosing the Best Man for the Job, as if there were scores of eager applicants. Maybe there were, and most had never climbed a mountain. They used to choose their friends in those days too. But before he chose his friends for the job, he felt he had to tender a good reason. This is a peculiarly masculine trait. I have been called an honorary man, (as in Honorary Consul rather than Hon. Treasurer), with temporary membership of this gentleman's club, so I will do my best to imitate Colonel E. F. Norton, *circa* 1924, and reflect upon the nature of my companions.

First our leader, of whom I can speak no ill. When we return home again I shall become Mrs Harry Lennard, and Harry will find a means of reading this diary, *malgré moi*. (Insert here all the superlatives usually used to describe gentleman mountaineers.) He would no doubt wish me to mention that he was in the Bengal Sappers and Miners on a wartime commission and therefore strictly a 'temporary gent', too.

Tom Ormerod is our mascot. Every team must have a mascot. An infant prodigy from the smokestacks of 'Bruddersford', not born by the normal process but rough-hewn out of Yorkshire gritstone.

Then the Scotsmen, John Paterson and Jock McKie (Pat and Jock) who learned their craft on Sunday outings from Glasgow before the war, then pursued U-boats in the Atlantic for the duration. They are the solid bedrock that every team needs. Jock is almost as good at coaxing a fire out of damp wood as any of the Indian hillmen.

Donald Hayter is our doctor-wallah, thanks to his time in an ambulance unit in the desert. He is a rock gymnast of the worst type, preferring plimsolls to boots, and scrambling up any odd outcrop of rock along the way, simply to keep in practice. Legend has it that he made several first ascents on caravanserai walls and the ruins of desert forts.

John Amory is the photographer (he was something hush-hush on the Home Front), and the only one besides Harry who speaks any Indian language. He learned Urdu out of a book, as one learns Latin, so his pronunciation is the cause of much amusement among the porters.

And lastly the honorary gent. Like Tom, I was too young for the war (except for blackouts and rationing); unlike him I learned to climb with the Girl Guides. I have no house-wifely skills – for these you must apply to Pat and Jock, who can make themselves at home anywhere. I speak no languages, I cannot tie a bandage and I lack all qualities of leadership. What use am I to a team except as elegant luggage?

(Harry, reading this, will deny the 'elegant' in that last sentence.) My role is to write this diary. That completes the team, which was chosen not as a team, but because we had all climbed together and found it good. Colonel Norton are you listening?

29 July 1953

This first part of the trail does not inspire purple passages. The villages are thatched and dirty, and there are pigs and kine in the downstairs rooms. Some of the villagers will sell tea at a price. In this village, an old 'Quit India' slogan has not been erased from the wall. The women hide their faces, and the children pursue us in herds, out of curiosity. But these are the petty foothills, enshrouded in insect-infested jungle, and without grandeur of scale or distance. We move forward, step by step, bowed under the load of rucksacks and sleeping bags, thinking only of the next step and the next breath. When I do pause for breath, I think only of Munshu, far away and out of sight, seven days hence.

The day of departure was set for 17 July. Rowley and the Rat were going out a week early, to get the equipment through customs in Bombay. Daz, Ieuan and Tom were working up until the last minute, because they all had jobs they meant to come back to. Petra and Diane gave up work at the end of June, and helped to pack Rowley and the Rat on their way.

It was a fine English summer, warm enough to go about in T-shirts and shorts. The girls managed to fit in several climbing days between the last-minute shopping and rucksack-packing. It was an expectant time, but relatively calm compared to the months that had gone before. There was now nothing to be done except to travel to the mountain.

Tom rang Petra on 10 July.

'There's something you can do for me. I can't get down to Somerset before we go. But someone has to go, and both you and Diane are free.'

'Somerset?'

'I wrote to Harry Lennard. We haven't met or even written for years. He wants to talk about the expedition.'

'Why?'

'It seems obvious to me.'

'No. Why did you write?'

'He deserves to know that we are returning.'

Petra thought for a moment, but still decided to put the question. 'You think he'd try and stop us?'

'He would have if he'd found out sooner. He may still try.'

'But what can Diane and I do?'

'Tell him what you told me.'

Reluctantly, Petra agreed to go. She was still not quite sure what could be achieved. This was a rather unsettling task to have to perform so soon before setting out for the unknown. It was as if she had turned over a page in a book, and the story was not what she had expected.

Diane came too, for moral support, but also out of Diane-type curiosity. Petra was staying with Diane and Daz in Manchester, having given up her room in Llanberis. They borrowed Daz's van – a decrepit Austin 1100. By the time they came off the M5 in Somerset, the van had boiled once on the motorway, and Petra had a streak of oil on her dress from when she had removed the radiator-cap. Both Petra and Diane had taken the unusual step of putting on dresses, as a vague gesture towards appeasing the unknown. They were trespassing on Hannah Kemp's mountain, and Kemp and Lennard had been inseparable names all those years ago.

Lennard lived in a large thatched house on the edge of a village of creamy yellow stone houses. The green grass verges showed never a dandelion, and roses and honeysuckle climbed up nearly every wall. Lennard's front gate was a rustic archway, and the name 'Manchet House' was carved into a block of stone on the garden wall. Diane parked the car in the lane, and they went in through the gate and knocked at the front door. The doorknocker was a heavy ring held in a lion's jaws.

A woman answered. She was in her fifties, and very well groomed. She was wearing pearls, even though this was a Saturday afternoon at home.

'We've come to see Harry Lennard. We're going on the Himalchand expedition,' said Petra. They had been kept standing on the step.

'I'll ask if he's expecting you.' The woman closed the door. They could hear her calling 'Henry!' Finally they were allowed in, and taken straight through the house to a verandah at the back. Petra caught glimpses of antique furniture and carpets. The place smelt of woodsmoke and beeswax.

'Henry, these young women are from the expedition.' There was a decided note of disbelief in her voice.

'That's right, Sally.' Lennard got to his feet out of the garden chair. He had a stiff leg and had to use a stick.

'Misses Merriman and Ponder? Well, well.' He was a big tall man with a bluff manner. He had the kind of bulk which had once been muscle but which had turned to fat. 'Sit down. Sally will get us some tea, won't you, Sally? Girls, this is Sally, Mrs Lennard.'

They all shook hands. Petra was reminded of her headmaster at school. She could see no sign of the man who might have put up the Cave Route on Ben Ewe, nor yet of the man whom Hannah Kemp had dubbed 'a temporary gent'. She recalled that Harry Lennard was now a bank manager.

'I was intrigued by your little pamphlet. Very professional job. "Expedition Himalchand." Photographs of everyone. Quotes, I notice, from my expedition. How did you produce it?'

'Photocopier,' stammered Petra. 'They let me use the one at the Centre. Mr Gobert-Jones helped a lot.'

'But all these biographical details are true? Alpine seasons, winter ascents. Merriman aged twenty-three, Ponder aged twenty-four. You have crammed a lot in. I just wonder what made you set your sights on Himalchand?'

Petra and Diane replied simultaneously. 'It was obvious.' 'It was Hannah Kemp's diary.'

'Ah.' Lennard had a copy of the expedition's prospectus, presumably sent by Tom. He let the flimsy paper dangle between his finger and thumb.

'Hero, or rather heroine-worship, can lead to disappointment. I ought to tell you what has been left out of the description of that mountain.'

'Tom Ormerod filled us in a lot.'

'Tom? He was younger than you are when we went. And I still doubt if he has any appreciation of danger. Even with these particularly good credentials which you have as lady mountaineers, I doubt if you will do anything but fling yourselves hopelessly at the mountain.' It was said softly, almost pleasantly, but there was an almost overpowering air of condescension. Harry Lennard smiled, and continued. 'Hannah, you understand, was exceptional. And she came to grief because her ambition burned too bright. You are not the first group of young people to come to me. There has been a lot of interest since the border controls were lifted.'

Petra interrupted. 'Tom told us that too.'

'I am no enemy of youthful endeavour.' He continued as if Petra had not spoken. 'I admire your resourcefulness. But you cannot hope to succeed where the likes of Hayter and Amory failed. Even the Scotsmen, who had no imagination at all, had to turn back.'

'What do you mean?' The garden, which had seemed so full of sunshine, suddenly seemed cold. Diane shivered. 'You make it sound spooky.'

'It was, in a way. You have been caught by the lure of the mountain merely at second-hand. The superstitious might call it a force outside nature. I was caught by it too, and I was thirty-two, not twenty-three, when I first heard of

Himalchand. A party failed on it two years before we made our attempt. Did you know? I met them at the old Alpine Club. They were absolutely certain that the route would go. Two of them had had frostbite. The mountain is only 22,000 feet.'

'I don't get it,' said Diane.

'Simply put, that mountain, more than most, seems to encourage people to stick their necks out further than is wise.'

Petra declared doggedly, 'I don't think that'll put us off, actually.'

'I know.' Lennard smiled, not quite pleasantly. 'But you will forgive me for making the attempt.'

Petra found herself staring at his hands. The knuckles were enlarged by arthritis. They gripped the knob of his stick, that other sign of disability. Harry Lennard was no more than ten years older than Tom, but he seemed to be of another generation. He had removed himself to this Somerset garden and forsaken the mountains. He had been one of the great climbers of his generation. And he had disappeared from the record after Himalchand.

'Why did you ask us here?' Petra spoke quietly. 'Was it just to try and put us off?'

Lennard's hands gripped the stick. 'I realise argument is hopeless. You think you've staked too much already.'

'Five hundred pounds,' put in Diane cheerfully.

'Five hundred pounds apiece and seven people. That's a smallish stake against the next fifty years of a lifetime. But age never cuts much ice with youth, unless he appears as an outrageous child like Ormerod. I won't waste any more breath. Just this.' He gripped the stick harder. The air all about them was full of birdsong and the scent of flowers. 'Just this. If you go up the Munshu glacier after all these years, you may find Hannah. Her body was never recovered. You will ensure my gratitude if you keep any such discovery a secret. A sensation of that sort would be quite intolerable.'

The girls stared at him, then glanced at one another.

'Of course,' stammered Petra. She was relieved that he had at last come to the point. 'We wouldn't want to cause trouble. We wouldn't expose her like that.'

But even as she spoke she did not believe that there would be any problem; she could not believe that they had any chance of finding Hannah Kemp's remains on the vastness of the mountain face or the glacier beneath.

Lennard said simply: 'Thank you,' and then his wife brought in the tea.

Three days later, Petra phoned her parents. She could hear the televison turned up loud in the background, with the racing commentary.

'When are you coming home?' asked her mother.

'Can we stay the night before we catch the plane?'

'When's that?'

'July the sixteenth.'

Her mother shouted above the television noise, without trying to mask the phone. 'Dan! Dan, when are the Rotary coming next week?'

The reply was inaudible.

'There won't be room, not with all the rubbish you'll bring.'

'Fine.' Petra could still be surprised at her mother's ability to quench family feeling. 'I'll see you in the autumn.'

'I don't know why you want to go to Nepal anyway. You'll catch something nasty.'

Petra did not even trouble to explain yet again that she was not going to Nepal.

CHAPTER 4

These days there is a bus to Munshu. Travellers do not have to march for eight days through the foothills. The bus runs from the railway terminus at the edge of the Plains.

They had been riding in a jolting train for three hours in the middle of the night. Petra knew that the sun had risen, but she was sluggish about opening her eyes. Sleep seemed an infinitely desirable memory.

'Pet, look!' Diane had the window seat, a flat wooden board beside a barred, glassless opening. Dust swirled in through the window.

'What?'

'The *Himalaya*.'

She looked out, and found that she had to look upwards a long way. The mountains began suddenly. Dark green foothills, clothed in forest, rose straight out of the flat cultivated plain. Above them was the dawn sky, and floating between sky and hills was the pearl pink shimmering line of the Great Snows.

'It's real?' asked Petra.

Diane leant against the bars, staring dreamily. 'It's real.'

The seven climbers waited at the bus station with a great pile of luggage. There were stout cardboard boxes, small crates and bulging kitbags, as well as their multicoloured rucksacks. The total weight of gear was of the order of half a ton, and it included none of the base camp or porters' rations. This was a modern, lightweight, Alpine-style expedition.

The weather was incredibly hot, despite the low-lying cloud which hid all but the nearer hills. The mountaineers were clad in shorts (for the men) or baggy cotton trousers (for the girls, bought in a hurry in a Delhi bazaar). They had subsisted for several days on tea and chapattis. Everyone was determined to arrive in the mountains without having contracted Delhi belly.

The bus was a long time in coming, but there was a general atmosphere of holiday which prevented anyone, even Rowley, from complaining about the delay. The Rat had tried to start a sweepstake on the departure-time of the bus. He had not been able to find out anything useful from the bus company office. This may have been because his method of communication with Indian officials (acquired rapidly but by hard experience at the customs in Bombay) was to say the same simple phrase over and over again, very loudly. The effect was to make the official promise anything one asked, provided one came back later.

'Winner takes all if the bus doesn't go by ten,' stated the Rat.

'Why ten?' asked Rowley idly.

'It's called 'gate rules'. It's a local rule to stop two buses meeting in a narrow stretch of road. A one-way system for large vehicles.'

'How do you know?'

'I've been talking to the first-class passenger. He's a schools inspector. Very informative. He says the bus is late starting because the bus from Munshu isn't in yet. The road has probably been swept away.'

'What?' exclaimed Diane.

'Apparently it's a regular hazard.'

'But what do they do?'

'About a hundred men with shovels come and dig out a bit of new road.'

Daz was picking at his insect bites. He was sitting on the crated luggage as if anxious that it might disappear if he looked away. 'How did you manage to talk to him? None of the bus station people speaks any English.'

'Oh, he speaks English. Here he comes. Mr Karia. I think he's going to want to be introduced.'

The Rat hailed a short dapper gentleman, an Indian in a pale grey pyjama-suit with a high buttoned collar. His only luggage appeared to be a small tin trunk. Despite the heat and dust, Mr Karia was as clean and fresh as if his clothes had just come from the laundry. Petra, who, like the others had spent all night on the train (to save hotel bills), was conscious of her own scruffiness.

'Good morning, good morning,' said Mr Karia. He made the Hindu greeting, hands together as if in prayer, with a slight, self-deprecating bow. It was oddly ceremonious, for a chance meeting in a provincial bus station.

'I am very happy to be meeting such intrepid mountaineers. I myself have made some small treks when I was in Officers' Training Corps at school. I was at Mohinder Kaur Academy in Chandigarh. May I ask which school you attended, Mr Radinsky?'

It was an odd question, but then an education inspector might be expected to map out the world in terms of the locations of people's schools.

'Peckham Lower School,' replied the Rat. He introduced everyone by name, together with two further Peckham Lower Schools and one each of Oldham High, Lady Wheatcroft School for Girls, Tranearth Welsh School and Huddersfield Elementary School.

Mr Karia shook hands with Tom. 'You are the uncle of the young persons?'

'Only by adoption.'

'I admire such very intrepid young ladies. May I ask if it is usual for ladies to climb mountains?' He had avoided looking directly at Petra or Diane, out of respect for them, or his own modesty.

Tom kept a straight face. 'It's unusual, but not unheard of. Are you going to inspect a school at Munshu, Mr Karia?'

'No. There is only village school at Munshu. Twenty-four boys and four girls. Sadly, girls are not often educated in these backward places. I myself am on vacation. I hope to obtain botanical specimens but also to breathe the healthy mountain air. If weather permits I shall admire the view of Himalchand.'

'Is that a famous view?' Tom spoke slowly, as if surprised that Mr Karia had even heard of the mountain.

'Oh, certainly. She is incarnation of a goddess, one of the manifestations of Parvati, the daughter of the mountains. There is a small temple at Munshu. I shall be paying my respects there also.'

'I heard the goddess was a moon-goddess,' said Tom.

Petra blinked in the dusty sunshine. It was quite peculiar to hear Tom, with his utterly down-to-earth Yorkshire voice, talking seriously about moon-goddesses. That was something from ancient Greek myth, like Athena or Helen of Troy – the kind of subject which had been hastily skated over at Peckham Lower School as a piece of rote learning.

Petra had only vague ideas about other people's superstitions. The Asian kids at her school had been either resolutely irreligious or unprepared to talk about it. She had not been prepared for this kind of culture-shock. Or for India. There were so many people. The streets and fields and stations were full of them, all hurrying busily to scrape a living. It had been the enormous number of people which had astonished Petra most when she emerged from the airport at Delhi: not the heat and dust, or the baroque, unintelligible script of the shop signs, but the huge numbers of foreign people in pyjamas and saris, and their incessant activity. Someone had once told her that the pace of life in the East was slower. After one near-miss by a Vespa scooter on a street crossing, and the experience of hurtling across Delhi in an old Morris Oxford-type taxi, she had concluded that life moved slowly only because most people had to walk. The Indians were busy, and absorbed in their own lives, and a party of English mountaineers was merely a matter of passing curiosity.

But beneath the busy material world was this astonishing closeness to the spiritual. Himalchand was not merely a mountain, but also a goddess. Mr Karia took the matter seriously, but in a practical fashion; rather as a Catholic might discuss their patron saint; or as if discussing a friend or neighbour whom one had a duty to visit. He was also keen to explain, schoolmaster-fashion.

'Indeed Himalchand is identified with the moon, and with the goddess Parvati. At certain seasons, the moon may be invoked at the shrine in Munshu, for the perpetuation of the seasons. This is merely a local tradition. The manifestations of the goddess are many and will change from place to place.'

And so on. But at least Mr Karia had informed them as to the cause of the delayed bus. And the cause for the delay was the forces of nature, not some petty form-filling officialdom. This served to reassure Petra that they were nearing the heart of the matter, even if the bus was delayed by a monsoon landslide on the road, and the journey might indeed have to wait until tomorrow.

Mr Karia, warming to his subject, invited them all to take tea with him at a nearby hotel.

'Can't leave the luggage,' said Diane.

'That is no problem.' Suddenly Mr Karia seemed to have adopted them all. 'I will arrange a porter.'

'What about *baksheesh*?'

'I will pay the man what is customary and you may repay me. Come.'

What Mr Karia had referred to as a cup of tea turned out to be something rather more substantial. The 'hotel' was an eating house and meeting place, patronised by the off-duty bus drivers and their waiting passengers. There were no other foreigners in the room. The place was an open-fronted shop in a concrete building from which the upper storey was missing. The flat roof bristled with the ends of reinforcing bars. The sign 'Mahal Hotel', red on black in English and Hindi (proprietor A. S. Singh), hung slightly crooked. At the entrance, a fat man in a turban sat at a till. Opposite him was an enormous clay-built cooking range with a fire burning inside, and various pots sitting over holes in the top. When a pot was removed, flames would shoot upwards. A vast black kettle boiled away, together with stew pots and a slowly expanding mound of rice. A small thin man, shirtless and covered in sweat, was busily frying things in a deep pan of oil. His hands moved quickly, throwing little three-inch-wide chapattis into the oil, watching as they expanded like small crisp balloons, and then flipping them over with a skimmer to crisp on the other side.

'You will take some of these *puri*? With vegetables?' Mr Karia gave the order. The tea came in small glass tumblers, boiled with condensed milk. The vegetable was an intense potato curry which was no match for the tea. The puri were quite delicious.

'Next best thing to a chip butty,' remarked Daz.

They sat on benches around a table, on which a Fablon tablecloth was punched with cigarette burns. Someone had painted stars on the ceiling. Very politely, Mr Karia found out all there was to know about each of his new friends. But he was also extremely informative about himself. He was thirty-five years old, as yet unmarried, with aged parents at home. He was a city type through and through, interested in films and music and books. He had to travel long distances in his work, and stay away from home in government rest houses, and this gave him lots of time to read. His particular passion was for Thomas Hardy, an author with no connection whatever with Chandigarh.

Ieuan turned out to be the most valuable member of the team in this context. The only other person who read fiction was Diane, but her leanings were towards costume romance. Ieuan had read a bit of Thomas Hardy, and Dickens and Thackeray, despite being the product of a Welsh school. It seemed that a young doctor, stuck in medical residences and unable to leave the hospital when on call, had similar opportunities to read when not actively involved in saving lives.

But a passionate interest in Thomas Hardy was not the reason why Mr Karia had chosen to spend his vacation travelling to Munshu.

'Regarding this mountain, I have read also that very excellent book *New Moon of the Snows*.'

Ieuan nodded. Tom, who had been wryly sipping his tea, put down his glass very carefully. 'Aye. What's that, Mr Karia?'

'You are Thomas Ormerod. I am very fortunate to have met you. It is a remarkable coincidence.'

'Aye. I should have guessed.'

'I speak most seriously. I have read this book many times. It has a strong spiritual sense. It is no mere adventure.'

Tom spread both hands wide on the plastic tabletop, palms downward. 'It was a long time ago. There's no magic to it.'

'Then may I ask why you are returning?'

'I want to climb the mountain. That's all. We all want to climb it.'

Mr Karia smiled politely, and did not press the question. Nonetheless Petra had an idea that he had not given up his notion of the spiritual quest of the expedition. She even entertained the idea that he might be right, in a way, although the climbers used a different vocabulary.

Ieuan, by way of diversion, said, 'I take issue with you over the question of coincidence, Mr Karia. You're following Hardy's notion of the fates taking a hand in everything. Our chance meeting here – we'd have to meet here because it's the only way up to Munshu, and this is the season to travel there, and there are eight first-class seats on the bus. There, it's pure logic.'

Mr Karia agreed, but with the same evident reservations as before.

Here it ended, because a man came in to announce that the bus was ready to depart: 'Harigarh, Kalam, Udinath, Munshu.'

They all hurried out to reclaim their luggage and move it on to the bus. Nothing had been stolen. Mr Karia was left behind at the hotel until the very last minute, arguing with Ieuan about who should pay the bill.

The road to Munshu was an eight-hour drive, which would be accomplished within the hours of daylight only with difficulty. The bus was packed full, with the eight 'first-class' seats in two rows at the front, and another twenty-odd people on longwise benches at the back. The floor was stacked with bags and baskets (although there was no livestock). The expedition kit was stacked on the roof-rack. The bus was built like a lorry, with handmade coachwork consisting of tin-plate panels nailed to a wooden frame. The framework was slightly flexible, and thus the bus tended to creak while cornering. Each panel was painted with a different design or motto. The rear doors had 'Horn please' in Hindi and English, painted large. Across the windscreen a number of icons and models of gods hung suspended beneath a multicoloured tinsel fringe. There were two horns: a loud one for pedestrians and goats and a softer, more respectful one for wandering cows. The driver was a small wiry man in a khaki uniform. His hair was greased down, and he smoked incessantly while driving. Evidently he found his job quite exciting.

Petra had thought that she was accustomed to danger, but here she found that danger could take a number of forms. The road had 8,000 feet of ascent overall, but multiplied this by at least three by climbing over spurs and ridges above the river valley. It achieved the ascents and descents by means of tight hairpin bends. Sometimes there was a clear 3,000 feet down to the river, a drop made the more perilous by the shifting, unstable nature of the mountainside. The hairpin sections were often those where there was evidence of earlier landslips, and occasionally quite large boulders sat in the middle of the road, having fallen from above. Sometimes, where the road had been buried by a previous landslide, the tarmac surface was replaced by loose shale.

The driver once attempted to light his cigarette while in the middle of one of the more exciting sections. This required him to strike a match (no question of a cigarette lighter). After two matches had failed to ignite, (both hands off the steering wheel), Mr Karia, who was sitting next to the driver, offered to do the job for him. The cigarette was lit just in time for the next bend, and the driver swung the bus around in fine style. Because of the gradient, and the laden condition of the bus, it was necessary to accelerate into each bend, with a last-minute clash of gears as the double-declutch just failed to match the revs.

The back-seat passengers burst into a chanting prayer from time to time, accompanied by the ringing of holy bells. The mountaineers hung on to the seats, or the superstructure, or each other, and invoked their own gods.

'Hell's bells.' Daz, on the seat next to Mr Karia, had the best view of the gear change. Diane sat on the offside seat and squeaked from time to time as the bus appeared to overhang the very edge of the precipice.

Rowley had the seat behind her. 'Look, Di, there's a burnt-out jeep in the river bed.'

She put her hands over her eyes. 'I wish we'd walked.'

'There!' Tom, sitting next to Rowley, leant across to Diane and pointed. 'Look, you can see the old track on the other side. That's the path we took. It looks as if it's not much used now.'

They all leant across to peer through the mud-spattered window. The hillside opposite was steep and green, low scrub dotted with larger pine trees, the upper slopes disappearing into the cloud. A tiny village was perched among precariously terraced fields, about 2,000 feet above the river. Below the village, the hillside sprouted a series of black outcrops of rock. There was a tiny wooden bridge across the torrent in the river bed. A faint green zigzag led from the bridge to the village.

'There are forty-seven bends on that path,' said Tom. 'We counted every one. It's the way over the hill, which avoids the gorge in the next bit of river.'

'The Kala gorge?' Rowley peered upwards, into the concealing cloud.

'That's right. The road blasts a tunnel through, nowadays. I guess we'll hardly see the gorge.'

He was wrong. The bus swung around the last uphill bend, and a hundred yards or so of level road was visible ahead. The road crossed a tributary river on a Bailey bridge, skirted a few lesser spurs of the mountain, and made a last sudden turn to disappear into the hillside.

'I can't see the tunnel entrance,' remarked Daz.

'It's up there.' Diane pointed.

After a moment Daz whistled through his teeth, craning his head. 'Sweet Jesus.'

The road had been obliterated for twenty yards or so by a fresh landslide. The tunnel entrance was half a dozen bends further on, a small black O in the green mountainside. The landslip was a seething, mobile cone of grey shale, brought down by a minor torrent from the mountain far above. Small fountains of water spurted among the stones. There was already a traffic jam on both sides of the obstruction. The outwards jam consisted of a taxi, two mules, a lorry and a party of women carrying sickles. The inwards jam included a herd of goats, several men with umbrellas, a jeep, another lorry and the bus.

Everyone got down and went to look at the problem. This was clearly not the first landslip at this site. More loose shale was piled up against the hillside below, right down to the river. It had dammed up the river to form a small lake.

'Well, we get a good view of the Kala gorge,' remarked Tom.

'I'd rather see a bulldozer.' Daz kicked at one of the stones. This started a minor landslide of its own.

'Don't do that.' Diane clutched at his arm. Other passengers were peering at the mound of stones, exchanging remarks in the local language.

'What shall we do?' asked the Rat.

Mr Karia, picking his way fastidiously through the mud in his city shoes, shook his head. 'This is big problem. A road gang will come tomorrow. The people are saying we will have to spend night in bus.'

'How far to a village on the far side?'

'Too far. Besides the tunnel is very dark.'

'We've got torches. Maybe some of us can get across on foot. Maybe that taxi could be persuaded to turn round and take us back.'

'It is possible.'

Just then Rowley shouted 'Yeek!' and pointed upwards. There was a horrid rumbling noise. Everyone turned and ran back towards the bus as more stones came singing past through the air.

The mountaineers collapsed, panting, at the roadside. The back-seat passengers got out their holy bells again and began praying.

'Not that way, I would suggest.' Tom was sitting on a reassuringly mossy boulder.

'Then we sit in the bus till the roadmen come?' The Rat was disgusted. 'Well, we can't get all the gear through by carrying it ourselves. We'd need a car, or porters, or horses. The gear has to stay with the bus.'

Daz chucked another stone over the edge. 'Well, Rat, you're the logistic wiz. What's your idea?'

'Who wants to walk?'

Diane groaned.

'Well, who really doesn't want to walk?' continued the Rat.

'Not over that stuff. It's lethal.'

'That wasn't my idea.'

'Oh?' Diane, and everyone else, looked hard at the Rat.

'If Tom can find where the old path goes down, you can get to that village. It's got to be better than camping in the bus. There's a couple of hours of daylight left. Then tomorrow we can meet up again in Udinath.'

'Brilliant,' said Daz ironically.

'You need the exercise.'

'No I don't.'

'Then you'd volunteer to stay with me at the bus?'

Petra gazed at the mountainside, and the vast deep cleft of the Kala gorge, and the tiny precarious traces of man's habitation there. She suddenly wanted to get away from the crumbling muddy road and the rickety bus. She wanted to get away from the atmosphere of argument and frustration.

'Let's take the old path. Tom?'

He nodded his head.

'Ieuan, Rowley, Diane?' Then, out of politeness rather than expectation, 'Mr Karia?'

Mr Karia declined. He would stay with Daz and the Rat and the luggage, and would help with any communication problems. But the other five would take the walk.

The old way led down from the road by the Bailey bridge, a hundred yards back. It followed the slanting bank of a ravine, before running along beside the river to the old bridge. Thereafter, even though the travellers were very lightly laden, the upwards track was pure, relentless toil. Hannah, as ever, had described the route better than Petra ever could. Petra recognised landmarks as they went by.

8 August 1953

> The Kala gorge is a great cleft in the mountain, where a black cliff diverts the eastward-flowing river to the south. The left bank is a sheer precipice, 4,000 feet of black rock, interrupted by waterfalls. The right bank is a nearly vertical green meadow, with a jigsaw puzzle of tiny field terraces. We lunched at the river crossing below the gorge. We left the porters there, cooling their feet in the stream in the heat of the day. The English (and Scots) walked uphill through a series of forty-seven zigzags on a green path two yards wide. The stones of the path were very ancient. Where a *nala* or side torrent had destroyed part of the path, it had been repaired with meticulous stonemasonry. The traffic is light at midday, but one may see shepherd boys and girls with their flocks, and women working in the fields. A sort of vertical Arcadia, though the local grown men seem to be somewhere else. Perhaps they are portering across the Tibet border, or employed in road-mending. Perhaps they sit

around under an apricot tree in the village, smoking, in one of those endless *panchayats* which seem to be the equivalent of a Parish Council hereabouts. I wish that I shared the language; not as Harry or John Amory do, for shouting at porters, but so that I could understand how the people can live from day to day in these villages.

We came into Kala village just as the sun had gone behind the black cliff opposite. It was still some time until sunset, but the loss of the direct rays made us all feel cold after sweating our way out of the valley. Harry says this is the only way to acclimatise to altitude. While we sat on a wall by a millet-field, Harry went to see the elders to talk about camping-sites. The son of the village chief brought tea, and stayed to chat. He is a slim youth of about fifteen, with a fine pencilled moustache. The tea came with salt and butter, in the Tibetan style. Kala marks the boundary between the true mountain people of Udinath and Munshu, who live by trade with Tibet, and grow only a few potatoes and millet, and the pastoral, rice-growing folk of the lower valley. The boy wore a sheepskin coat and baggy breeches, and had the face of a Central Asian, almost Chinese. His breeches were tied with a red sash, giving him a bandit-like swagger. Lesser villagers wear homespun, but many of the women have silver jewellery, or gold rings in their noses.

The boy wants to come with us. Not for pay, but for the thrill of it. His excuse is that he has cousins in Munshu, two days' walk away. But he confides to us that his ambition is to be the one to show us our first sight of the mountain. I have lent him my support, though the leadership are expressing their doubts. They are afraid they will have to pay him.

He has paid me a compliment. He compares me favourably with their goddess, who has an idol at Munshu. The boy's name is Kotai Singh. We call him 'Tai' for short.

Fate, in the form of a landslide, had sent Petra and her friends on a diversion to Kala. The view of the black cliff was the same, a massive promontory of unstable rock, now punctured by a 400-yard tunnel and scarred by the many landslips associated with the road. The path still had forty-seven bends, but the storm damage was no longer so neatly repaired. In places the path was a fine-beaten line, snaking across the debris in the bed of a *nala*. The village itself still had an apricot tree in the square by the temple.

The boys and girls were bringing home the cattle when the climbers arrived in the village. The mooing of the cows provided a bass note to the tinny clinking of their bells and the shouts of the children.

'I need a beer,' remarked Rowley, as he dumped his rucksack by the tree.

People began to gather. They chattered and stared, and for the first time since Petra had arrived in India she was conscious of being at the centre of attention. All the women clustered around, making a gesture with their right hand, passing a finger across their lips and pointing up the gorge.

'*Ke upar?*' one asked.

Petra shrugged her shoulders. Other women were gathering around Diane, touching her clothes and making admiring noises about her auburn hair.

'Himalchand,' she said, and pointed to the north-west. This provoked a whole burst of conversation, none of it understandable.

Ieuan and Tom had arrived ahead of the others, and they were already the target of attention from the men.

'*Angrezi?*' The speaker was a gnarled old man with an embroidered cap and waistcoat. He walked with a staff, but perfectly upright, as if the staff were a badge of office.

'*Hanji*,' said Ieuan, who had picked up a few useful words. '*Panchayat hai?*'

The old man pointed at himself. '*Sirdar hum. Sri Kotai Singh.*'

Tom, who had been sitting down on his rucksack, looking

tired, levered himself to his feet. '*Tai Singh*? I'm Tom Ormerod.' He put out his hand. He was a head taller than the other man. But Tai Singh, now the village headman, had that air of eminence which is conveyed by advanced years. He was definitely an elder, and proud of it. He was probably five years younger than Tom.

'Do you remember me?' Tom made no attempt to jump the language barrier. There was no need. Tai Singh leapt forward and clasped Tom's hand in both of his.

'Tom Sahib. *Accha. Accha. Shabash*.' The handshaking went on for several minutes. Then: 'I remember so well. We are both old old men. These are your children?'

Rowley gave a snort of laughter, then covered his mouth with his hand.

'No. Young friends. We're going to Himalchand. Tomorrow.'

Tai Singh let go of Tom's hand and spread his arms wide. 'Tomorrow, Himalchand Pahar. Today, *bara tamasha*.'

'What's that?' Rowley interrupted.

Ieuan whispered in his ear: 'It's a big party. Maybe you'll get that beer.'

'Good,' declared Tom. '*Bara tamasha*. Eh, it's good to see you again, young Tai.'

Petra saw, as probably none of the others did, that Tom was no longer present in the here and now. He was back in the Everest year, a young man again, with no tally of failures. And Tai Singh had been a friend of his then. It was really an extraordinary piece of luck that they had survived to meet again like this.

Sri Kotai Singh gave orders to right and left. Many of the younger people present were his sons and daughters. He presented each of them by name to Tom, who stayed under the apricot tree as if holding court. The apricots were pale and unripe, as they had been when Hannah came through Kala.

'This is magic,' said Rowley. He had got his breath back,

and his face was not quite such a bright shade of red. 'It's a sight better than staying by the bus.'

'I expect there are little biting things in the beds.' Ieuan was still trying to maintain his lugubrious face, but was failing; the strong vertical lines spread into a smile. A goat was trying to nibble his shirt and a tiny girl tried to pull the animal away. 'The folk seem friendly enough, though we're a bit of an invasion.'

Diane, slightly cross from all the probing fingers, said: 'We're a show at the fairground. I bet this is the most exciting thing that has happened in years.'

Petra had been enthralled by the whole scene, just as Rowley was. 'Well, it's the most exciting thing that has happened to us so far.'

'Pity about Daz,' said Rowley.

'And the Rat?'

'Ah, he's got logistics badly. He's much happier organising a landslide.'

Another small child appeared, balancing turned brass tumblers on a tray. '*Chang*,' it whispered.

'What's that, Taff?' Rowley had unjustified faith in Ieuan's understanding of the language.

The doctor peered into the tumbler which he had taken from the tray. The contents were pale grey and opaque, with nameless lumps floating just below the surface. There was a fine white line of froth at the rim; the odour was of school disinfectant.

'*Chang*. Fermented god-knows-what. It's like beer mush, which hasn't grown into beer yet.'

'Is it safe?'

'It'll probably kill you as well as the bugs. You wanted beer, Rowley. Drink it.'

Diane sipped her portion. 'Peugh.'

Rowley, true to his reputation for heedless courage, drank the lot. His chubby face went pale, almost green. 'That's a man's drink all right.'

Ieuan, the object of everyone's attention, now followed suit.

His efforts at not blinking an eyelid were plain to behold. Petra, finding it was her turn, took a mouthful. The taste was of something dead, preserved for years in embalming fluid. She swallowed quickly, before the taste could make her sick.

'I hope there's something else at this party besides *chang*.'

Some men began to clear a space on the threshing floor in front of the tree. The ground was paved with irregular flat stones and there was chaff in the chinks between. The terrace was surrounded by a low wall, upon which people sat. Outside the wall, the ground was a mixture of mud and animal dung. The houses surrounding the square were built of rough stone faced with mud, with the same large irregular flagstones on the roofs. There were two storeys to each house, but the lower storey housed animals and storerooms.

It became apparent that the ground was being cleared for dancing. Petra put down her cup and went over to Tom under the tree.

'Have you found out where we are to sleep?'

'I imagine this'll go on all night.' But he asked Tai Singh, accompanying the question with a pantomime of sleeping. The headman laughed and gestured largely towards the biggest of the houses around the square.

'Take my house. I will go to my brother.'

Tom demurred.

'You also are my brother,' declared Tai. 'As Ana was my lovely big sister. She is in heaven.'

'Aye,' said Tom. He made no more argument.

The expedition members watched the dancing from the balcony of the house. The supply of *chang* went round and round, apparently inexhaustible. Petra discovered an advantage in being a female. She was not really expected to drink. Tai Singh's sister brought *puri* and a kind of vegetable curry called, apparently, 'budgie'. For the teetotal there was tea with butter. Petra found that this was actually rather nice, certainly compared to the *chang* – it had a savoury, salty taste like warm soup.

The dancing went on and on. The *chang*, though only weakly alcoholic, had a sleep-inducing effect, particularly after the long climb up from the river. The music was a mixture of drums, cymbals and bells, played rhythmically in accompaniment to a chanting voice. The effect was almost shockingly foreign. As it got dark someone lit a hurricane lamp, which shed a pool of light in one corner of the square. Otherwise torches made of resinous wood, in the medieval style, provided the only other source of illumination.

Petra, cross-legged on the balcony, stared wide-eyed.

'It's like we're on another planet.'

Ieuan was at her shoulder. 'We're the aliens.' His voice was very sleepy.

'But at home there are lots of Indians. And Mr Karia was just like any of them. They're not different like this. Even Tai Singh, in daylight, didn't seem part of this.'

'They're uncorrupted.' Ieuan's accent, usually unclassifiable, had taken on a distinctly Welsh flavour. 'They're the *paharis* – mountain men. I'll bet the Welsh were like this before the Chapel got 'em.'

The music, very fast already, developed an almost frenzied rhythm. The dancers accelerated, and the chanting became a continuous high-pitched ululation.

'They'll be worshipping the old gods,' said Ieuan.

'You're guessing.'

'Sure. But isn't that how it feels?'

Petra peered into the crowd of dancers, then she glanced back at the balcony. Rowley and Diane were leaning over the rail, clapping their hands. Tom was out of sight, in the dark at the back wall.

'We all feel it differently,' said Petra

'And you?'

'I believe it's a dream. I'll wake up. I don't believe it's me here. It'll all disappear when I turn my back.'

'You're superstitious?'

'I suppose so. I can't help remembering what Hannah said.'

9 August 1953

They worship the mountains as gods. Not as the abode of gods, like the ancient Greeks, but as actual deities. I have found out that the *paharis* think that we are on a pilgrimage, going to make some sacrifice to Himalchand. It is hard not to be affected somewhat by this knowledge. We are all capable of mountain-worship to some degree. I remember the summer before the war when I was taken to Scotland with the Guides. The two leaders were called Bea and Muff (Bea with a red fringe and Muff with a dark fringe, both liking to dress alike). We took the train to Mallaig and went over the sea to Skye. It was not your usual sort of guide camp. Bea and Muff were climbers, of a generation in which there were too many spare women, because of the First World War. They were hoping to instil their enthusiasm into the four girls who accompanied them. With me they succeeded. I remember a long day out on the Pinnacle Ridge of Sgurr nan Gillean. It was not an easy route, and not a sensible place to take novices. One of the girls had the heebie-jeebies at the top of the abseil pitch. But I loved it, slippery wet rock and all. I slid down the rope in a state of sheer abandon, trusting myself entirely to the anchorage on the mountain. I crept over the loose mossy pinnacles, and jammed myself into chimney-cracks, and finally ran down the scree below Am Bhasteir. I might as well have been flying. The Cuillin of Skye were blue and jagged, and the mist drifted on and off the peaks, like a veil. I said to myself: 'I shall return.' I say this to every mountain. But I have never yet repeated the Pinnacle Ridge. Maybe I shall one day, when I am old, and have a novice to inspire. But for today I am not finished with new peaks. I must pay my respects to Himalchand. I have a feeling that Mrs Harry Lennard will not be going climbing in the Himalaya. This is my last great peak. *Ave* Himalchand!

The party faded away when the dancing ended. Petra had fallen asleep where she sat, and she had to be shaken awake.

She blinked her eyes open, and saw the last of the torches retreating down the narrow paths of the village. The music had gone, but its cacophony still echoed in her head. The night was very still and dark.

Diane was still shaking her. 'Come on, slug. We have to creep into our sleeping bags.'

'It's too warm.'

'Well, we have to creep indoors anyway. The gents are lying on the verandah. Someone has let slip that we aren't married to any of them. We have to seem respectable.'

'How Victorian. I'll bet no one cares.'

'Tom says to be a bit careful. We need their help with porters and things.'

Indoors was very dark indeed, and stuffy, smelling of woodsmoke and onions. Petra's hand-torch revealed a pile of rugs in the corner, a pile of cold charcoal in an old oil-tin, two cooking pots, a Hindu holy picture and some half-finished knitting. There was no bed or other furniture. The knitting, on closer inspection, was being done on old umbrella-spokes. The wool was the same grey homespun that the men of the village wore. Petra's sleeping bag, spread on the earthen floor, was a garish mix of orange and purple. Her small rucksack, meant for lightweight travel, contained nearly as many possessions as the whole of Tai Singh's room. And he was among the more affluent of the villagers.

She went to sleep again, her sleeping bag spread directly on the hard floor. Tai Singh's rugs would certainly contain fleas. Besides, it seemed that the expedition was already accepting too much of the headman's hospitality. Petra balked at making use of his bedding too.

Diane, snuggling up beside her, whispered, 'This is out of this world. Fancy us being here.'

'It's only the beginning.'

'But you don't think we'll really manage to climb the mountain?'

'Let's wait and see.'

'It seems more and more impossible the closer we get. I shan't really mind if we don't. Did you see the dear little girls with their silver earrings? And the babies being carried slung on mother's back, with just their little faces showing?'

'Broody, Diane?'

'I was just being appreciative. You never look at anything that's in front of your eyes. You're a star-gazer. I hope you won't be too disappointed if the mountain won't go.'

Petra was silent. The way to the mountain, which had seemed so straight and true when seen from the distant hills of Scotland, had now become a maze. But each turning brought something new. And there was no thought of turning back.

Udinath was back on the main road again. The village street was a strip of tarmac road, bordered by muddy ditches, and faced by a double row of stone or concrete buildings. Behind one row of houses, the mountainside fell nearly sheer to the river; behind the other was the usual terraced slope, dotted with deodar trees.

Petra, Tom, Ieuan, Rowley and Diane came down the old path through the fields in single file. The day was fine, and they had started early from Kala. By walking on the old, high-level path, they had seen views of the gorge and the mountains which would not have been possible through the windows of a bus. The landscape changed slowly as they progressed: the impossibly steep hillsides were becoming more wooded, with no room for cultivation. But there had still been no sighting of the snow-mountains. Munshu, and the path to Himalchand, was now less than five miles distant as the crow flies. But the walls of the gorge and the lower, nearer peaks still stood in the way. And although the walk was splendid in its way, it was an incomplete recompense for the frustration of losing a day in the approach to the mountain.

Udinath was in sight from time to time, but was lost to view during the final steep descent. The last part of the path formed a flight of steps, down to a valley between the houses. At the top of the steps, Petra came to a halt and Tom nearly ran into her.

'The place is full of lorries. Does that mean the roadblock is open?'

'Which way are they facing?'

'Up.'

'Can you see the bus?'

The narrow street was one great traffic jam. The lorries were painted in the same gay colours as the bus, and there was a good deal of engine-revving and horn-blowing. A crowd of people surrounded the vehicles, and some of the cargo was already being unloaded. Some of the people had evidently come just to watch. Petra counted seven lorries. The bus, if present, would have to be around the corner of the street.

'Let's go and look,' said Tom. As they wove their way through the crowd, Petra realised that some of the people coming the other way had been on the bus with them. The people were in an uncharacteristic hurry, and were carrying bundles and bags. In the crowd, the five climbers became separated, but Tom and Petra arrived together at the bus.

The driver had the engine open, and was wiping his hands with an oily rag. A cigarette still dangled from his lip. The expedition luggage was in a heap in the middle of the road. Beside the heap, Daz and the Rat were arguing and gesticulating at one another. The Rat had lost his cap and his curly hair stood on end. Daz had his hands in his pockets and was drooping slightly. Whatever they were shouting about was not audible in the general din of engines, horns and people. Mr Karia, looking disconsolate, stood at a distance, with his tin trunk at his feet.

'Daz!' There was no response to Petra's shout. Tom elbowed his way forwards. When the young men saw him they stopped shouting. The Rat turned on Tom instead.

'At last!'

'Well done getting here,' said Tom.

'We've been here since nine. The bus to Munshu is at the far end of the street. We'll miss it.'

'Hang on, lads. A day won't matter one way or the other.'

'What if there's another landslide?'

Petra realised the effect the night at Kala had had on all of them. The Rat, stuck with the luggage and the bus, had not had the chance to slough off the pressures of civilisation. He was still in a hurry.

'Fine.' Tom sat down on one of the boxes. 'We'll have to make two trips.'

'Where are the others?'

'They're on their way.'

Petra put down her own small rucksack. 'We had an interesting time in Kala.'

'Lucky lot,' snarled the Rat.

It was some time before the other three arrived. They were laughing, and eating something out of a paper bag. The bag was greasy, and appeared to have been made from old newspapers. Daz growled at Diane. She blinked at him, and offered the bag. 'Have a *pakora*?'

There was only one left. The Rat refused his share. 'I've got the shits,' he said gloomily.

They got the bus in the end, despite failing to bribe the driver to wait for them. Mr Karia was not on the bus. He had decided to spend the night in a government resthouse in Udinath. 'I will see you tomorrow?' he said brightly. They said goodbye, but did not expect to see him again.

One passenger was even later catching the Munshu bus than was the expedition. He actually ran down the street after the bus and clung to the ladder which ran up to the roof-rack at the back. Someone opened the rear door and pulled him inside. He fought his way up to the front, and tapped Tom on the shoulder.

'*Namaste!*'

It was one of Tai Singh's sons, on his way to Munshu. His appearance on the bus did not seem to be mere chance. His attitude was benevolent, but his English was even worse than Ieuan's Hindi, and no one could be quite sure if he had come along specifically to lend a hand. There were '*namastes*' all round.

This evidence that local help had been recruited was the only thing which could have made Daz and the Rat realise that there had been some use in what they persisted in referring to as the 'outing' to Kala. They had had a very bad night, and needed the encouragement of continued progress.

At last the journey's end, the cluster of houses at Munshu, came in sight. It was nothing like Kala. A few dozen low houses occupied a promontory by the side of a subsidiary gorge. The road crossed a metal bridge below the village, and the bridge had a military guardpost beside it. A soldier with a rifle stood at the far end of the bridge; his home was a brown tent by the roadside. The soldiers saluted the bus. Then the bus roared to a halt outside a teahouse. A few shabby men were hanging around at the bus stop, without any apparent reason for being there. A dog sat outside the shop, scratching itself.

The luggage came down off the roof-rack and formed its usual heap. The mountaineers stood by the roadside, stretching their limbs.

'What now?' said Rowley.

There was a small silence. It was like a pause for breath, as the journey's end turned into the beginning of something else.

CHAPTER 5

10 August 1953

We have come a weary way from the Plains, and still have not seen the mountain. Munshu is no metropolis. It is a kind of staging post on the trail which leads to Tibet. Here the caravans of yaks halt after a day's march, during the season. The passes are not yet open, so there are no travellers from the north as yet. But in a week or two they will come past, bound for the market at Harigarh. The Tibetans bring salt, to trade for Indian cloth. This we are told by Tai Singh, whose family makes a yearly investment in the trade. These bare hills could not support the people by farming alone. Tai Singh has a dagger with a silver hilt, and he is free to come adventuring with us, without needing to work for wages.

We find Munshu short of men, the best of them having gone across the border to join the caravans. Men can cross the passes a week or two before they are open to yaks. What remains in the village is a pack of women: sturdy independent women with kilted skirts and plaited hair, and yak-hide boots sewn with beads. They crow at the beauty of Tai Singh, and ply him with sweets. The rest of us they ignore. They do not speak Hindi – at least not the Indian Army Hindustani in which Harry addresses them. Thus we have to use the boy as a go-between, although all my fellow Britons are suspicious of him. They have the hearty sportsman's dislike of fine clothes and male beauty, as if it were something degenerate.

We have been promised some horses and a horseman to carry our loads up to the glacier. The porters who have been carrying for us from the Plains are adamant that they shall go no further than Munshu. Their contract does not extend to venturing into the abode of demons.

Harry and John Amory have wasted a good deal of argument in trying to persuade them differently. But now they are glad that no reluctant followers will have to be coaxed up to base camp.

Today Tom and I went with Tai Singh up to the temple above the village. The rest of the company are oiling their boots and talking about ice-axe technique. All that remains to be done is to have some grain milled into flour, to supply the last of our food. This is meant to be a day for rest and recuperation, but we young ones find the prospect irksome.

We have been rewarded for our energy. The day, which started with the usual dismal mountain mist, has blossomed into clear skies and blue distances. We are the first to have seen the mountain.

The expedition drew half-a-dozen porters from the muddy dwellings of Munshu. The men were idle during the low season for road construction. They were used to carrying loads, but no one made the trek into Tibet any more. Tom, seated among his young friends at the roadside teahouse, provided an explanation.

'The Chinese Army, as you ought to know, invaded India from Tibet in 1962. They got most of the way into Kashmir.' He sipped at his tea-with-condensed-milk. The only other fare available at the teahouse was a kind of malted-milk biscuit, rather stale.

'That's why the bridges are still guarded. The Indians sent a defensive force, but both sides were hammered by altitude sickness. It was the mountains which won the battle. But then the Indians built this road, and set up permanent military camps near the border. The border itself was slammed shut. No more yak caravans.' He gestured towards the low houses with their corrugated iron roofs. A woman was filling an empty oil can with water at one of the roadside rivulets.

'I can't believe how this place has changed. There aren't any more bright colours.'

The woman, indeed, was wearing black plastic sandals. No more yak-hide boots. The men, when they showed up for work, were in ragged trousers and homespun jackets. Their leader wore a woollen cap, but the rest were bare-headed.

Daz and the Rat went to negotiate. The pile of luggage was composed of units of about sixty pounds each, the recognised standard load for a mountain porter. No one had any weighing scales, but the porters' leader seemed to be able to estimate the weight by feel.

They were all small men. Even the Rat, who for all his chunkiness was no taller than Petra, stood several inches above the tallest. Daz, at over six feet, was a giant. The leader, or sirdar, was a very dark-skinned man with the flat, Tibetan-style face which they had first seen in Kotai Singh. His name was Jumna Singh. He spoke a useful amount of English.

'Twenty rupee,' was the opening gambit.

'Not including food. No food.' Daz made eating gestures and shook his head.

'No food, twenty-five rupee.'

'Twenty.'

'Foreigner-wallah bring food? Twenty.'

'No food.'

Jumna Singh picked up one of the loads, grimacing at the weight. 'Very heavy pack.'

Daz muttered something to the Rat. Jumna Singh began to roll a cigarette.

It was all rather disturbing. Petra knew that this ritual of bargaining was somehow essential. But they were still only talking about a distinction of about forty pence a day per man – the price of a bag of chips at the café in Llanberis.

At home, the expedition members had had to scrape together money for the trip. Petra, who had a low-paid, often seasonal job, had always thought of herself as a frugal person. Every spare penny went on climbing gear. She had come to

India with her worldly goods in the rucksack on her back. It was not much, this collection of rainbow-coloured nylon, and it had a transient lifespan. But it was a clear indication of wealth to the barefoot men in homespun.

Ieuan was sitting next to her. He echoed her thoughts. 'Why not settle it, for God's sake?'

Tom raised a hand. 'It's necessary. For mutual respect. We all know they get twenty-five rupees if they bring their own food. There have been enough expeditions here lately. Daz knows to settle for twenty-five rupees, and then throw in free tobacco and sugar.'

'And when we're halfway to base camp, doesn't everyone go on strike?'

'That's usual. You've read all the books.'

'I can't see it does much for mutual respect. What does Tai Singh's son say about it?'

This young man was happily engaged in chatting to the shopkeeper. The only thing which distinguished him from the porters was the fact that he wore shoes. He had no embroidered jacket or silver dagger. He was probably twenty years old; thin, dark and wiry.

'That lad? He's our credentials.'

'How?'

'He spoke to Jumna Singh. It'll keep the haggling to a minimum.'

'I still don't like it.'

'The pay's good. A road-mender gets five if he's lucky.'

'It's still exploitation. It's the North–South split.'

Rowley put in his oar at this point. He was slightly green about the face, because he was suffering from gut-rot, like his friend the Rat.

'Ah, cut the soggy liberal rubbish, Taff. Right, we're exploiting. So what? They get money, more than any other way, and we get the mountain. It's life. I didn't see you refusing free food from Tai Singh yesterday.'

'That was different.'

'How? Because it was the ancient tradition of Eastern hospitality? *Arabian Nights* stuff?'

'No.'

'You'll go all cultural over the ethnic dancing, but you won't do business with them, is that it?'

'Shut it.'

'Or is it because Tai Singh is a gent and these fellows are just peasants?'

'I said shut it.'

At that point Rowley groaned, leapt to his feet and dashed off into the bushes. A few minutes later he returned, looking still more unwell. 'Sorry, Taff, the local speciality was getting to me.'

'You want a pill for it?'

'No. Better out than in. It was probably the *chang*.'

'Eastern hospitality?'

'Let's leave it there.'

11 August 1953

The hired horseman has chosen his moment to strike for more pay. I, a mere female, have not been involved in the negotiations. It has been a mutual test of manhood between Harry Lennard, John Amory and the horseman. Tai Singh, our self-appointed guide, seems to have no authority. On a three-day march, the strike has been timed for the evening of the first day, already beyond the logistical point of no return. Harry says, 'If we cave in today, he'll strike again tomorrow, to see how far he can go.' But of course it was different in practice than in theory. There is no way Harry can stand firm while the expedition lies around the upper pastures of Munshu, hopelessly stranded unless the horses do the carrying. It was a question of timing the cave-in. Harry's first threat was that the man would get no money for the day he had already worked.

And so it went on.

Petra had come to believe that the mountain was chiefly a logistical and technical problem. The rocks and snowslopes were made up of so many rope lengths, so many blows from the ice-axe. If the climbing team kept the organisational problems well in hand, and they had average good luck with the weather they would get to the top.

They left Munshu on the day following their arrival. By the time they left the village it was about noon, and all the upper valleys were full of grey cloud. It was not a pleasant walk. The path led upwards in a series of zigzags, first through the potato and millet fields of Munshu, and then into the native forest. The altitude was already very high. Munshu was nearly 3,000 feet higher than Kala, and the initial ascent from Munshu was very steep indeed. No one had slept well during the night. They had camped in their tents by the roadside. Rowley and the Rat had had to keep getting up to go to the toilet, and everyone else except Daz had picked up fleas. At seven o'clock, when the sky was barely light, some lorries rumbled by on the road and woke everyone who was still asleep.

The porters did not arrive for work until eleven, by which time the climbers had been packed up and ready to go for some time. When they finally set out, the clouded sky had begun to send down a thin drizzle.

Within an hour, everyone was wet. Despite the altitude, it was too warm to put on waterproofs. The air was totally humid, so sweat would not evaporate. Petra found that her thin cotton clothing had become drenched both inside and out, and her rucksack was stuck firmly to her back by the damp. Her hair dripped into her eyes. Diane, who had plaited her long hair to stop it tangling, had a drip on the end of each plait. Rowley's curls were shimmering with dewdrops.

'Beware leeches,' said Tom.

They all kept a nervous look-out for them. They were rumoured to be able to get through the lace-holes of boots and said to inhabit the trees and drop down on to unwary passers-by.

'They're little beasts, about an inch long. Black and slimy, like small slugs. They swell up when they're full of blood, and then you can see them more easily.'

'Yergh.' Diane shivered. They had stopped for a rest after the first hour of marching, during which they had climbed relentlessly uphill. No one had much breath for humour.

'What do you do about them?' Petra found that her legs were weak from the exertion, and she could not imagine bearing anything further in the way of misery.

'You put a lighted cigarette on their tails.'

'We don't smoke.'

Ieuan had been holding his head in his hands. His wet hair was plastered over his head like a skull. 'If they leave a bit behind, it rots in you. They don't carry disease or anything. But it can cause a nasty sore.'

'Yergh.' Diane batted at her arms and body as if trying to ward off mosquitoes.

'This is the jungle, you know. Jungle is just the Indian word for a wild wood.'

There was still a path, because the route to the glacier lay first through the upper summer pastures used by the villagers of Munshu. The porters knew the way well, and had set off at a great pace, despite their heavy loads. Once they were out of sight, and when even Daz had ceased to attempt to keep up with them, there was nothing but wild wood all around.

The next halt was by a stream. Petra and Diane, arriving last, plunged their faces into the water with cries of joy, but they were almost too weary to be refreshed. The water was the clearest and coolest that they had yet encountered. It was the first source which might be expected to be safe to drink, because it tumbled straight out of the wilderness. The stream bed was rocky and mossy, and various green plants grew there in the dampness. By the stream there was daylight. The steep woods were dark. The trees were tall, and most were evergreen, so there was little undergrowth. The ground was a mat of pine needles covering slippery mud. Without the path, the ascent would have been nearly impossible. Where the tree branches dipped low, strands of Spanish moss hung down like enormous cobwebs. These gave the impression of neglect, as if no one had done any housekeeping for years.

Hannah had never written about this part of the approach. Perhaps it had affected her endless optimism. And Petra was troubled by the darkness and gloom. She felt that this was a place where she was not meant to be, as if by travelling through it she would become haunted by some ancient and unpleasant spirit.

In truth she was very weary, as they all were. Toil, sleeplessness and discomfort all served to shorten tempers and banish tolerance. They set out again, strung along the track, and Petra and Diane fell behind once more.

From time to time Rowley or the Rat would have to stop for hygienic purposes, and then would catch up again. On one occasion Rowley dangled a strand of moss on the back of Diane's neck and said, 'Oh look, leeches.'

The girl screamed, predictably. Only Petra's grip on her arm prevented her from taking off down the steep hillside.

'It's just a joke,' declared Rowley.

'That's bloody unfair. And dangerous.'

Diane, still whimpering slightly, felt at the back of her neck. 'You sure it's gone?'

'It was just Ben being juvenile.'

'Well, if you can't take a joke ...' Rowley stumped away up the path, waving two fingers.

'What got into him?' Diane had recovered her composure completely.

'Dunno. He calls me ma'am sometimes nowadays. Christ, I've known him since we were eleven. If I can't call him things, who can?'

'You don't know about managing men.'

'I don't want to.'

'So you put them off? Have you ever had a proper boyfriend, Petra?'

'What do you mean, proper?'

'You know.'

'Well, nothing very thrilling.'

'And you with your chances.'

'You mean Ben Rowley? Give me a break.'

'I thought he was your oldest friend.'

'So?'

Diane made a knowing, 'Aha! There was something, wasn't there, Pet? Ages ago before Daz and I met.'

Petra shrugged her shoulders. 'It wasn't anything great. Anyway, I wouldn't have a man running my life for me.'

'Hmm.'

'Well, think of Hannah. Could you imagine her married to grumpy Harry Lennard?'

'Maybe he was gorgeous when he was young.'

'But look what he turned into.'

'Maybe he was so upset when she died that he went all nasty.'

'He was an Army officer. I come across dozens of ex-Army types in my job. They are revolting chauvinists. They'd never let a girl breathe. I can't understand ...'

Petra stopped. The thought had only just entered her head, but now it took possession. In that wild wood it was very easy to think uneasy thoughts.

'What?'

'I never understood why she was engaged to Lennard. I mean, Tom would have been more her type. And he was the same age.'

'Well, maybe there was something. Are you going to ask him?'

'No.'

'It might explain why he has come back.'

'Tom? I doubt it. You don't need that kind of explanation. The mountain itself is enough reason.'

'But thirty-odd years ago it might have been different.'

'No. It's ridiculous.'

'But mightn't that have been one reason the expedition fell to pieces, why they were so ready to publish official facts? So that questions wouldn't be asked?'

'You're digging dirt.'

'You thought of it first.'

Away up in the wood, someone shouted their names.

'Coming,' Petra yelled back.

Diane made no move to shift her discarded rucksack. 'I wonder why I'm here. I'm not going to get up Himalchand. I'm 'base camp manager'. Women and children last. It's different for you, but most girls only get what they want by persuading some man to take them.'

Petra was surprisingly nettled by this. 'So? What makes me different?'

'You challenge them at their own game, 'just like a boy'. That's why the Army types slaver over you.'

'You're disgusting.'

'Ho ho. Just joking.'

There were more shouts from above. This time the girls shouted back in chorus. They shouldered their rucksacks and after that the toil of climbing prevented them from talking at all.

Camp was pitched at sunset below the pass. The sudden darkness was made absolute by the persisting blanket of cloud. But just before darkness fell it was possible to see that the wood was opening out into a meadow. The deodars and pines had given way to small juniper bushes and rhododendrons, and there was tussocky grass underfoot.

The weather was too damp for sitting around a campfire, unless one had to. The porters lit a fire, but only through liberal use of paraffin. The rhododendron branches were barely flammable and the juniper twigs flared up and died, and were useless for sustained warmth or cooking.

The porters had no tent, so the fire was their only protection from the weather. They crouched around the fire, wrapped in thin homespun blankets, while moisture dripped off the branches of the trees to sizzle in the flames. The mountaineers, equipped with easy-drying modern clothing, had cosy mountain tents into which to crawl.

But that was the deal. An expedition provided tents only for high-altitude porters or Sherpas. Porters for the valley or the approaches brought their own gear. That was how it had always been.

Everyone woke early. The sun, so long hidden behind cloud, came bursting out. By seven o'clock the interior of the tent was unbearably hot. Petra crawled out, blinking her eyes at the brightness. All over the green meadow, blankets were spread out in the sun to dry. The porters were cheerfully drinking tea and smoking beside their crackling fire. The dreary tiredness of yesterday evening had disappeared, as if evaporated by the sun.

And there was the mountain. The pasture where the expedition had camped formed the shoulder of a lateral ridge, and other, similar ridges intersected in a zigzag as the river wound between them. At the source of the river was the Munshu glacier, now invisible in its basin. But the mountain occupied the V-shape where the last two ridges met.

Petra had not expected to be surprised. She knew the topography of Himlachand so well from photographs and descriptions. She had expected to recognise the peak, to be impressed by its grandeur, but not to be surprised.

Yet that first view, coming on the first bright morning after the monsoon, was like a vision of the unreal. The unexpected, almost shocking perfection of the snow-cone left Petra almost breathless. She had no thoughts to match it, let alone words to describe.

The sensation was one of pure, unreasonable happiness. Although the most difficult part of the expedition was still to come, and although the human element was already proving an impediment to progress, still the mountain was reason enough for joy.

'Come out!' Petra shouted. 'Come out, everyone, and look! We can see Himalchand!'

She went round and rattled the poles on all the tents.

One by one her friends came out, sleepily rubbing their eyes. One by one, they were brought up short, gasping at what they saw. Even Tom, who had been within a few hundred feet of the summit, even he looked like a man who had never seen a sight like this before.

'I'd forgotten.' He stretched and yawned involuntarily, as if the sleepiness brought on by the thin air was hard to disperse. 'You don't expect to be shocked twice. And I was young then. But there is, there really is nothing like it.'

He sat down on a rock. Vivid red flowers were growing in clumps about his feet. The grass was perfectly green, sparkling with dew. The sky was blue. The mountain ridges were black. The mountain was pure light. But all this was nothing to the wonder on Tom's weatherbeaten face.

'I'm back. I'm glad I came back. Thank you, lads.'

'Nowt to do with us,' declared Daz, hands in pockets. But he was looking not at Tom, only at the mountain.

Petra saw that Tom's eyes were sparkling. There was the same catch in his voice that she had heard that first day in Scotland, when he had talked of the glamour of Himalchand which had been born of the disaster, not the triumph.

It was true. It was true. No matter how much he remembered, or how hard he might have tried to hold on to the vision, the glamour would fade with time. The sight of Himalchand was a remembrance.

Diane, with her hair loose about her shoulders, was striding about the meadow, kicking the flowers in the air in her exuberance. Rowley and the Rat stood with their heads together, pointing out the mountain's features to one another. But even in this pretence of nonchalance, they could not help smiling.

Ieuan had been very quiet. He was staring at the mountain as if at a spectre.

'Well?' Petra wanted him to acknowledge the mountain, to thank her for it, as if she had given it to him as a gift.

'What did she write, the girl who died? "The mountain keeps its own peace ..."'

'... "under the centuries of snow."'

'How can you dare to climb it? It'd be like going to the moon.'

'No. We put one foot in front of the other. It's just like a Scottish gully, only longer.'

'You believe that?'

'Oh, don't be philosophical. It's a marvel just to look at. If we fail on the climb that's just the name of the game. We don't need to book our failure in advance.'

'It's a terrible size.'

'OK. I am afraid. That's the challenge.'

'What kind of fear is that? That you love to be afraid? Here's Tom, more than thirty years later, enthralled by the memory of a fear. The mountain isn't beautiful at all.'

Petra did not know what to say. As usual, Ieuan had taken the debate out of her depth. She still could not fathom why the Welshman had come with them. He did not seem to fit anywhere into the jigsaw. He did not even love the mountain.

While the mountaineers stood staring at Himalchand, the porters were going about the meadow picking up stones. They built a huge cairn, and upon it they hoisted a prayer-flag, a long scrap of coloured cloth tied to a pole. The incessant wind blew the flag through all points of the compass.

Ieuan, more interested in people than mountains, squatted on his heels to watch.

'I wonder if they're claiming protection, or warding off danger?'

'Ask them.'

He shook his head. One of the men, the dark, wiry youth who was Tai Singh's son, had brought a little bowl of flour mixed with butter and was spreading the mixture onto the stones. The men began to sing, a reedy ululating chorus. They had their own particular way of dealing with the vision.

The peak appears above the horizon like a strange planet rising. In the eastward early morning light the outline of the mountain is perfectly clear. It is blue, transparent, and cold. Seen from the green pastures below, it does not seem to be attached to the earth, but seems rather to be part of the sky. It is fleshless, otherworldly, and surely unattainable.

We feed off fear. We have no other gods.

The way to the mountain was a winding path, rising and falling as it skirted mountain spurs or turned through the stream beds of the ravines. The first spur, traversed soon after leaving the camp on the pasture, was the highest. It formed the pass into the upper Munshu valley. The party did not set out again until near noon, by which time the sun had become ferociously hot. There was no wind. The air was bright and clear, and by now it was very thin. Already the path was at a higher altitude than most Alpine summits.

But if anyone had had breath to spare, there would have been singing. The day kept its perfection well into the afternoon, and by evening there were only a few cotton-wool clouds around the summits of the mountains.

One by one, the other peaks came into sight, the other points on the Himalchand ridge. Petra counted them: Munshu peak (19,000 feet), Kandar (21,000 feet), Gopalkand (3 peaks, I 20,200 feet, II 19,300 feet, III 18,130 feet). Then Himalchand (22,250 feet), then the larger but less immediately impressive giants to the north-east: Auraz (22,910 feet) and Tengdatta (23,000 feet). The latter two peaks had been climbed from the other side, by Americans, some time in the sixties. Munshu peak had had many ascents; it was a gentle walk from the pass. Kandar and Gopalkand were fragile, crumbling horrors which no one had felt justified in attempting. Himalchand shared solider rock with the two large peaks. And its position at the head of the valley gave it a dramatic quality out of proportion to its height.

That night they camped on a rock platform above the river. There was no soil to speak of, and the only tent which could be pitched was the tiny high-altitude dome. The climbers chose to bivouac, like the porters. The night was cold, but not wet, and very clear. Above their heads the narrow wedge of sky was punctuated from time to time by shining smears of light, shooting stars passing between the fixed ones. The sky itself was very black, and the mountains were only in evidence as a blackness without stars.

The woods in the ravine were darker still, and the continuous rush of water in the river imposed silence on all other sounds. Even the crackle of the campfire was inaudible from a few paces distant. Supper was rice, boiled interminably over the brushwood fire. The air was so thin that the boiling-point of water was significantly lower than normal. The rice came out in a solidly caked lump.

The climbers and porters sat together on large stones around the glowing fire. The plain rice was shared out, with a little crushed chilli and salt for flavour. The expensive mountain rations were tucked away in the climbers' packs. After a day of enormous exertion, plain rice had a savour which it had never had before.

The Rat had brought his mouth organ. It was an instrument which had often been banished from climbing huts into the outside snow. But here, on this ledge pitched between cliff and river, any music would have seemed friendly. When he took it out of his pocket, his face asked the usual sheepish question 'Will you have a tune?' expecting to be roundly silenced. In the rushing darkness, no one refused him.

He played 'Old Kentucky Home' because his taste ran to country and western. To everyone's surprise the porters clapped politely. Their leader handed out cigarettes. One of the number produced a wooden flute. This instrument, played with a kind of nasal ululation, was a fair match for the mouth organ.

It was as if no one wanted to go to sleep, under that dark sky. The exhaustion of the day's marching had settled down to mere numb indolence. The effort of crawling into a sleeping bag was too great to contemplate while the fire lasted.

The Rat played through his repertoire. Sometimes, if his friends were familiar with the words, he was accompanied by singing. But this was no boisterous campfire round. The reedy mouth organ, and the equal but opposite reply of the Indian flute, were merely a means of pushing the silence back a little way.

Ieuan sang something in Welsh, quite competently, in a minor key.

'What's that?' asked the Rat, testing out some chords on his instrument.

'Welsh song from school. I don't know what all the words mean. I thought I'd forgotten it till just now.'

'The name?'

'It means 'The Well of St Winifrede'. I told you it was from school.'

'Right. Trad. folk.'

The sirdar cleared his throat. The piper started a rather more rousing tune. The porters all broke into a song with a repetitive chorus and actions. The sirdar led the song, like a shanty. It was not difficult for the foreigners to pick up the chorus and join in. The song had a martial, marching feel to it. There were about fourteen verses.

Then the silence came back.

Tom Ormerod rose and stretched his arms. 'I'm for my pit.' He had kept out of the fireside chat. Now he turned and went to the place where his red sleeping bag lay, outside the circle of firelight. People called 'Goodnight'. But it was not long before everyone else took to their beds. As Petra nodded off to sleep, she heard the faint rumble of thunder in the distance. But she slept nonetheless.

The next thing she knew was a rough shaking, and a note of panic in someone's voice. She opened her eyes. The dark was absolute.

'Wake up, wake up.' Ieuan had gone very Welsh in his agitation.

'It's still dark.'

'The river. It's come over the place where I was lying, and it's still rising. Wake all the others!'

'How?'

'A storm perhaps, in the mountains. I was lying awake. I was worried because I could hear everyone breathing, really irregularly, and then stopping from time to time. It's the lack of oxygen. You can hear people stop breathing completely for a whole minute. It's the way very sick people sound when they're about to die. And then I felt my sleeping bag go damp. The river has crept up at least two feet since we went to bed.'

'It's meant to stop rising after dark, when the sun goes off the glacier.'

'It hasn't read the books. Get up.'

She crawled out of her bag by feel, and turned on her torch. The limited circle of light showed a rushing whiteness a yard or two away from where she lay.

The others were lying variously nearer the cliff, having chosen spots of ground where the boulders were least protuberant. They were all hard to rouse. Sleep at high altitude had a stupefying effect, due to the lack of oxygen. It was Ieuan's luck that he had been awake when the river reached him. He might have been floated away downstream without waking up.

There were noisy complaints as people woke, followed by muted shock. The ledge where they lay was ten yards wide. The way out was a steep path up into the woods.

'What's the time?' Daz tried to give an impression of taking charge.

'Four o'clock.' The Rat had a waterproof watch with a built-in light.

'Two or three hours before it gets light.'

The Rat shone his torch all round the ledge. The porters, protesting at being woken, had gone into a huddle under the cliff.

'We'll lose a lot of stuff if we try to move in the dark. It'll be dangerous. And none of the porters will help, I guess.'

Tai Singh's son had gone home after the first night's camp. His ambition had been to view the mountain and make the necessary prayers. It was not his job to manage porters on a trail.

They went and asked. The head porter said that the river would not rise. It would not rise dangerously tonight.

Tom, who had been here before, remembered that the Everest year had been a particularly dry season in these parts. His own expedition had camped here, on this ledge. There were so few areas of flat ground in the approach.

'There's no undergrowth here, and no trees.' He shone his torch all around them. The flat ground was boulder-strewn, but the green things which grew there were all small plants, mosses, ferns and grass. 'Maybe it does flood. That river rose suddenly enough.'

Diane shivered. 'What if there's a tidal wave?'

'Unlikely.'

They were all silent, listening to the roar of the water. Ieuan was wringing the water out of the toe of his sleeping bag.

Rowley scratched at his flea bites. 'This looks like a job for mountain logistics.' He volunteered no further ideas. The Rat was entirely silent.

Then: 'It could be bloody dangerous,' declared Daz. 'If it floods in bad weather it could cut off our return.' He dug his hands into his trouser pockets. (They had all been sleeping fully clothed.) 'Real *Boys Own* stuff, eh?'

'It's part of the hazard.' Tom spoke quietly, and the roar of the flood nearly drowned his voice.

'What's that?' Daz asked.

'It's just another thing we'll have to take into account when we're on the mountain. We don't have time to search for another way back.'

'What'll we do now?'

'Trust the men, I'd say.'

'Isn't it wishful thinking?'

'Maybe. But we risk more by trying to carry the loads up

into the woods. We could get back to Munshu in what we stand up in. We're not in danger yet. But if one load gets dropped in the river, that's the mountain finished.'

'Oh, sod it.'

'We can stay up the rest of the night, watching the river. You can change your mind if it gets closer.'

So that is what they decided to do. It was difficult to decide upon inaction. There was nothing else to do but watch the water and worry for the next three hours until day. To save the torch batteries, they sat in darkness. Somebody rekindled the fire, but it burned only sluggishly.

Ieuan had marked along the stream bank with lines of whitish stones. Each line was six inches further from the river than the last. *Boys Own* style, it was designed to measure the rate at which the level rose. From time to time he would get up and inspect the installation with his torch. Each time he returned to the fireside, his face longer and his expression more lugubrious.

There was no singing around the campfire now. No one could think about anything but the prospect of having to abandon the mountain before they reached its base. Except the problem of having their retreat cut off if things should go badly on the climb. The stakes for success or failure had increased dramatically.

The porters had all curled up in their blankets and gone back to sleep. Their reliance on fate was impressive, but then they did not own the half-ton of luggage. And they had never had any prospect or ambition to climb Himalchand.

By five o'clock, the atmosphere was rather like that in Allin's Hut in bad weather. No one was worried by the danger any more; they were irritable from frustration.

Tom tapped out his pipe on the hot stones by the embers. 'I remember Harry Lennard used to say that mountaineering was the moral equivalent of war.'

'That sounds like right rubbish.' Daz was not to be diverted from his gloomy contemplation of the dying fire.

'It was a common enough notion, after the war. Find something else for young men to do, apart from slaughter each other.'

Petra, no happier than anyone else, took Tom up on the point. 'Young men? What about the women? We don't slaughter each other.'

'Well, there's that.'

Rowley had wrapped his sleeping bag round his shoulders like a shawl. He growled, 'You would too, given half a chance. I've seen girls at discos in Sheffield going at each other with their handbags over some fella.'

'Well, it takes a man to do that.'

Diane giggled. '*Cherchez l'homme.*' They had taught French well at the Lady Wheatcroft School for Girls.

'I don't think mountaineering is a substitute for anything else, actually.' Petra was in her mountain instructor mode. 'It's an end in itself.'

Tom was cleaning out his pipe now, with a frayed pipe-cleaner. 'Now that's what I used to think.'

'And now?'

'It's part of the journey through life, like all those other things. War, old age, religion.'

'Sex,' put in Diane.

'That too.'

There was a pause while Ieuan got up to inspect the flood gauge. His torch flickered up and down the margin of the river. Then he tramped back to the fire.

'It's holding.'

'Oh good!' Petra felt unusual relief.

Ieuan did not smile back. 'It's not falling, though. And there's another hour at least until dawn.' He sat down again. 'Do we get more on the philosophy of climbing?'

'Yer gets to the top.' Rowley hitched his bag up around his neck, so his blond head emerged as a tuft out of the billowing red nylon.

The Rat made a rude noise on his mouth organ.

'Thanks.' Ieuan picked up a stick and poked at the embers of the fire.

'It's a way of passing the time,' declared Petra. 'And I've heard you, Rowley, and the Rat too, holding forth in bars about why you choose to climb.'

'Well, it wasn't anything to do with religion,' declared the Rat. 'I started for the same reason you did. To get away from home life and my dad always sitting in front of the telly shouting at me to wipe my feet when I came in.'

'That was just the start. There's more to it now, isn't there.'

'You tell me. Your mum still put doilies under the cakes? She still hoover the garden path? And that frilly toilet-roll cover? I definitely remember a frilly toilet-roll cover.'

'Bollocks,' said Petra.

The Rat tooted his mouth organ again. 'Frilly. Blue satin. With a bow. Avocado bathroom suite and a bidet.'

'Really?' Diane suddenly took interest in the conversation. 'I don't think I ever used the upstairs. But I remember the doilies. And the electric gadget which absorbed harmful ions out of the air.'

'Well, what about the Rat's place?' Petra was determined to get in a return blow. 'Photographs of all the Radinsky ancestors in Homburg hats. The Rat's sister practising the violin. She wore her hair in plaits out of choice.'

'Oi. Unfair,' said the Rat. 'She plays the violin quite well. It was Pa who used to bug me. If I came in wearing new shoes he wanted to know how much they cost. Not cos he was broke, but out of interest.'

'And Rowley,' continued Petra. 'His dad had *Encyclopaedia Britannica*, all twenty volumes. He used to quote bits all the time. And there was a metal crusader to hold the fire-tongs.'

'Yergh,' said Diane.

By now people were laughing, even Ieuan. Various improbable anecdotes ensued.

'I had an uncle,' said Tom, 'who used to keep coal in the bath.'

'No!'

'We didn't. We had no bath. Nobbut a tin tub by the fire. Ee, times were hard. The bog was a shed down the yard, with no catch on the door, so you had to sing to tell other folks you were in occupation.'

He tamped the tobacco down into his pipe. 'Mind you, my mother would always put a tablecloth on the table. And it was more than our lives were worth to come indoors in our boots. When the war came there was more money and frills started appearing everywhere. Mind, I don't remember there being one on the toilet paper.'

'Oh?'

'We used sheets of the *Sporting Life*, torn up. You'd call it recycling, nowadays.'

Ieuan said, 'We sometimes had bits of the *Daily Telegraph* at school. That was probably a political statement.'

'Oh yes.' Petra found herself remembering all sorts of irrelevant facts. 'Our loo rolls at school had 'London County Council. Now wash your hands please.''

'Dirty business, politics,' said Ieuan.

Daz had been dozing, apparently, while his friends exchanged notes on domestic arrangements. He lifted up his head now. 'I thought we were staying off sex, religion, politics and why we climb. My dad used to get my mum to polish the soles of his shoes before he went to church. And the bog paper was Bronco, 350 leaves to a box. What with mum's cooking, the box would last us three weeks.'

Diane nudged him with her elbow. 'Such refined manners! Your mum used to tell me off for tipping up my plate when I was finishing my soup.'

'And your 'mummy' – didn't she ask you "Does he take sugar?", not me directly, because of me having a northern accent and being a bit of a foreigner?'

'She never.'

'She did.'

Petra shivered. She had had about five hours' sleep, and the proximity of the glacial river made it very cold. She suddenly felt very distant from all the other people. The discussion on the finer points of urban and suburban life had served to distract everyone from the prevailing gloom. But it was still there, hovering outside the circle of light. She got to her feet, stretching her limbs. Ieuan was up too, ready to go and have another look at the flood meter. They walked together along the river bank. Ieuan's torch was glowing with a yellowish light, as the battery threatened to fail.

The white stones showed one by one out of the darkness.

'I can see them. Well beyond the torchlight.'

Ieuan flashed the feeble beam upwards and it was lost in the sky. But the white stones could still be seen. The darkness was now slightly grey.

'And the stars.' Petra looked upwards. 'The stars have gone.'

They stopped at the end of the line of stones. The level of the river still held steady. The night was over.

'It's only the beginning.' Ieuan doused his light.

'Dawn comes quickly.'

'I mean, this is only the first danger, isn't it? Are you beginning to realise you've bitten off more than you can chew?'

'I'm not going to give up, just because you're a pessimist.'

'It's not just the mountain that's dangerous, is it?' Ieuan insisted. 'It's the way you lot scrap when things get difficult.'

'We don't. I mean, it's like a family. We re-do the same arguments over again. It doesn't mean anything.'

'Then will you get Ben Rowley off my back? What is he, a working-class hero?'

'His dad works in the council offices.'

'Well, it's a pose that doesn't suit him. My father is an agricultural mechanic. He made bloody sure I didn't go the same way.'

'You think Rowley's a waster?'

'He's wasting something.'

'He's climbing. That's enough for him. And me too.'

'And you think it's enough, to live for the day?'

'Jam tomorrow? You mean I should marry a nice boy and put doilies on the cake plates? No way.'

'There are alternatives.'

Even in the few minutes while they were speaking, the sky had gone from black to dark blue, and the people around the fire could be seen as blurred grey shapes. Petra started back towards the others. 'You don't understand. This is our life. This is the alternative.'

'Isn't there a middle way?'

'A compromise? Sunday outings to the Peak District? No, you don't understand. Let me be corny. It's better to have lived and lost. It's the risk that keeps us alive.'

They were back at the fire. Colours were now back in the picture. The red sleeping bags, the dark-blue pile jackets, the livid green of the ferns under the cliff.

'The night's over.' Petra did not sit down again. One by one her friends stirred and stretched themselves. Tom tapped out the cold ash from his pipe.

'We'd best be going.'

With daylight, the tension had gone. Petra felt very tired all of a sudden. She yawned. Rowley unwrapped himself from his sleeping bag. 'Well, it was all just a panic then.'

Ieuan kicked the nearest of the marker stones into the river. 'Someone's got to be cautious.'

No one else said anything. They were all beginning to stow things away in their rucksacks. Rowley and Ieuan glared at each other for a moment, then Ieuan shrugged his shoulders and went to pack away his own sleeping bag.

Rowley stayed put. It was the Rat who said, 'Cool it, mate. We're on holiday.' When Rowley tried to say something else, he handed him a billycan and said, 'Fill that with water. Come on. I'm mountain logistics, remember. I have to get this camp moving.'

Rowley obeyed, probably out of sheer surprise that his friend should assert himself so. But then the Rat was the one of all of them who would stop at nothing to get to the mountain.

Petra felt slightly ashamed, as if the whole thing had been her fault. She was fairly sure that she could not have got Rowley to shut up as effectively as the Rat had done, even though they knew each other just as well. Daz was supposed to be the leader, but he seemed to be daunted by the task of managing the separate personalities. He was a climber, happiest doing practical things like sorting out loads and finding the route. He was already up in the woods looking for the path. And Ieuan had been silent all through their hurried breakfast. When he had finished eating he went to have a word with the porter who was carrying most of the medical supplies. And when they set out up the steep path into the wooded ravine, he walked fast, and was soon way ahead of the rest of the party.

12 August 1953

> Himalchand is not a delicate, pretty mountain, as it appeared in the distance from Munshu. You meet some hint of the ruggedness to come as you creep out of the river bed up to the moraine of the Munshu glacier. The river pebbles are great boulders, the size of cars or houses. While we rested at midday, Donald put on tennis-shoes and tried out rock problems on the boulders. The horse man from Munshu thought that the shoes must be magic, to convey apparent levitation in this way. He made it clear that he would accept the gift of these shoes as part of his baksheesh. I am sorry to say that both Donald and Tai Singh encouraged him in this view.
>
> Everyone is getting very excited. It takes each of us in different ways. Harry becomes increasingly dogmatic and leader-like. We have to remind him that this is not a British national assault on Everest. Tom Ormerod becomes even more silent than usual, and whistles a tuneless dirge under his breath. The Scotsmen argue with one another. And John Amory polishes his boots. These poor items of footwear must have absorbed the grease from a hundred dead geese

since we left Bombay. He is afraid that the heat will dry out the leather and crack it. He has to be reminded that he is expedition photographer.

There was a photograph of the 1953 team at base camp, on the shore of the Munshu glacier, perched upon an improbable ridge of moraine. They were well out of the way of any avalanche from the steep faces of Auraz and Tengdatta. This black-and-white image was the only picture of the whole team. It was consciously posed, and included the horses which had carried the loads up from Munshu.

Harry Lennard, handsome and clean-shaven, was in the central position. The Scotsmen, square, bearded and alike as twins, formed the second row. Hayter and Amory leant on their long-handled ice-axes in a studied fashion. Tom, looking about fourteen years old, was squatting on the ground next to Tai Singh. Hannah, wearing an open-necked army shirt and tweed breeches, stood rather stiffly next to her fiancé. Her broad-brimmed hat shaded her face so that only her chin was visible. It was impossible to see her features, let alone her expression. The tone of her diary, up to that stage in the expedition, had remained relentlessly cheerful.

The new base camp was as near to the old as could be managed. Tom's incomplete memory, and the sketchy maps which existed from that time, did not allow any exact interpretation of the topography. The glacier had changed. The route through to the snowslopes of Himalchand would have to be reconnoitred as if for the first time.

They crossed the river under the glacier's outflow. Here the melting ice gave rise to a wide clear stream bubbling between pebbles, as innocent as the River Aire at Malham in the Yorkshire Dales. They could splash across with their boots on, without getting wet feet. This was at about ten o'clock in the morning. Later in the day the river would have risen, as the ice on the glacier melted in the sun. But so early in the day it was hardly a barrier.

The glacier itself at this point was a mass of dirty boulders. The glacier had scraped along the mountainside, over thousands of years, and cracked these boulders away from the underlying bedrock. The boulders had then been pushed along, like a dust-heap, to form the great mounds of the terminal moraine at the end of the glacier. Some of the rocks had been left behind at either side, to form the hundred-foot high ridges of the side-moraine. It was up these moraine ridges, distinguishable as three parallel lines curving along the hillside, that the climbers were able to ascend the glacier. The grey rubble underfoot was a very uncomfortable surface upon which to walk.

Everyone was tired after the alarms of the night, and energy was hard to come by now that the mountain itself loomed overhead every minute of the day. Each forward step was also an upward step, and the air grew thinner with altitude. Petra found that breath was hard to come by, but even that was not the limiting factor. She found that her heart was beating so furiously that she had to stop from time to time to let it slow down. Her progress was thus a matter of short dashes between pauses. The Rat, who had made it his business to bring up the rear, kept running into her. His comments were essentially unprintable.

'Try and get into a rhythm.'

Petra got her breath back and protested, 'I'm not a machine.'

'Well, I'm not carrying you.'

'Well, you don't have to dog my heels, Tim. I'll get to base camp. The porters are still behind.'

'If you're overloaded I'll carry something for you.'

It was Petra's turn to say something unprintable. The Rat muttered something about women on expeditions. They stopped for a full-scale slanging match, such as they might have indulged in when in their teens. On the open expanse of the glacier there was no need to worry about raising their voices.

It was an exhausting business. They both had to stop to get their breath. For a moment they glared at each other, then burst out laughing. At that moment the first of the porters trudged past. He grinned, gap-toothed beneath his squashy felt hat.

'*Namaste.*'

Striving for a straight face, Petra returned the greeting. The man continued without pausing, but ten paces on he stopped, breathed heavily for a few seconds, and then continued on.

'He's doing it too,' she remarked.

'What?'

'Dashing and pausing. It's the only way to cope with the altitude. You can't get into a rhythm – there's not enough oxygen.'

'Oh. Where d'you hear that?'

'Ieuan said something.'

'Uh. Taff knows it all, doesn't he?'

'I don't know why you and Rowley have got it in for him.'

'He's not a climber.'

Petra knew exactly what he meant, but would not admit it. She was beginning to realise that the reason she had begun to seek Ieuan's company was precisely because he was not a climber. He was not making a competition of it, like the others. But this she was not going to tell the Rat.

'Oh, don't let's argue. It's bad enough without. I wish I could guess how far we have to go.'

'It's a place where the ridge flattens out. Where the South Munshu glacier comes in to join the main one. There's supposed to be a change in the colour of the rock.'

'I hope we can tell.'

'Shouldn't be hard. Munshu is granite. Pale and solid. The rest is just chossy shale.'

Petra looked up. At this distance from the mountain she had to crane her neck to see the summit. 'Do you think that's it? There's a stripe of pale rock on the face of Tengdatta. It must loop down under the glacier.'

'Could be. Just keep looking at your feet.'

They came to the camping-place in the evening. Ieuan had found it, because he had continued to lead the way. By the time Petra caught up, the light was too poor to assess any subtle alterations in the colour of the grey rubble. But Tom, who had been there before, seemed satisfied.

Five red domes sprang up on the crest of the moraine. They were dotted at intervals along the ridge, making use of tiny level patches of ground. The largest levelling-out was the site of the campfire, and the site of the largest of the dome tents. Daz and Diane slept in this tent, but it was also to be used as the 'mess-tent' for meeting and eating when the weather was too poor for sitting outside.

Sleep was harder than ever. The thin air gave rise to that irregular pattern of breathing which Ieuan had noted at the river camp. As a result Petra woke up several times, choking and gasping for air. Her little solo tent was halfway along the line of tents, and from where she lay she could hear everyone snoring. From time to time, each sleeper by turn would stop breathing entirely for half a minute.

Just before dawn, all the porters got up and headed back home to their village. By starting early they could make the entire journey in one day. They did not argue about their pay, and the Rat had provided the recognised quantity of baksheesh. He saw them on their way.

Petra heard the whole loud exchange through the nylon wall of her tent. Sleep had become entirely impossible. She crept out and stretched herself. So near the snowline, everyone was sleeping in their clothes for warmth.

Her first glance was for Himalchand. The mountain now loomed almost vertically above them. The summit and the crescent-moon snowfield were now out of sight beyond the lower slopes. The bulk of the mountain seemed lumpy and shapeless.

Petra turned away and stared down the valley. She could see

where the green of the juniper woods began, and the splash of white water as the river flowed through the lower boulder field. This was all more than 3,000 feet below where she stood. She could see the dark figures of the returning porters already crossing the stream, although it seemed only a minute or two since she had heard them departing.

Soon even the distant figures were lost to sight. The seven climbers were alone. Their last link with the everyday domestic world was now severed entirely.

The weather was clear, which was more than anyone could have expected. Tom, it seemed, had already been on a dawn reconnaissance. He came back when everyone else was sitting on the boulders making breakfast. Diane offered him a cup of tea. He sipped. Then he took a large swallow of the freshly boiled liquid. 'Hmm. Seventeen-thousand-foot tea.'

The stuff was warm rather than hot, and had the tinny taste of tea which is made from sub-boiling water.

'I made it on the primus. You were right. It is the only stove that really works up here.' Diane's hands were sooty, and she gave out a gentle odour of paraffin. 'But it took a lot of pumping to get it going.'

Rowley was squatting beside a very small gas-cylinder stove, using up matches. 'This bugger won't light.' He scratched his chin, which was just beginning to grow a gold stubble.

Daz was sitting very close to Diane, with his bootlaces undone and his long hair straggling. None of them had been able to wash.

'Shake it, Ben. That's the trick with butane.'

Rowley shook it.

'Or stuff it down your shirt, to warm it up.'

Rowley shook it again, with his ear to the cylinder, listening for the sloosh of liquid gas. 'I've got to get the trick. This is our high-altitude stove. It's supposed to have extra-chunky gas that won't freeze.'

Daz took the next cup of tea from Diane. 'I read about one

expedition where they used to pee on the gas bottle to warm it.'

Diane sniffed. 'Don't be repulsive.'

'Honest, it's true.'

Rowley swore. 'It's the matches too. They break when you strike them, and then they won't burn.'

Tom, who had finished his tea, wiped his mouth on his sleeve. 'Wax vestas.' His voice was muffled by his jumper.

'You what?' asked Rowley.

'Wax vestas. That's what we had. They burn longer than wooden matches.'

'Now you remember.'

'I still use them for my pipe. Better in wet weather in the Lakes.' He patted the pockets of his breeches. 'I've a box here.'

'Is that all?'

'And another dozen in my pack.'

'You sod,' said Rowley, without rancour. 'Now hand 'em over. You can have the Hanuman brand cheapo Indian safety matches for your pipe.'

'I feared that would be the case.' He threw the yellow matchbox. 'All for one and one for all. I think we've camped about 200 feet too low. But there's nothing to do about it now. I'm glad to say that the way across the glacier is obvious.'

13 August 1953

Base camp at last. This is the beginning of the climb. But I feel as tired as if we had already climbed the mountain. If all this travel is simply the means to an end, the goal itself will have to be tremendous.

All of us feel it – that the fever which impelled us here has now burned out. We are listless. Hayter says it is the altitude that makes us tired. It is the lack of oxygen in the air and the cold wind off the glacier. This is the mechanical explanation. I believe that our enthusiasm has faltered because Himalchand is no longer a dreamt-of goal but an all-too-solid reality. From our camp in this bouldery desert we can hardly see the mountain. It is too close.

Tai Singh has volunteered to stay with us and help carry some loads. The leadership thought about this a good deal, because the supplies will have to stretch to accommodate one extra mouth. There is still a lingering suspicion that he will expect to be paid. And a stronger suspicion that a minor lordling of this sort will not be up to the hard work and will let us down at some crucial moment. I backed him, because I have heard all those same arguments levelled against the inclusion of women on major mountaineering ventures. Tai Singh would like to climb Himalchand. He knows he will not be allowed to, but he will still try to get as far up the mountain as possible.

The glacier crossing was the first true mountaineering problem of the expedition. From base camp, the main arm of the Munshu glacier could be crossed above the point where the smaller South Munshu glacier joined it. This allowed the climbers to reach the face of Himalchand with a minimum of glacier travel. The upper reaches of the Munshu glacier were a tumbled mass of snow-covered ice, issuing from the base of the curved wall which formed the north face of Auraz. For a short stretch thereafter, the glacier levelled out, still snow-covered, but with the horizontal cracks of the main crevasses easily visible. Then the snow covering was lost, and the surface of the glacier became a jumble of rubble pocked by huge craters. Tom Ormerod had seen immmediately that the most straightforward route lay across the middle portion. The danger from the crevasses was largely visible. The snow covering evened out the roughness of the bouldery surface. They would still have to proceed roped together, because the snow could still hide bottomless pits of various sorts, but once they had been back and forth a few times there would be no further problems with route-finding and the going would be relatively easy.

'We should go and look at it now.'

Daz, who had finally got the gas stove going, looked up

from his squatting position and shaded his eyes. 'All of us? We're knackered.'

'It's a clear day. We may not get another for a week.'

'Good point.'

'At least three of us, to test the glacier. Who's got the best eye for ground?'

'Me,' said Daz, 'but I'm knackered.'

'I'll go,' offered Rowley.

Surprisingly, the Rat did not volunteer. He was rather quiet this morning. 'I've got the runs again.'

Petra felt horribly weary. It was the effect of altitude, of course. But the desire to see what was beyond the horizon remained strong. 'I'll come. You can send me first over the crevasses. I'm the lightest.'

No one suggested that Ieuan or Diane might wish to participate. This was the point at which the mountaineers split off from the support team.

Petra swallowed her lukewarm tea. She had been slopping about the camp in unlaced mountain boots. Now she sat down to do up the laces. 'We'll need crampons and axes. Is there any water up there?'

Tom shook his head. 'The last water is in the pool below this camp.'

'Isn't it a thermal spring?'

'That's right. That's one reason it tastes odd, and why it's still flowing when everything else is frozen.'

'Didn't Lennard call it "*aquae sulis*"? After some Roman thing?'

'Aye. It's grand for washing your feet after a march. You folk who are resting today should try it.'

Daz groaned. 'It's 200 feet downhill from the camp.'

Diane kicked him. 'Gerrup, lazybones. Someone has to fetch the next lot of water.'

The reconnaissance team filled their bottles with the water that remained from breakfast. The trek to the little blue pool of the warm spring was too much to add on to a serious march.

They shouldered their packs and set out, step by step, up the ridge. When Petra first looked back, the red tents of the camp were out of sight.

The day was interesting, even though they did not achieve all they set out to do. The surface of the glacier, smooth from a distance, contained many more obstacles upon close inspection. There were a few dangerously balanced structures of snow which had to be avoided by a wide margin. No one fell into a crevasse, but there was one point where Petra felt the ground fragmenting beneath her feet. She leapt back, to see a black hole the size of a dust-bin lid appearing in the smooth ground. There was no guessing how deep it was. The party made a large detour around the spot.

It became evident that they could not cross the glacier and return safely within the hours of daylight. They stopped for some lunch at about two o'clock and perched themselves on the highest point in the vicinity, so that they could complete the reconnaissance while eating.

'The snow is still hard,' remarked Rowley.

The sun, so bright in the morning, had disappeared into a haze of high cloud. The wind had become colder. Petra chewed at the cold chapatti which constituted their lunch. She had no appetite and less inclination for talking. Tom answered Rowley's unstated question.

'We'll have to keep regular crossings to the early morning, when we can rely on the snow. I remember it used to get very soft with the sun on it.'

'Camp one where?'

'Last time we put it on a rock island, out in the glacier, well away from the face. We had to watch out about wandering on to the glacier in the night. You could fall down a crevasse in the dark, going for a leak.'

'No pissing beyond this point? That wasn't in the book.'

'No. Not in '53. But we did still piss. There's less snow this year, I think. It should reduce the risk of avalanche from the face. We won't have to camp so far out on the ice.'

'It looks a bloody terrible face.' Rowley had some binoculars and was scanning the nearest slopes of the mountain. The start of the real climbing was perhaps half a mile distant. 'It's steep snow with rubbish falling down from above all the time.'

'Not as bad as it looks. The angle allowed step-cutting. And most of the debris from above shoots down on to the South Munshu. The band of rock at the top of the face is very solid indeed.'

'Camp two?'

'At that band of rock below the snowfield. There's room for a bivouac tent.'

'Three?'

'On the main ridge.'

'And then a dash for the summit. I suppose we would reckon to snow-hole in an emergency?'

'Have you ever done it?'

'Once, in Scotland. It was rough.'

'I wanted to ask you – ' Tom paused, and took another bite of chapatti. His eyes were still on the mountain. 'Petra, do you reckon at all to Daz's idea of trying a new route?'

It was Rowley who shook his head. 'No. This is enough. It's a stunner.'

'Petra?' Tom asked again.

She was chewing at the grey leathery chapatti, which was sticking hard in her throat when she tried to swallow. She shook her head. 'Not now we're face to face. This is going to be hard.'

'I think so. Even without the step-cutting.' Tom too shook his head, but it was as if he were trying to shake something loose. 'I keep not believing I'm back here. So much of it is so bloody familiar.'

There was a sudden crack and rumble. All three climbers leapt to their feet. They saw the tell-tale smudge of white on the face of Auraz. Then the sound of the avalanche echoed all around the mountain sanctuary.

'Christ,' exclaimed Rowley. 'We'd better get back.'

14 August 1953

Forty pounds or so in a lump, piggyback, is like carrying a reluctant child home after a day's walk. The load becomes heavier and heavier, and slumps down your back as the shoulder-straps bite in. The newer packs (as carried by Hayter and Amory) have an extra strap that does up like a belt. This distributes the load more effectively. However, on rough ground, the pack is harder to get rid of if one falls. We have seen the dapper Amory sprawled like an overturned tortoise, pinned to the glacier by his load. The porter's habit of carrying the sack on a rope strap around the forehead makes more sense under these conditions. It is hard on the neck, but no doubt the knack can be learned. It means that porter and load can part company easily, and no porter will be seen following his load down a precipice. I see that both Hayter and Amory now undo the waistbelt when there is a chance of a minor slip resulting in severe danger.

Because of the glacier crossing, we have to make an advanced base camp (known as Camp One) before tackling the face. This camp must be supplied, and the supplies must be carried piggyback. The horses, with their man and boy, have gone home. We are in territory where no invention of men is any use: we must use our own legs and our own backs. But I have the privilege of a smaller load than the others, because I am the girl. It is a grudging kind of chivalry.

All at once I have become afraid that I shall not be allowed even the chance of the summit. I cannot pay my way in hard labour. And if I were a strong man, would I labour to put the frail, female mascot on the mountain-top first? Has this intention been there all along, that I would be allowed on to the lower slopes but not carried to the summit? I suspect that they would not know it themselves; such plotting can be unconscious.

But I shall not be put off my ambition. No one will be able to climb this mountain unless they do so as part of a team. I shall not relinquish my place out of some sense of inverted chivalry. The menfolk may claim the summit out of right. My rights are no less. I find I am arguing against myself, against an inborn sense that men were made to lead and women to follow. I thought my generation had grown out of that curse. But the purely physical challenge of the mountain sends us all back to the stone age.

I must remember, over and over again, that the climb depends on skill as much as strength, and that there will be no successful ascent unless each member of the team works to that end. I am not a passenger. I am not a passenger.

Petra had those words on the brain as she trudged back and forth across the ice over the next three days: 'I am not a passenger.'

The weather held, remarkably. At the end of three days, the team began to suspect that this was not simply a window in the monsoon weather, but the beginning of a new season.

On the third day, all four of the younger men carried extra loads to make sure that everything was in place. Just a few days at altitude had enabled them to begin to adjust to the thin air.

In the evening, with base camp left behind them, a sentinel speck of red on the far moraine; the climbers sat down to wait for the water to boil for tea, and they talked more freely than had been possible for days.

'You think this is the post-monsoon?' asked the Rat.

Tom, thus addressed, nodded and chewed at his pipe. 'I hope so.'

'So we've got a month or six weeks of clear weather?'

'If we're lucky.'

'If not?'

Tom looked up at the sky, with its few pale pink clouds; and at the crisp line of the ridge, which obscured the sunset.

'Happen we'll have the luck they had on Everest in '53. It was a good year for weather. So were the seasons the couple of years before. The four biggest peaks were climbed in three seasons.'

'You mean Nanga Parbat?' said Daz.

'Aye. And Annapurna, and K2. That was bad. The Germans, the French and the Americans all had their peaks, so Everest had to be British.'

Ieuan grunted in derision, 'British? A New Zealander and a Nepali.'

Petra remarked: 'There was a lot of hype about that, wasn't there?'

'British expedition,' said Tom, unperturbed. 'They suppressed the news so that it would break on Coronation Day, June the seventh. I was there.'

He looked up again at the mountains, now fast-fading in the rapid tropical night. 'I was glad to leave England when we did. But we'd have been luckier going to Himalchand in the premonsoon. More snow, but a longer season. We were particularly unlucky.'

The others were silent. They wanted to hear what Tom said, but this was a subject upon which no one, not even Ieuan, cared to ask questions.

After the pause, Tom continued; he was still talking about the weather but he had changed tack.

'These last few years have been bad, again. We're due for a change. Given a couple of good seasons, every peak worth climbing will have had its ascent. There are no political restrictions to speak of any more. The gear's unbelievably better, even than five years ago. There's enough money swashing about to float a battleship. In a year or two they'll be selling tickets for Everest.'

'You reckon we've got in ahead of the crowd?' said Daz, with enthusiasm.

Tom smiled slightly. 'There will be other years.'

Petra caught his eye: 'But this one's special?'

He smiled again: 'This one's special.'

Petra found herself praying to all the gods of the place that this autumn season would be the clearest and brightest and longest for a hundred years.

16 August 1953

We navigate head down through fog, following the prints we made yesterday on the snow. The snow is mucky and yellowish. The air is not much better. A warm wind (a cousin of the Alpine föhn?) is blowing from the tropics and turning to fog in the cold air over the glacier. The glacier basin seems to act as a funnel, concentrating the warm air. The monsoon snow-covering has melted, and the old snow is showing through. All through the afternoon we listen to the avalanches on Auraz. But luckily (and we hope that this luck is dependable) there is no evidence of avalanche activity on our own mountain. The slope only gets the sun in the early morning. The snow is crisp and icy, and slow to melt even under these conditions. We are all waiting for the weather to change, so that we can attack that snow-ice with our axes. But even Tai Singh has lost his outward enthusiasm. Young Tom has stopped talking at all. They seem to have entered a competition to see which of them can make the glacier crossing fastest, so they are always back at base camp early. They hang around the camp, untidily, like unemployed men on a street corner.

No one talked about hurrying, but hurry was in the air. Three days of load-carrying had established the upper glacier camp. They had made the necessary leap. They had their foothold on the mountain, and it was as if the mountain was drawing them upwards. Rowley and the Rat were self-selected to take the first ropes on to the face.

CHAPTER 6

17 August 1953

Here, above the snowline, the world keeps its ancient shape. The raw clash of wind and weather against the immovable rock creates a landscape of perpetual turmoil. Beyond this point, no human being has ever set foot. Ever. No one has made their mark, even by a footprint. These last 5,000 feet are one of the few places on earth where nature remains uncorrupted by artefact. It is as if we were setting out on to the surface of a new planet.

The desire to be the first to claim that wilderness for human kind is a sickness for which there is no cure.

We keep our desires secret from one another. Except perhaps the Scotsmen, who mutter together at the edge of the camp, and then stop talking if someone enquires their business. It is a curious truth that we who were such excellent friends in England, the companions of happy mountain days, we discover that the impulse towards the mountain is stronger than any mere human tie.

Here the diary records a blank.

The Rat had brought along his copy of the book. In the chilly camp the night before the climb, he asked Tom the reason for the missing entry.

'Did you cut the pages?'

Tom denied this. 'She must have ripped them out herself. Or never written anything.'

'But what happened?'

'Do I need to tell you? There was a row.'

19 August 1953

Climbing pairs for the ascent to Camp Two. Pat and Jock, Hayter and Amory, Kemp and Ormerod, Lennard with Tai Singh. We form ropes of four over the last part of the glacier. The Scotsmen have crampons with front points. The rest of us hack steps. If I had known that front-pointed crampons allowed one to walk on water I would have sold all I possess to buy a pair. As a saving in energy, they are equal to a day's food and several thousand feet of ascent. Hayter and Lennard are both veteran cutters of steps in steep snow. They use three swift, accurate blows from the adze-head of the ice-axe. Each step takes a second or two to cut, sufficient to take the teeth of the crampons which protrude vertically downwards from the boot. But the Scotsmen have two more points, horizontally under each toe, so they could theoretically stand on vertical ice. It means they can walk up the steep slope, with both hands free.

The team all had front-pointed crampons, these having become the only available style. Rowley and the Rat did not have to get their footwear made specially by a blacksmith as Pat and Jock had done. They set out in the first glimmer of dawn, when the ridge was just visible as a dark edge against the grey sky. Huddled together in the mess tent, they forced themselves to eat some breakfast – tea and porridge oats.

'I'll have jam on my oats,' Rowley said.

Appetite was a problem. The early hour, the altitude and the anticipation of danger, all conspired to produce a revulsion against food.

Diane doled out a spoonful from a tin. 'We should have brought more jam.'

'Can't you make some out of whinberries?' Daz was still in his sleeping bag, saving his strength.

'Magic I cannot,' replied his girlfriend.

The Rat swallowed the last of his porridge with a visible gulp. He drained his tea.

'Let's go.' He used an American-cop-movie voice, making a joke of it; he was not managing to smile. He unzipped the tent and crawled out. The tent-flap opened on to a grey world.

Petra drank the last of her own tea, cool, tinny and tasting of earth. She was wearing fleece clothing all over, topped off with a duvet jacket, but still she felt cold. Rowley crawled out of the tent after his friend. After a couple of minutes Petra followed. Diane and Daz were putting on another brew, and Diane was back in her sleeping bag. Petra zipped up the tent behind her, to keep the interior warm. There was a slight chill wind off the snow. But the air was crackling with cold and all the avalanches were silent.

Rowley sat on a rock at the edge of the camp, strapping his crampons. The Rat was pacing about, all ready to go. They both carried sacks full of rope and gear.

'Have a nice day,' said Petra.

The Rat was humming a tune under his breath. '"Dream trog. Oh my essential space walk. Dre-eam."'

'What?'

'It's a track from Antifreeze.'

'Right.'

Rowley tightened the last strap and tucked the end in under his gaiter. 'Beam me up.'

'Bye.' Petra stayed put as the other two set out across the snow. They were so self-absorbed that she might as well have been standing behind a sheet of glass.

As they walked away towards the mountain, they went out of sight from time to time because of the uneven ground. Then, as the dawn turned to daylight, the Day-Glo colours of their clothing became visible against the blue snow, and the line of sight remained unbroken. Slowly they crept up the slope. There was a pause, fifteen minutes or so, then one figure started to move alone.

Tom, coming up behind Petra, surprised her as his foot caught against a loose stone. He put out a hand to steady himself.

'Halfwit,' he muttered, as he caught Petra by the arm. 'You all right, lass?'

She nodded. She had glanced only briefly at him before turning her eyes back to the climbers.

'I should've looked where I was going. I was looking up and trying to walk at the same time. I've got the field glasses.'

Petra took the binoculars and held them against her eyes. She needed a moment or two to find the focus. The blank smooth snow-face had no point of contrast on it by which she could gauge depth or distance. To begin with, the objectives showed only a white blur. She concentrated on the rocks in the foreground, and made herself look from rock to rock as if stepping towards the mountain by giant-size leaps. A tiny part of the way up the face she saw the Rat. He was recognisable by his lime-green Goretex jacket and his mirror-glass sunspecs. He was standing in a bucket-step in the snow, with his legs hidden from the knee downwards. He was looking up, with his hands at his belt controlling the belay device, and his body curving up and around backwards. His neck was bent so far back that his face was almost horizontal. His mouth was slightly open.

The rope ran straight upwards, a fine dark line drawn by a mapping pen on cartridge paper. Balanced on the top of this line was Rowley, the leader.

Petra saw the red jacket, the hunched shoulders obscuring the head as Rowley moved up on his ice-axe holds. Then his hands moved up: one, two. A pause for breath, head hung. Then a brief glance upwards and the feet followed. Petra had a glimpse of blond hair sprouting out around a red headband; then the shoulders were hunched again.

He was moving quickly, considering the altitude. Within half an hour, the rope was fixed and the Rat was climbing up behind him. The rope was 150 feet long. The mountain, from glacier to peak, was 4,000 feet high.

Petra let the glasses fall. She was feeling slightly giddy with the concentration. She tried and failed to calculate the ratio between 150 and 4,000.

'It never gets easier,' remarked Tom.

Petra raised the binoculars to her eyes again. 'What doesn't?'

'The green-eyed monster. You want to be up there first, don't you?'

'Oh. You want to look through the glasses? They're moving like snails. What is he doing?'

'The glasses,' said Tom. Reluctantly, she handed them back. 'Thanks.'

He looked for a while, in silence, and Petra stayed beside him. The great scoop of the glacier basin was filled with silence. Even the ant-like figures on the snow-face appeared to be making no noise. The clear clipped line of the mountain ridge divided the white snow from the blue sky, a statement of simplicity.

'This really is a stupendous place,' said Petra.

Tom was still looking through the binoculars. 'An unearthly beauty.'

'What do you mean by that?'

'It doesn't have much to do with us mortals, beavering away at the climb.'

Petra, hearing the meaning behind the words, replied: 'I expect we won't scrap so much now we've got something to do.'

'Don't take bets.' He lowered the binoculars, but did not take his eyes off the climbers.

Petra found herself talking again. 'Well, I've read all about it in the book. All that jostling for position. But aren't we different?'

'Not that much. We're all climbers, just the same.'

He looked at her at last, but there was not much to read in his expression. 'It's catching up with me, I guess.'

Petra realised how very isolated they were, in that scooped-out bowl among the mountains. In such a place, a hand might be stretched out to the most unlikely source of reassurance. And even Tom Ormerod might need someone to talk to.

'You're remembering just how you felt at the time? Was it Hannah you were thinking of?'

'Aye. And that tyke Tai Singh. He was wild about her. Seems he still is. To him she's completely identified with the mountain.'

'Well that's true, she is.'

Petra's words fell into another silence. She was aware of a faint sense of disappointment. Tom was staring again, not at the climbers, but out at the distant rim of the glacier, beyond which lay the valley.

'That's it, I suppose. Plain envy on my part. There aren't many mountains that belong for ever to one person. Where else does it happen? Herman Buhl on Nanga Parbat. Shipton for Nanda Devi, though he didn't climb it. Mallory and Everest. Either you write the book or you leave your bones on the mountain. Hannah did better. She did both. But she wouldn't have planned it that way.'

Petra waited. She knew better by now than to ask any more questions.

'She told me she was too restless to be happy anywhere. It was when we were at Camp Two, while the Scotsmen pushed the route. She said – and it's a funny thing, she's always going on about stars and planets and heavenly bodies in that diary, but I never heard her talk about it except that one time – she said, wouldn't it be great if we could climb to the moon, and look back on the earth from outer space. The mountain-top wasn't enough for her. She always wanted the next thing. I'd have been glad enough of the peak. Glad enough to go home and hang up my boots and never try anything of the sort again.'

'But you wouldn't be beaten by her?'

'No. I wouldn't be beat.'

He was silent for a moment, but he did not lift the binoculars again. 'It's nothing to do with her being female. I've got a lot of time for females who go climbing in general. It was something about her which would've been the same if she'd been a great hairy Scotsman.'

Petra smiled, and Tom echoed the smile. 'I can't put it in words. But you're not like her, not at all.' He handed her the binoculars. 'Keep an eye on them. I'm going to report to the leader.'

He picked his way back through the morass of dirty snow and clinker which paved the camp. Diane was outside the tent by now, brushing her hair.

Petra could not look back for long. She soon had the binoculars trained on the climbers once again. Her eyes were blurred with all the staring. She thought of how far they still had to go before the summit. She thought of Hannah, wanting to leap on towards the moon. Perhaps it was Hannah's quality of imagination that had left Tom feeling so uncomfortable, and so determined not to be beaten in the more earthbound competition. Hannah would not have known what the earth looked like from space. She had died before the days of moon travel. But she had been out there in her imagination and had seen it.

Like Tom, Petra envied her.

21 August 1953

Peculiar coincidences happen in these mountains. Some make the encounter between Oedipus and his stepfather seem quite plausible. But the paths by which people come and go are few, and certain families breed true. When Harry was a boy, before he went to school, he was brought up in India. There was one summer he used to tell me about when the family went out to the hills, avoiding the hot weather in the Plains where his father was district officer. He remembers a morning when he rose early before the rest of the family and was astonished to find a hillman sitting on the steps of the verandah, patiently waiting for the master of the house to emerge. The young man, with his fearsome old muzzle-loading rifle and bandolier, said he was a shikari. Young Harry thought that was his name. In fact, a shikari is just the Hindustani for a huntsman. The hunter had come to take Harry's father shooting. What Harry never included in this tale is that this rather unfashionable hill-station was in the foothills of the Kala valley, east of Harigarh. It seems that the shikari was the father of Tai Singh.

Now this is remarkable enough (although Tai Singh has fifteen brothers and sisters, any one of which we might have encountered), but it is more remarkable in the effect on Harry of having known Tai's father. It is not quite so great a recommendation as having been to school with the man, but it confers a respectability which no effort on Tai Singh's own part could achieve. Harry has taken him in hand and is teaching him to climb.

I am not sure that this is the right time or place.

I am burning my heart out with all this ferrying of gear. I envy those pre-war Everest expeditions (and even the self-advertising juggernaut of 1953) who have Sherpas or Dhotials to do the donkey work on the lower slopes. But it has been pointed out to me, none too subtly, that she who carries her own equipment bags a place on the summit push.

Hayter and Amory are ready to find a way through the rock-band at last. They reckon this will crack the climb and we'll all sail on to the top. But I believe that the rock-band is not the hardest part of the climb. The summit ridge is a knife-edge, and beneath the snow it must be less solid than the rock-band. The tell-tale notch in the skyline which allows us to gain the ridge is a sure sign of a weakness in the underlying structure of the rock.

I look forward to the climbing, as a glutton looks forward to a dish of spring asparagus when he has eaten too many Bath buns. The lower snowslopes, repeated too often under too heavy a load, have acquired a daunting sameness.

At evening, Rowley and the Rat burst upon the camp with howls of joy and triumph, and white powdered snow encrusted on their clothes and hair.

'It goes, it goes!'

Daz, like all of them, had been watching through binoculars on and off all day. He had to shout louder than his friends to get them to calm down.

'Report, Mr Spock.'

He got the expected answer from the Rat.

'Star-date ten zillion. Site identified for camp, and ropes fixed.'

'What, all of them?'

'No, just a couple of pitches where it begins to steepen. There'll be a bit of donkey-work further on. But it's a plod up to there.'

Their excitement was palpable and infectious. Petra realised that she had not really expected the route to be still there in the same form, more than thirty years later.

'You got to the rock-band? I didn't see you.'

'Not quite,' admitted the Rat. 'We did a snatch of the last few pitches because we were out of time. But we were way up the snowslope, and the ledge for the camp is obvious.'

Rowley struck an attitude. 'It is a horizontal island in a sea of verticality.'

'Prize for poetry,' growled Daz.

'Aren't you going to say "Well done, chaps"?'

'Jammy buggers. I'll be jumaring up those ropes tomorrow – just you wait.'

Diane, shivering in her fleecy boiler-suit, muttered: 'Didn't know it was a race.'

'It is, darling, it is,' crowed the Rat, and gave her a smacking kiss. 'You'll love Camp Two. Nice day out for the ladies.'

'Bollocks,' replied the lady, wriggling free.

'How about some food?'

The day, already at an end, suddenly turned into night. It was a matter of minutes after the triumphant return that Petra realised that she could not see beyond the circle of light from the camp's storm-lantern. All the colours disappeared, even the Rat's Day-Glo jacket.

Dinner was the usual tedious composite of boiled rice and something to help it down. At this altitude, the rice was taking longer than ever to boil, and there were gritty bits among the grains. The sauce was something out of a packet. The two pioneer climbers, once the exhilaration of their feat had died down, were almost too tired to eat.

They crept away to bed. The rest of the party discussed who should follow up and consolidate the climb on the morrow.

'Typical,' remarked Daz. 'They snatched the last few pitches instead of sticking up another fixed rope.'

'That's sour grapes,' insisted Diane. 'You weren't there.'

Petra, picking over the last of her unpalatable plateful, waited for Daz to make some statement about the plans for the next day. He was meant to be the leader, after all. But he turned to whisper something in Diane's ear. She giggled.

'So.' Ieuan had been the only one not visibly excited by the substantial gains from the first day's climbing. 'Does that mean it's going to be easier than we thought?'

There was a patch of silence while the climbers considered how to reply to this absurdly naive question.

'No,' Tom said at last, quite kindly. 'But luck was on our side today.'

Daz was sitting cross-legged, slightly hunchbacked under the curved roof of the dome tent. He slapped his hands down on his splayed knees. 'Well, Tom?' he asked decisively.

'I'm easy. There'll be plenty of other days.'

Petra, looking down into her plate, kept saying to herself, 'I will not ask. I will not say 'Take me too'. I never have and I shan't now. I am one of the lead climbers in this outfit.'

After slightly too long a pause, Daz found the grace to say, 'Do you fancy the job, Pet?'

She looked him straight in the eye and replied, 'I'm easy. There'll be plenty of other days.'

Diane laughed. 'Good on yer.' But she was looking at Daz, not Petra.

'OK. Feminine bloody conspiracy. Are you coming or aren't you, Ms bloody Merriman?'

Petra looked at him and smiled. 'You won't be disappointed.'

Everything up to that point had been a means to an end, even that last piece of manipulative behaviour. But at dawn the next day, even while the valley was in the blue shadow of the sunrise behind the eastern peaks, Petra would set out axe in hand, looped coils of rope in the other, across the last of the glacier and on to the face of Himalchand. She lay down at night with that image crowding her mind.

As the night progressed, the sound of the avalanches died down, until by midnight the snow had been frozen into silence. But Petra could not sleep, because of her anticipation of the day to come. This was the push for the summit: the final thread in the complex tapestry of preparation.

As she lay there, she could hear the sound of breathing. Everyone in the circle of tents would snore raucously by turns, and then subside into silence, as if holding their breath. There was no other noise in the universe, and the night was completely dark.

'Daz?'

'Mmm.'

From the big tent, five yards away, even the quietest speech was now audible.

'I don't want you to go.'

A groan.

'You've heard the avalanches. I'm just afraid you'll go up there and never come back.'

'Diane, please, let me sleep.'

There was a few minutes' silence, which was broken by a sniff.

'Oh, for God's sake, Diane, don't cry.'

'I'm not tough. I'm not a heroine like Petra. I couldn't bear it if you fell off. You must be very careful. You will be careful, won't you, Daz? And you'll look after Petra?'

'What's got into you now? I need my sleep.'

'You don't care, do you? You don't understand. I've got to wait down here, not knowing what's going on, not being able to do anything. It's worse than being in danger, the not knowing.'

The sobs started again. Too late, Petra put her fingers in her ears. She did not want to be reminded of her own mortality.

She did not want to lose the image of the mountain. All she could hear was the irregular, quick rhythm of her pulse.

22 August 1953

This is written at Camp Two, which is the first camp properly on the face.

Tom made the suggestion. We carried spare mountain rations up 2,500 feet of steep snow. The lead climbers are through the band of rock and should be setting up the top camp by now. Tom and I are meant to retreat back to the glacier camp at the end of the day.

The campsite is on the rock band above the lower snow-face. It is a perilous situation. Avalanches course down the diagonal gully above, but they seem to have a tradition of not overflowing the banks. The flat shelf where the tent was pitched is perhaps ten feet square; elsewhere the ledges are no bigger than one's footprints.

'This is a wild place,' Tom said when we arrived. He was in a strangely garrulous mood. I concurred with his view. Then he added: 'Your old man's lost interest, hasn't he?'

I was shocked to silence by these words of wisdom from the lips of our usually silent and oracular mascot. He thought I was shocked for some other reason, so he blushed very nicely, and tried to explain. He said: 'That native youth. Harry's teaching him to climb, just like he taught me when I were a lad. I doubt he's concentrating on being an expedition leader.'

'Indeed,' said I, still astounded at his verbosity.

He went on, 'Hayter and Amory and the Scotsmen have bagged the summit attempt, right?'

The lad was reading my mind. I grinned at him, a horrible sight no doubt. 'Right.'

He grinned back. 'So we're staying the night here, like?'

We stayed the night. As daylight was fading, I peered out through the doorway of the tent and made the mistake of looking vertically down. There was a curious illusion. The snowslope was so featureless that the camp below seemed small rather than distant, as if one could stretch out a hand and seize one of the tiny figures.

As never before, I felt that we were suspended above the world, like ethereal beings. Below us these ant-like people creep across the grey glacier. Beyond, fold upon fold into the distance, the earth is blue. Like the sky.

Petra, unladen and eager, embraced the climb as if it were her own treasured child. For the day, the mountain was her own, even though others had been that way before.

The first part was the easiest, because the slope curved inwards in a parabola. Rowley and the Rat had said they had left fixed ropes anchored in place from the point where solo climbing ceased to be prudent. Thereafter it was a question of climbing the rope by artificial means.

Daz let Petra take the lead on the first fixed rope. She threaded the rope through the camming system of the jumar-clamp. The handle of the clamp had a trigger device to allow it to be pushed up the rope, but which clamped shut immediately if the jumar tried to slide downwards. Petra checked that the clamp was on the rope the right way up, then she clipped it to her belt. For fixed-rope climbing she needed only one jumar; in a place where she might have to climb a free-hanging rope, a second jumar with a tape-loop for the foot would be added. It was a system which essentially allowed self-belaying, and was the standard way to get a large number of people quickly up a fixed rope.

Daz followed close behind Petra. They reached the snow-stake to which the top of the fixed rope was belayed; they looked in vain for the lower end of the next rope.

'They haven't bloody fixed any more ropes!' growled Daz. 'God knows where they went. We'll have to find the route again.'

Fine powder-snow had filled up all the footprints. It showered gently down from above, like dust.

Daz cut some larger footholds and stood in them. 'You'd better take the lead.'

'I wonder how far they did get. How many snowstakes do we have?'

'I don't f—ing care.'

"We're doing well, anyway.' Petra would not be daunted by Daz's bad humour. She was sorting out the coils in the lime-green rope, which was to be fixed on the upper part of the slope.

'We'll have to haul the sacks, further up.'

'Look, aren't you too puffed to lead through?' suggested Daz.

'No.'

She spoke sharply. The strength lent by excitement was a precarious thing. She dared not let Daz call it into question.

'OK, OK.'

Petra drew a deep breath. The air was perceptibly thinner and very cold. The sun was hidden behind a layer of high cloud. 'I'm climbing.'

Daz settled himself on the belay. 'Look out for lost abseil points.'

23 August 1953

> I have been thinking seditious thoughts. I am the pack pony who decides to lead the battle charge. I have always gone second or third, or sixth – never at the pinnacle of this human pyramid linked by rope. Yet it is there I must stand, whether I deserve it or not. I have no argument to offer which is based on anything that my friends would call reason, and none of us has any breath left for argument. Like the draught-horse in battle, my only chance is to go mad and run the wrong way by accident. I must cheat.
>
> How the cold encircles us! I can feel it embrace us like a giant unfriendly hand. The primus splutters impotently and melts a little grey snow. The tea tastes of solder. The only warmth is inside our sleeping-sacks.
>
> We fear the end of the summer season. Already the avalanches on the cliffs of Tengdatta are smaller and less

frequent than before. The mountain, which thawed a little in the monsoon, has begun to freeze solid again. The snow conditions, always a little precarious, have become perfect. And today the Scotsmen set out from the camp on the ridge. They will reach the summit.

And our purpose? As Tom tends the melting snow, and I wrestle with the congealed straps of my crampons, I fear it would be bad luck to reveal our purpose now.

Petra was at the apex of the human pyramid. For the distance of one rope-length she was the pioneer. The snow-slope in front of her was innocent of any human imprint. If the lads really had come this far the day before, all sign of their progress had been obliterated.

As she began the rhythmical upward movement, she had a sudden thought of the kind that Hannah had always been so good at expressing. For Petra, thought did not take the form of eloquent words. But she could feel the mountain as if it were a living creature; this mountain, and all the other mountains she had ever climbed, formed into an army of omniscient but capricious giants. She could have addressed them each by name: Rothorn, Dent Blanche, Dru, Cima Grande.

She had the feeling, never so clearly felt before, that to climb any mountain was the ultimate in hopeless endeavours. She, and all her predecessors since Mummery, had wasted effort in ascending to summits whereon they would leave no record of their passing. But untouched snow was a perpetual and irresistible temptation.

Petra, putting the thought into words, said aloud, 'I'm going to get to the top.'

The words were whispered, because of the thin air and the breathless effort of climbing. They were snatched away and scattered by the cool wind.

After two more steps, her mind closed down again. The altitude, which had robbed her brain of oxygen, first created fantasies and visions, and then blinded the inner eye. She became an automatic creature. One, two, three, four – each limb moving slowly and singly, leaving three stable points of contact on the slope. No trace of human intelligence was required for this exercise.

All the time, the rope was being paid out behind her, a fine streak of green on the snow. As a rope's length increased, its usefulness, except in a most unimaginable disaster, decreased. At the end of 150 feet, that rope was merely a means of chaining the climber to the earth. It weighed heavily.

Petra stopped. She was now higher above the earth than she had ever been before. The summits of the Alps, even the highest of them, would barely have protruded above the rubble in the glacier.

She let the breath catch up with her. Briefly, she felt the wonder of it all. She was hammering in another belay, clearing snow away for a stance, clipping karabiners into loops of rope. The business ended with the three sharp tugs on the rope which signified a safe belay, the big-mountain equivalent of the craggers' 'Climb when you're ready.'

Daz had seen her halt. He started climbing.

In the end they fixed another five pitches of static rope. They did not reach the site for the next camp. It was evident that Rowley and the Rat had not got anywhere near the rockband the day before. They had reached a minor outcrop at about 1,500 feet up the face, and had drifted from the direct line of ascent.

Daz and Petra left some gear at the highest point, then abseiled all the way back down again. The ascent, which had taken the better part of the day, was reversed in a little over an hour. Back at the camp Daz immediately took the Rat to task for having failed to fix ropes.

'Unless you were such a pair of wallies you lost your way on a blank snowfield.' As recriminations go, it was nothing like Daz's best, but it was hardly fair.

'Too right.' The Rat shrugged, and did not attempt to inflame the argument.

Rowley muttered through the folds of his red duvet-jacket something like 'stuff it'. He was not happy, but even he appeared to have become conscious that any full-scale row would endanger the whole project.

Petra tried to divert attention away from the question of who had done what wrong. 'I got all light-headed. It must be the altitude. I was seeing things.'

'What, little green men?' snarled Rowley.

'No.' She rather wished she had not raised the subject. 'Sort of shapeless visions. Did you get that?'

'No, I didn't. And you're beginning to sound like Hannah.'

That night she dreamed. The unrestful, fitful sleep of high altitude was a breeding-ground for dreams, but usually they left no memory behind. A strange taste in the mouth, or a shapeless feeling of unease, or the now-accustomed sense of suffocation: these were the usual consequences of dreaming. But the day after her high point, Petra remembered the whole night of dreaming more clearly than she remembered the details of the climb. The colours and shapes of things remained bright and clear, superimposed upon the background of the tent's roof, even after she had opened her eyes. For a few minutes she dwelt between vision and reality. It was something that had not happened to her since childhood.

She was afraid. It was not the exciting, invigorating fear of physical danger, but a more primitive emotion. The old ghosts, returning from her childhood and her ancestry, had come back to remind her of the precariousness of her own fate.

It had been Rowley's brother-like remark, getting his retaliation in first, which had sunk in rather deeper than Petra would voluntarily have allowed. He had compared her directly with Hannah. Petra found she was having the climber's death dream of falling. Always falling but never coming to rest. Each time she felt that she had reached the ground, she would fall again, in an endlessly repeated sequence. And each fall was a little different from the last – from rock, or snow, or high buildings, or tall trees, or out of an aeroplane. Each time she fell, she experienced a sense of escape, and relief, immediately before the fear gripped her.

She did not tell her dreams to anyone. Rowley might have laughed. Diane was nervous enough without taking on Petra's fears. Ieuan, ever since the camp by the river, had not made free with his own thoughts, and Petra felt that she could not impose hers without invitation.

That day the Rat was out of sorts with his gut again, so Daz and Rowley went to fix the last of the ropes and set up a tent at Camp Two. Petra, after her troubled night, was in no fit state for lead climbing.

Diane chose to be cosy and make pancakes using a dried mix from a packet. Ieuan had shaken off his mood enough to help her. Tom sat on a boulder and polished his boots again.

Petra sat on a more distant boulder and did not watch the climbers. She was thinking over Rowley's remark, 'You're getting just like Hannah.'

Almost, she wished she were. Hannah had become more than a name to all of them. She was company on the climb. She was the element of imagination which the new, young, tough style of climbers had never learned to express. But imagination was the enemy to hard, painful achievement because it made one question the single-minded need to get to the top of the mountain.

The weather was a little worse, with uneven cloud collecting in the V-shape of the Munshu valley. Petra watched the cloud, and after a while Tom came clumping along with his boots unlaced. The leather of the boots was dark brown with oil, and the red bootlaces were encrusted. He sat on the next rock and took out his pipe. Petra stared at the boots.

'You haven't thought of getting plastic boots, like us?'

'No.'

'They keep your feet warm.'

'Warm and sweaty. I had some once. You can't feel your toes. I was tripping and stumbling all over.'

'Less chance of frostbite, of course.'

'I'll take my chance. I've survived thus far. Did I ever tell you about the traverse of Punta da Cerro?'

'No.'

'I went in '64. Nearly came unstuck at the start because there was a revolution in Bolivia and the customs didn't want to let all our metal gear into the country in case it was used for making bombs.'

'What did you do?'

'Hayter bribed the boss. Hayter generally knew how much to bribe people. A wee bit like your Rat. No illusions about humanity.'

He paused, and chewed at the stem of his pipe. 'He were past forty then, and devil-may-care. That were the last time he went high. He used to climb afterwards in odd little boots with round toes, because his feet were short from having his toes chopped off.'

'Eugh,' said Petra.

'You didn't see his feet after we came down from the Punta. Black and stinking. The Bolivian doctors didn't have any penicillin, so the only safe course was to amputate. Hayter asked to keep the toes, as a memento.'

'You're joking.'

'I'm not. He kept them in a pickle jar, like so many little black gherkins.'

'He kept them?'

'He would have, but the customs at Southampton confiscated them as a health hazard.'

'You're pulling my leg.'

Tom grinned. 'Nobbut a bit.' He took off his left boot and began to peel off the grey woollen sock underneath. Like all of them, his socks had been without washing since they left the valley. The sock had moulded itself perfectly to the contours of his foot.

'See here.' He wiggled five pasty white toes. Or rather four and a half. The smallest toe was missing its tip, including the toenail.

'Frostnip,' said Tom. 'That's my souvenir of South

America.' He put the sock and boot back on.

Petra felt a little sick. 'If we get frostbitten, will Ieuan have to cut off our toes?'

'I don't think so. I believe there have been medical advances in twenty years. Frostbite in March, and amputate in October. Or so Ieuan's book says.'

'I'll have to ask him.' Petra frowned a little and turned her gaze back to the billowing mass of valley cloud. For a little while there was silence, then came the rumble of an avalanche on Tengdatta. She shivered.

'Ieuan hasn't spoken to me for days. That's not good for the expedition, is it?'

Tom gnawed at his pipe, which had gone out. The air smelt of damp tobacco.

'It depends on how you mean that. Did you have a row?'

'I don't think so.'

'You'd know if you had. The lad is preoccupied. He takes the business of medical officer seriously. He thought, before we set out, that he might be in a position to save lives. Now he knows he won't. When you're up above Camp Two you might as well be on the moon, as far as he's concerned.'

'So what'll he do?'

'I'll tell you what, and you can moot it with the others. Make sure Ieuan gets practice using fixed ropes on the face. Get him carrying loads. He's got the muscle for it.'

'He's never done it.'

'He got up the cave route with us, that first day. I wouldn't call that amateur.'

'OK. But he was concentrating hard, all the time. When he loses concentration, he trips. You've seen him.'

'Hmm. And you never trip up?'

'Never. I've spent seven years getting it right. It's instinct, like walking.'

Tom laughed, and his laugh was drowned by the booming roar of another avalanche. 'The certainty of youth!'

'You calling me arrogant?'

'Well, aren't you? That, or ignorant.'

'Is that what Ieuan thinks?'

'You tell me.'

Petra sat very quiet and still. 'You really do think that? Then why aren't you slamming into Rowley too, or the Rat, or Daz? They're all totally ignorant and bumptious with it.'

It was Tom's turn to look down the valley. 'How do I say it? The world is made up of all sorts and types of men and women, but life isn't a perpetual competition.'

'It is,' insisted Petra. 'It is now. We're climbing a mountain.'

'We'll only do that as a team. We've got no room for solo heroics. Go and get Ieuan working with a jumar, so he can carry loads up the fixed rope. Get him joining in.'

'Why? You tell him.' Petra knew that she was sounding thoroughly ungracious, but this talk with Tom had snatched her out of the peculiar dream-like state in which she had dwelt ever since the start of the climbing. She was not grateful to him for being practical.

Tom tapped his pipe out on a convenient stone. A wisp of smoke rose from the dottle.

'I'm not the leader.'

'Nor am I.'

That double denial stopped the conversation in its tracks. But the silence was readable. Tom looked at Petra, and neither of them was smiling. There had been no mutiny in the expedition, but Daz continued to show no inclination to try to build a team. He had been elected leader, rather than volunteering for the job. He was one of the lads. Perhaps he believed that the friends could carry on in the same old way on Himalchand as they had at home. Tom Ormerod was not going to upset that consensus.

'OK.' Tom shrugged his shoulders and got to his feet. 'We'd better have a look at progress on the mountain. That cloud'll be with us in an hour.'

24 August 1953

Back at Camp One. Utter disgrace. Lennard furious. Tom sulking. The summit ridge of Himalchand is a line of light.

25 August 1953

Lennard is right, of course. Tom and I should not have even attempted to climb to the ridge. There was not room for us in the tent at the ridge camp with the other four, and the supplies were meant to be carried upwards, not consumed on the spot.

Let me set it down here. Tom and I, eschewing the wisdom of the leadership, spent the day before yesterday battling our way through the rock problems on the band. It was mixed snow and ice work, requiring concentration, but our friends had left a few rock pegs. We got to the upper ice-field, and saw the ridge curving up to the summit, and then down came the cloud. We might have crawled on up to the ridge camp, which was as full as it could hold of Hayter, Amory and two Scotsmen; and thus we would probably have ruined the expedition's chances of success.

It was not nobility of mind, but caution about the weather that made us turn back. Lennard's fury upon our return was born out of anxiety at our having gone missing for two days. I fear he may also have shouted at Tai Singh, who is looking cowed. Tom is ominously silent; he is no doubt regretting his caution, since the threat of bad weather came to nothing. My job seems to be to pick up the pieces of everyone, applying spiritual balm and sweet tea.

But the Scotsmen have planned another go at the summit today. The weather favours them, and the greater part of the route has been reconnoitred. For the first time in four days, that creeping fog is not coming up the valley during the morning.

And once Pat and Jock have been to the summit, the hunger for success will be quenched. The expedition does not exist to put all its members on the summit. It exists to put someone (or two) there.

I keep in mind that image of the ridge, dipping, twisting and curling back on itself, sinuous, white and breathtakingly thin. At times one can see through it like frosted glass.

Was that vision enough for me? By the will of the expedition, I should not even have seen that.

Three days on, Camp Two was in existence, with the prospect of the push up to the ridge ahead of them.

Daz, in a moment of rare decision, had concluded that the man who had been there before, however long ago, should be entrusted with the initial difficulties of route-finding along the rock-band.

'If Rowley and the Rat can get lost on a blank snowslope, they'll be helpless on mixed ground.' He made the statement to a dinnertime meeting of the entire team in the mess tent. The Rat was still rather ill with his tenacious stomach-upset, and twice he had to excuse himself from the meeting.

Rowley, shaggier than ever, and with the beginnings at last of a downy beard, growled his disapproval.

'Well, Ben?' asked Daz.

'This ain't a democracy. What'm I supposed to say?'

'You'll get your chance later.'

'Sure.'

Everyone sat in rather uncomfortable silence. Petra felt that anything she might say would only make matters worse.

It was Ieuan's job to do this, however.

'Who would you want with you?' he asked Tom. He spoke in the peculiarly expressionless fashion which had settled on him at high altitude. It was as if he alone, lacking the physical imperative of climbing, felt too sluggish to think clearly.

Rowley interrupted. 'Not you, Taff, I hope. I don't fancy digging you out of a snowdrift.'

'I wasn't volunteering.' He did not even look Rowley in the eye. He had been doing a conscientious job, taking gear up to

Camp Two along the fixed ropes, but his imperviousness to the inspiration of the mountain and to the challenge of the summit had never been more evident.

Rowley of course took the whole thing as a sneer. 'This isn't something you volunteer for. It's a diktat from the Führer and the worst you can do is look keen. Shit, I made one mistake. I was doped up by the altitude. I'm going to be more careful. I'm still a good climber.'

Petra looked down at the ground. The blue nylon groundsheet was muddy and scuffed and dotted with bits of dinnertime rice. She thought of the squalor that was the inevitable companion of climbers. She thought, but did not say to Rowley: 'It only takes one mistake'. Even in her own short experience, she had seen friends forced out of climbing by serious injury; a few more distant acquaintances had died. The Himalaya were particularly lethal. Rowley's urge to be first was potentially as dangerous as Hannah's. Except perhaps that it was clearly and repeatedly expressed. Hannah seemed always to have kept her own ambitions a secret.

Petra spoke up. 'I'll come with you, Tom.'

'Fine.' Tom's answer was out, almost in the same moment as Daz's 'Hey!' and Rowley's more flamboyant expletive.

'Votes?' Diane asked brightly.

'She's got mine,' said Ieuan. 'But this isn't a democracy.'

'Why?' Rowley demanded.

'You said so yourself. Daz is the dictator.'

'No. Why vote for Petra?'

'Because she's bold. And I haven't heard her complain yet.'

Rowley glowered. 'You think we boss her about? You're joking!'

Ieuan seemed ready with a reply, then visibly thought better of it. The faces in the lamplight were all looking at him.

At that moment the door-zip opened and in crawled the Rat from his hygienic excursion. He was beginning to look thin about the face, and his pasty complexion was scabbed by tufts of dark beard.

'How's things, Tim?' Daz asked.

The Rat put a hand to his tummy and made a face. 'Montezuma's revenge, I believe.' But he had not missed the atmosphere of the meeting, and was not prepared to be used as a diversion. He sat down carefully, cross-legged on the ground.

'I've got my opinion too.'

'What?' demanded Daz.

'If we don't start to pull together we're going to fall apart at the seams. And if I sound like Gobert-Jones then so be it. This mountain isn't going to make allowances for seven weedy little climbers. I've realised that if this gut of mine doesn't shape up I won't get up to the top. But I'll be pissed off if no one gets up the mountain because we're all scrapping. And I don't mean just Ieuan and Rowley. I know there are ideological differences there which won't go away. I mean all of us. Probably me too. I'm probably making things worse by making a speech. But I've talked to each one of you, by turns, and everyone seems to think it's the other guy's fault. Even you, Tom. You can't help being the experienced mountaineer, but how are the rest of us meant to catch up? I've got a proposal. Send Tom and Pet to make Camp Three on the ridge. With a chance to snatch the summit if things go smoothly. Ieuan and I keep the lower camp supplied. And if we have brilliant weather for several days, we can do a shuttle in twos and threes and all go for the top. But this way Pet and Tom get the first go but Daz and Rowley get the best chance. And I guess the rest of us stay out of the contest.'

It was a long speech, and was met by a strenuous silence from the climbers. This was Radinsky the lawyer, the son for whom the Rat's Jewish father had hoped in vain.

'Christ,' muttered Daz.

Petra and Rowley both spoke at once.

'We didn't.'

'We aren't.'

They both stopped in mid-sentence. Petra blushed. She

could feel herself doing so. Rowley scratched his head.

'Look. I've known you two longer than anyone. And the name of the game is competition.' The Rat had clearly got the bit between his teeth. 'When you were sixteen years old you'd go and practise in secret on a problem which the other one had failed on. That's why you climb better when the other one isn't there. But I've never thought you'd give up being friends because of it.'

He looked expectantly at Rowley.

'Stop picking on me,' said his friend.

'I'm not. I'm picking on whatever it is which makes you and Pet pull in opposite directions.'

'We don't,' stammered Petra. The tent, under its round red dome, seemed very close and airless. All around her the unsteady lamplight seemed to make her friends' faces indistinct. The tent was very full of people. Outside, beyond the fine nylon skin of the tent, there was nobody, only the darkness and the mountain.

'We won't any more, will we, Rowley?'

'You think the Rat's right?'

'He's got a point. We did used to go probleming in secret, trying to get better than each other. We've hardly climbed together for years. Maybe it stops being fun, competing like that, if it gets in the way of real climbing.'

'I'm not afraid of being beaten by you.'

'Yes you are. I am too. I'm really afraid of being beaten to the top by you. I'd think twice about going on the same rope, in case we got into a discussion one pitch from the summit. Tim's right. We've got to leave it to chance.'

Thus Petra, borne upwards by the web of fixed ropes, set out for their highest camp. She had Tom with her, which gave a peculiar sense of security to this increasingly dangerous climb. He had been there before. He had seen how internal competition could wreck an expedition. But Tom was the one who had come home.

25 August 1953

A second diary entry for the day. Since noon we have been watching the grey clouds roll in from the south, a new and slightly peculiar direction for the wind. The cloud has poured over the side of the Munshu valley, obscuring the lower hills but making no attempt to come up to the glacier.

We do not know what it means, but most changes in the weather are bad luck for climbers. I hope, I do hope with all my heart that the summit team has already got there and is on its way down. I have been wishing my rivals too much ill. I don't mean it. My envy is not towards them but towards the chances they have had.

'Better get in our pits. It's getting dark.'

Tom and Petra were crowded into the entrance of the tent at Camp Two. The lower snowslope, now deep blue in colour, began instantly at the edge of the tent, so there was no security out of doors. The camp was one small round tent on a shelf of snow. They had had to excavate the tent-platform out of the ridge of a small spur which stood out from the lower edge of the rock-band. Its situation was designed to allow any possible avalanche to be diverted to one side or other of the spur.

Petra shivered. 'It's much colder here.'

'There's more snow than last time.'

Petra looked up at the slope above, where the first of the parallel diagonal stripes of rock could be seen. These features, visible from the distance as dark stripes alternating with bands of snow, were each forty or fifty feet wide. She could see only the lowest snowslope, and the first few feet of jagged rock. The view was fast fading in the dim light.

'I guess we try to get back on to snow, then stick to the snow as long as we can. The rock isn't desperately solid.'

Tom grunted. 'It's better than on the ridge.'

'So we must be careful but we also mustn't hang around. What time should we retreat?'

'You tell me.'

'OK. Three o'clock. Depending. Are you giving me some sort of test?'

'I'm making sure we agree.'

Petra sighed. But even that reminder of the human turmoil which they had left behind in the valley was not enough to suppress her elation at the prospect of some really difficult climbing.

The business of making food and drink and getting to sleep took about five times as long at the high camp as it would have done at home. All the water had to be made from melted snow, and the feeble blue flame of the gas burner gave out no perceptible heat. The food was dried rations, so water had to be made to reconstitute them.

Petra, huddled up in her sleeping bag, remarked, 'I wonder if we'd save enough on fuel if we carried the water instead?'

'Hmm.' Tom poked at the little ice floe in the billycan.

'The Rat worked it all out in calories and kilos. With plenty over for an emergency. But you could die of thirst waiting.'

'Hm. Pass us some more snow.'

Petra topped up the billy. She stopped trying to talk. The point at which expedition members really begin to get on each other's nerves is when they are stuck two to a tent with no safe ground outside. There was evidence for this in every expedition-book, however superficially cheerful. Hannah's book was perhaps unique in that it told the truth about the destructive uncomradely forces at work within a small group of ambitious people.

A more practical point, which would not of course have been allowed into print when Hannah was writing, was the problem of sanitation. There was a bottle, and in Petra's case a large funnel. And an extremely rigorous set of rules for keeping that particular bottle out of the way of everything else.

It was perhaps fortunate that the relative lack of drinking water made peeing a once-daily activity. Tom of course looked the other way, although even that was difficult in a dome-tent.

Petra found the whole business rather funny, but there was no question of her sharing the joke.

When darkness came, they settled down in their sleeping bags, and the torches were turned out to save the batteries. But sleep was another matter.

After a restless half-hour, Petra said tentatively, 'Tom?'

'Aye.'

'How'll we get to sleep?'

'We will in the end. Have you got a headache?'

'No.'

'Not yet, then.'

'Have you?'

'Aye. It's the altitude, and the cold. I've felt this way before. It passes off with sleep.'

He turned over in his sleeping bag and writhed about a bit to get comfortable. Then he blew his nose. 'I remember when I was on a trip in Kenya, and we were really short of money and food. And the other bastard put marmalade on his porridge. We weren't speaking for days after that. We did a new route on Batian, on Mount Kenya. The other individual was a coffee-planter's son. Drank like a fish. He could climb, mind you.'

'What's his name?'

'Arthur Young. Young Arthur, we used to say.'

'What happened to him?'

'Bad avalanche on the Dru.'

'Oh dear.'

'Too many of my stories seem to end that way. You shouldn't get me talking. But things are a lot safer than they were. All this new gear. The last time I camped here, with Hannah, we were in a pup-tent with a separate groundsheet and no flysheet. Instead of all this Goretex clothing we had Ventile cagoules, which never would dry out. And the duck down in our bags went into lumps with the damp. And our primus went up with a three-foot orange flame and nearly set fire to the tent – it would have done if the tent hadn't been damp. Scorched the canvas.'

Petra laughed. She really could not believe in people coming up so high with equipment which she would have rejected for a Guide camp in Sussex. She was warm and relatively comfortable in her down-filled sleeping bag.

But she was lying awake, because no amount of equipment could compensate for luck in climbing. An avalanche would take no account of how good a climber she had once been. She wished that there was some good-luck charm which she could see or hold. In the darkness, waiting, there was no antidote to thought; she could not bury her anxieties in action.

'Tom,' she said again.

'Yes?'

'Nothing.' She had been about to ask him if he felt the same. But she knew immediately that no good would come of letting that particular imp out of the bottle.

Then, without realising that she had fallen asleep, she was awake, and the tent was red with the dawn.

Getting going was a lengthy process too. Outside the tent, the snow was pale pink and crisply frozen. All the footprints from yesterday were preserved intact, hard-edged. Petra and Tom had to put on crampons even to stand outside the tent. And their climbing sacks were heavy with the gear that would be necessary to protect the rock pitches.

Petra moved sleepily, hardly aware that she was out on the mountain. She and Tom covered the first snowslope moving together. The angle of the slope was now precarious, but speed was as important for safety as any arrangement of ropes.

At the first rock-step, Tom hammered a piton into a crack. Just as he had done that first day in Scotland. The hammering made a sound like a cracked bell, because the rock was fragile and unsound.

'Watch that. The rock seems to be held together by ice.'

'Will you try another placement?'

'I'll only waste time. Some belays are better than others.'

He led the pitch. Petra followed, rather too tentatively, because this was a place where neither the leader nor the second could afford to fall.

She slipped. The rope, tautening, held her solid. But her last foothold crumbled away and fell in fragments on to the snow-field. A single moment of danger, as suddenly gone.

There was no yelling. That was for local crags in England. Here, Petra was silent, amongst the silence of the mountains. She had no spare breath, for one thing. For another, a cry for help would have been useless. A cry of fear would have been a step towards panic. The tension of the rope echoed the tension in Petra's mind. She was frozen, seemingly for a long long time. Then the mind, attacking matter, told her that she must relax, because tense muscles cannot react to new unbalancing forces. Even the wind, so very slight for that altitude, might have tipped her off balance had she continued to cling hard to the holds.

She moved up, slackening the rope, and buried the pick of her ice-axe in the next snow-filled cleft. Then she breathed again.

CHAPTER 7

26 August 1953
The weather is foul. The ridge camp is abandoned, and the tent at Camp Two. No one has reached the summit.

27 August 1953
Council of war. Lennard has bravely put into words what we have superstitiously feared to say. This peak may be beyond us, not because we are feeble, or lack determination, but because we have not been blessed by the weather. The mountain is soaked in new snow, and the cloud creeps up the valley every day and hides the peak from us.

It is so near. In the clear air of dawn, we see the zigzag of the mountain ridge like the edge of a broken biscuit. It is so near that you could take a bite out of the crisp crest. It would be cool and pleasant, like the taste of a water melon. Here we sweat among the dirty snow and the foggy air.

Tom made a remark: 'T'clag's up again.' Clag is his word for this clinging mountain mist which breathes damp but will not rain.

Hayter and Amory have declared that the route will never go. They want to go and reconnoitre in the other valley, where the South Munshu glacier gives on to the west face of Himalchand. From a distance, the face seems to be one sweep of smooth steep snow up from the glacier. Hayter swears that the south-west ridge looks less jagged than ours. If that were so, it might promise solid rock. He means to go and look, just as a reconnaissance. Others of us thought the ridge looked particularly treacherous. We are not going to move camp. We are going to stay put at base, waiting for the weather.

Our own ridge, the north-east, is tortuous, steep and encrusted with snow. The Scotsmen have let us know why they failed.

'Pinnacles like a stickleback. Every one with a cornice or a sérac. And the ridge between is a knife-edge.'

'It was the wind. We could not stay upright.'

'Aye. A balancing act. Even with Jock's ballast.'

They are reasonable men. They have made a frank assessment of the risk. The far side of the ridge is a 7,000-foot precipice. But they make their excuses too loudly. They are still thinking about the ridge, and how temptingly close the summit was. We are reading each other's minds.

'We found the old tent.'

Petra, standing in the scuffed snow of the camp, announced this as her first words of greeting. Tom was still picking his way down the last of the snowslope, having come off the abseil rope last.

'Where?' Daz spoke sharply, as if ready to take notes.

'What was in it?' asked Diane.

'It's frozen solid into the snow. You can see the folds of material, all grey and crumpled. I thought it was rock, until the ice-axe sunk in.'

'Er.' Diane sat down. 'How peculiar.'

'It was peculiar. Tom went green.'

They all stopped talking as Tom covered the last few yards into the circle of the camp. He did not appear perceptibly different. But, he said, 'We fixed the ropes on the hard bit. We've put a tent on the ridge. It'll go.' Then he sat down. He began undoing his crampons. Petra was still geared up. She had not even put down her rucksack.

Ieuan, who seemed always to hover on the edge of things these days, came forward and took Tom's sack. He knelt down by his friend and began to undo the buckles on his other crampon.

'Petra said you found the old tent.'

'Aye.'

'Do you want to find if there's anyone still in it?'

Everyone was holding their breath. Tom shook his head. 'She's not there.'

He put his head in his hands, his crampons momentarily forgotten. 'You know. You all know the bloody story. We waited three days up there, in the bad weather. Longer, and we wouldn't have come back either. She fell. She must have fallen. The tent just contains abandoned gear. We didn't leave it for her. We were saving our own lives then.'

He paused. No one said anything. Petra looked at Diane. Diane looked back, long-faced. They were both remembering the garden in Somerset, where Harry Lennard had told them of his greatest fear. Hannah lost was a romance, at this long distance in time. Hannah found would be different, because it would fix that romance firmly to earth. It would plaster blood and flesh over the image.

'She won't be there. Would I have come here if I thought I'd find her?'

'Didn't you?' Ieuan was still the only one who would ask the question.

'No. No. I was laying a ghost, wasn't I?'

He looked up, seeing the circle of alarmed faces. He caught Petra's eye. She looked down.

'You're all young, aren't you? You're all so incredibly young.' He stood, bent down to pick up his crampons, and then went off to his tent without another word. Petra found that her knees were shaking, in a way they had not done when they had found the old tent on the ridge.

There was some coughing and shuffling of feet. Daz and Diane went off together. So did Rowley and the Rat.

Ieuan said, 'You should take off your crampons too, Petra.'

She sat, because her knees could hardly hold her. She put her head down between her knees. Ieuan put a hand on her shoulder.

'People are harder than mountains, aren't they?'

'What an awful cliché.' She felt sick, and it was not just because of altitude and exhaustion.

'But I'm still jealous of the mountain.'

'What?'

'It's that bond that you've all got, even though you spend the whole time fighting.'

'Oh.'

'And I've found I'm on the outside and can't get in. It's bizarre. I've found that studying people out of interest isn't enough. I find I want to change things. And that's fatal.'

'What d'you want to change about Tom?' Petra was barely interested. She was beginning to feel particularly vile.

'Not Tom. I wasn't talking about Tom. Petra, if you want to go soft, I'm the one to go soft on. You don't need to spend the whole time being brave.'

Petra laughed. Then she found she was feeling better.

'Diane said you were husband material,' she said to the ground between her feet.

'Stuff that,' replied Ieuan.

29 August 1953

Retreat. Even without making the decision, the heart has gone out of the enterprise. We are no longer thinking upwards. We have so far to climb again, even to look at the ridge, and we have all been overcome by an immense lassitude.

Lennard has begun to talk about his garden at home, and about Sundays on the crags. He talks, dear God, about village churches and weddings. I can see myself, sleek-headed like the Easter lamb, bowing down at the altar. Dear Harry, I must tell you the truth soon. I shan't marry you. You'll be happy to hear it, because I am too rough-hewn to be a garden ornament.

I shall have to find some other means of living, once we have climbed this mountain. I shall not be content to follow Harry for the rest of my life.

Now, when I am so near to losing the mountain, I can put the thought into words, the faint thought which has pursued me all this way: that I have followed Harry because he was going to Himalchand. The mountain comes first, and then another mountain, and another. And old age, I hope, in a garden somewhere, but not now.

Pat and Jock will go for the porters tomorrow. Hayter and Amory are still on the South Munshu. Tai Singh says 'Are we not going to fetch down all the tents?'

At his home in Kala, they never throw anything away. They sell it. He cannot believe that the abandonment of mere material goods is nothing compared to the loss of our dream. Two tents, 200 feet of line, twelve rock pegs, the odd tin of bully beef. Part-exchange for not reaching the summit of Himalchand. If the weather stays poor, the task of retrieving the gear will be too dangerous. Besides, Lennard has gone down with a gut-bug and does not want to organise anything.

The diary ends there. Petra borrowed the copy of *New Moon of the Snows* which the Rat had brought with him all that way. She read the last page again. It was as if Hannah had simply paused to draw breath. Then came a blank page. The Rat had written on it:

'Rs 550 for bus. Pay the driver.'

She closed the book. Tomorrow the entire team would make a concerted assault on the peak. All except Diane and the Rat. The weather looked good. There were no ominous signs, strange clouds or unnatural calm, which might portend a change for the worse. In two days, they would have the mountain. Or not.

Petra went back and read some of the earlier entries in the diary. She was in danger of learning the whole text by heart. But still she could not discover the reason for Hannah's sacrifice. The mountain, shining like a light, had seemed to grip Hannah in a way that no human contact had succeeded. If the story was to be believed, she had given up everything at that point where the diary ended. She had no untidy human ties which could hold her back from a bold last try for the mountain.

Of course the dismal reckoning in that last entry was not the final sum.

But thereafter the events could only be puzzled together, a jigsaw with too many pieces missing.

Petra picked up a pen, the cheap Indian biro that the Rat used for his accounts. She tore up the cardboard wrapper of a used packet of oatmeal breakfast cereal, and she began to write.

'Dawn. Ieuan quoting T. S. Eliot before breakfast. The Rat grim and grey, but beginning to eat at last. Tom calls us together. "No heroics," he says. We know what he means because we haven't been thinking about anything else. The sun is on the mountain. Bright orange. Flaming.'

Ieuan stamped about, declaiming from 'The Journey of the Magi', until Tom asked him to please be quiet.

They were in odd ropes: Tom with Petra; Daz, Rowley and Ieuan as a rope of three. They would spend a cramped night at Camp Two and leave Ieuan there in the morning. Ieuan had no ambitions to go higher. He was carrying spare gear, and would help the general effort, but he declared that he did not trust himself on the precarious ground of the rock-band itself.

'But,' he declared, 'I will return. I will go back to school in the lesser ranges, and in Scotland, if I'm not too old to start.'

'You're perfectly bloody good at it,' countered Daz. 'You're just a tad scared.'

'Not any more.' Ieuan's euphoria was almost as odd as his preceding gloom. Rowley and the Rat, who had taken to referring to him as Eeyore, now called him Winnie, as in Pooh.

Up they went. Thousands of feet of mindless slog, treading in footprints. The tent at Camp Two, meant for two or three people, was cosy for five, but that night was an unusually friendly one. Together they watched the sunset from 19,500 feet. In the morning Ieuan said goodbye. He did not look lonely. He was going to pack up his things in a leisurely fashion and go back down the fixed ropes alone.

Petra considered his ability to stop short of the goal, and thought it extraordinary. She would never have said, 'I have come so far. This is enough.'

Perhaps he was hiding the truth. Perhaps he was being generous. But by his action he had enabled the team to avoid any arguments. Two ropes of two was the best way to ensure success, since the team would be mobile and flexible. With the Rat out of action, Ieuan's help in load-carrying had made enough difference to boost them on their way. Further, he would have been a liability.

'Goodbye, Ieuan.' She was already preparing for the difficult, concentrated task of reclimbing the rocks above. If the ropes were still in place, the task would be manageable. If the ropes were buried by snow, they might yet waste a good deal of time, and not make it to the ridge camp before dark.

'Come back and tell me all about it.' He stopped. There was a particular note in his voice.

'What's that?'

He looked at Tom, and at Rowley and Daz. 'Good luck, you guys.'

They nodded.

'Maybe I'll wait here till you come back.'

Tom looked at him. There was already a detached expression in the veteran's eyes. He was already mentally set on the rock-climbing problem.

'Till Tuesday morning, Dr Price. We'll bring you a stick of rock.'

'Jeez,' muttered Rowley. 'I wish Tim was with us.'

Petra and Tom went first, because they had been that way before. Conditions for climbing were as easy as they would ever be. The air was cold, but not bitterly so. The icy snow held firmly to the underlying rock, and the climbers' ice-axes bit in with a satisfying thwack. There was an unusual lack of brittle ice or powder snow, and the freezing temperature kept the fragile rock bound together.

Tom led, clearing the snow off the ropes and finding the way. Petra followed. Then came Rowley, with Daz bringing up the rear. The climbing, which had seemed so desperate a few days before, had acquired a kind of familiarity. They were climbing the fixed ropes with assistance of jumar-clamps, with only one climber at a time on each free stretch of rope. That meant that Petra and Rowley sometimes coincided at a changeover point, because Tom in the lead always took longer to climb a pitch than anyone else.

Rowley whistled between his teeth, tunelessly. Petra stood close beside him, facing outwards, over the void, with the mountains stretching away into the clear distance. 'We're lucky so far.'

'Ssh. The gods, the gods, Pet.'

She was silent for a moment. Then: 'This is a long, long way from Harrison's Rocks.'

'Mm.' Rowley noted a sudden tightening of the rope, as Daz put his weight on the last stretch. 'I'm glad we're not old enough to look backwards all the time. Look at poor old Tom.'

'He's not old.' Petra made the statement with conviction.

'Well, he's no youth. But shit, if I can climb like that when I'm fifty.'

There was a tug on Petra's side of the rope. 'He's there.' She became very busy, checking her jumar-clamps and her harness.

'That's the really odd thing.' Rowley was still conversational. 'Being here in this place, along with you. Just like we were in the school playground. But I wish the Rat was up with us. He's got a hard nut.'

'Poor Tim.' Petra tugged at the rope, three times, in the agreed signal. Tom was out of sight beyond the bulging rocks. The answering tug came.

'Cheers, Rowley.'

'Cheers.'

She climbed. The rock, which she had climbed and descended once before, seemed easier on long acquaintance. It was a short sharp hard pitch, probably the technical crux of the whole ascent. At Harrison's Rocks it would have been a nice problem for a novice. At 20,000 feet, economy of effort and skill were required.

Petra had one hand for her axe and one for the jumar-clamps which provided her security on the fixed rope. She needed to be careful with her feet to stay in balance. The fixed rope hung taut, like a luminous-green harp-string. Crystals of snow sprang off it as Petra transferred her full weight to the rope.

She shifted her balance slightly, because the rope introduced a lateral force which tended to swing her away from the easiest line of ascent. She rammed her axe-pick into the ice, shifted her balance again, then brought up her feet, one at a time – piercing the icy covering of the rock with the hard steel points of the crampons.

After two moves she paused for breath. The wait at the belay had allowed her to rest a little, but she had already come a long way that day. She breathed hard, half a dozen times, then made the next move: jumar-clamp, axe, left foot, right foot. Her hands were cold in their three layers of gloves. Not dangerously cold, but enough to be uncomfortable. She was wearing thermal underclothing (gloves and socks included), a fleece-lined jersey, an anorak and breeches, and a windproof layer of luminous-orange proofed fabric. Her sack contained a sleeping bag and down jacket, as well as climbing gear. Only on the very last pitch, on the ridge itself, would the sack be lightened completely because by then the only source of safety would be speed of progress.

She heaved herself up again, and again. And breathed, and moved again. Her gloves were crusted with melted snow which had refrozen. Fine snow particles settled on her snow goggles, cutting down visibility. But she knew that to remove the goggles would be the most dangerous thing of all. In clear weather, even if there was no direct sun, snow-blindness was an ever-present risk. And blindness would turn a dangerous escapade into pure suicide.

She stamped and hammered her way upwards through the blur. She knew that if she kept her head down, in a matter of time she must come up to the snow-field below the ridge, where Tom was waiting.

31 August 1953

Dear Harry,

The voices of my upbringing tell me that I should stay at base camp and nurse you through this unfortunate illness. Forgive me, but I cannot pay heed to the virtues of good womanhood now. I shall see you again. But I find I cannot live without having climbed Himalchand. To leave now, or even to lose days of climbing weather waiting for the team to regroup, that would be unthinkable. I have been up to the ridge. I know the ground. My little tent is perched up there now, full of food and gear, ready for the summit team. I must have one try. And democratic processes will never award me the summit.

I told you last night that Tai Singh and I would go to Camp Two to retrieve some gear. You approved, on economic grounds. If you read this, it is because I spent last night at Camp Two, and tonight at the ridge camp, and tomorrow for the summit.

You will not be able to send anyone after me in time to stop me.

If you were I, you would do the same. If you cannot put yourself in my place, then I am sorry for it. But all the better then that I have not given up ambition for domestic duty.

You and I are of the earth, Harry. We are ordinary humans who must eat and sleep, and only talk about the stars. Up there, at the highest point of the earth, perhaps I shall reach out and touch the stars. I shall see the valley as the heavens see the earth, blue, misty and mysterious, just as we earthbound people see the skies. I shall stand there beside the planets in their orbit, clutching the moon in my arms.

Your ever loving
Hannah

Harry Lennard, in his passion of self-justification, had included even that last letter in the book.

The round red tent, burnt pink by the sun, perched like some extra-terrestrial object upon the horizon. Tom and Petra had hammered it into place during the few furious minutes they had spent at the ridge camp last time. Petra hardly remembered what the site was like; she remembered only the feeling of immense precipices on all sides.

It was a scoop out of the white snow, at the one place on the crest where the wind had not scoured the rock clean, or piled whirling snow into precarious pinnacles. That small snowfield marked a vortex of calm on the stormy ridge. That was why the old tent was still there. Because thirty years had failed to add an accretion of new snow. Each summer the winter's fall had melted or blown away, to be replaced again the next winter.

Petra looked down the other side of the mountain. The valley was so far away it was blue with the haze of distance.

'Seven thousand feet sheer,' said Tom. 'I've still got you belayed, but will you not jump off the edge?'

Petra stepped back. 'I'm testing my head for heights.'

Tom had rammed his ice-axe into the snow, and wound the rope round it in some kind of hitch, 1950s fashion. The belay would never hold a long fall. They were all learning that modern-style safety precautions were often too slow and elaborate for the speed needed in high mountains. Petra stepped away from the edge. Her crampons bit into the ice of the tent-platform. The white ice was creased here and there with folds of weathered grey canvas tent material. The old tent could last centuries, under conditions of perfect refrigeration.

Hannah's words echoed in the air – strangely windless air for a place that was almost as exposed as the summit itself.

'You and I are of the earth, Harry ...'

Petra took a new deep breath which had nothing to do with the high altitude. She breathed out. The mountain, and Tom, and the chubby pink tent were all still present. The air sang.

'What's up?' asked Tom. He had not unhitched his belay.

'Twenty-one thousand feet.' Petra sat down on the square yard of ground and lowered her head between her knees. Tom was near enough to touch but she kept her head turned away. She could not tell him the true reason for her faintness. She had seen Hannah falling, spinning away into the blue distance, a mile and a half away, straight down.

'No pain?'

'No.' She was still lying. She felt pain, but the pain was in no identifiable part of her body. 'I think I may have to try breathing in a bag. I'm overbreathing. Ieuan says we all do it.'

'Creep into the tent and lie down. I'll watch out for the others.'

His voice was unusually calm, even for Tom. He was one of those people who got calmer the more tricky things became. Petra edged past him, her eyes on the snow. This was not the place for a climber to get vertigo for the first time in her life. She hoped it was the altitude.

She unzipped the tent and grovelled inside, with her cramponed feet still kicking outside the door. She was conscious of the need not to rip the groundsheet.

Tom leant across – he was that near – and tugged at the crampon straps to undo them. Petra heard a muttered curse. The feet to which the crampons were attached seemed hardly to belong to her.

She giggled. 'I haven't got a paper bag to breathe into.'

'Then use the stuff-sack from your duvet, but get a move on. This isn't the place to muck about.'

Tom angry? The thought entered Petra's head and then went spinning around with the rest of the jumble of rubbish inside her skull.

He was muttering 'Blast, blast,' and rummaging in the sack. Petra's duvet jacket came out, billowing blue and red. 'Put it on.'

Her arms could not find the sleeves. She felt like a peg doll. Tom put something to her face. A bright blue handkerchief? It was the small nylon drawstring bag that had held the duvet jacket.

'Breathe.'

She breathed, somehow. The bag, close around her mouth and nose, threatened to stifle her. She had to take longer, deeper breaths. It was the treatment that the PE teacher at school had used on girls who used hysterical overbreathing as a means of getting out of games.

Petra's next breath seemed to smell of school corridors and disinfectant. She choked. The mud of the school field, the whirr of the mowing machine, the smell of clipped grass and people cheering. The scratch of chalk, the endless drone of the schoolmaster, the bars on the cage.

'Let me out.' She struggled. Tom held her tight. The sun, shining through the tent fabric, made everything rosy.

'Snap out of it,' he muttered. 'Keep a hold.'

He was holding her head. The bristles on his chin scratched her forehead. The warmth of his breath was perceptible. The rest of both of them was bundled up under six layers of clothing.

Petra was sick into the bag. Then she felt better. Tom was still there, cursing about all the mess, but still hanging on tight.

She muttered something like 'sorry'. Tom told her she was a bloody fool to go peering over precipices before she had got her breath back from the climb. For a moment, she clung, because Tom seemed to represent safety. At 21,500 feet the illusion still remained: that the danger is less if one is not alone.

Then came a noise like a beached sea-lion, and the crunch

of hardened steel on snow. Two final positive steps landed outside the tent.

'What the bleeding hell is going on here?' asked Rowley, and then he took several more huge deep breaths. 'You nearly killed me. Your fucking crampon came flying past and nearly fucking hit me. It caught in my jumar loops.'

Tom stayed put. 'Button it.'

'Oh yeah?' Rowley, inflated in size by his bulky clothing, his eyes hidden by mirror-lens goggles, looked positively menacing.

'She's off colour. Touch of altitude.'

'Eh?'

'Petra's been sick. Can you tip out the bag?'

'Jeez.' Rowley took the blue bag. 'If she's got Tim's bug.'

'Button it, I said. Did you catch the crampon?'

'Luckily yes.'

Rowley went off to get rid of the sick. The bag would have to be kept, because it was the only way the down jacket could be compressed small enough to fit in a sack.

'Shit.' Petra shivered. 'Tim bloody Radinsky's bloody bug.' She rolled away, to lie flat, looking at the bright roof of the tent. 'Shit, shit, shit.'

'And you button it too.' Tom hauled his own rucksack into the tent and began to undo his own crampons. 'We'll make a brew, get some fluid inside, get some rest. See what the morning brings. It's not like you to panic.'

'I'm not.'

'OK. Don't despair dramatically, then. Blast.'

'What?'

'My fingers are freezing to the crampons. Even with the inner gloves on. It must be way below zero already, and the sun hasn't set.'

Daz, coming up on Rowley's rope, crept into camp in the twilight. He was very quiet. When the two lads finally crawled into the tent, the sky beyond the tunnel entrance was royal blue and full of stars. Petra saw the new moon, fine cut and luminous, perched just above the ridge.

'You better?' Rowley asked.

'Um,' she replied. Things had stopped whirling, but her mind still felt considerably detached.

'Any gut-ache?'

'No. I don't feel sick now.'

'Good.'

Daz grunted greetings and began to pull his sleeping bag out of the rucksack. 'I'm for my pit.'

In the tent, everything was dark. Daz's headlamp flickered about the walls and the faces, and the heaped-up downy folds of the sleeping bags. It was like a series of individual pictures, snapping across a screen like old-fashioned magic-lantern slides.

Petra thought of how the images of this expedition would be stored for posterity as still photographs, without the movement, like those stiff, posed pictures from Hannah Kemp's time. No one would photograph the interior of a high-altitude tent. But this wordless, weary scene was very close to the heart of expedition life.

'Sleep.' Rowley pulled his sleeping bag up around him, twisting his body this way and that. Petra and Tom were already in theirs. Rowley zipped up the tent and arranged the cooking apparatus.

'Tea.' Rowley was tending the faint blue flame of the gas-burner. He put cubes of snow into the pint-size aluminium mess tin and stirred the mixture about as it melted. As the snow became slush he added more snow, bit by bit. Each block of snow made a tiny increase in the fluid level in the pot.

'Must have fluid.'

'Grrmph.' Daz's sleeping bag was over his head.

'Ieuan says.'

'Bugger Ieuan,' growled the sleeping bag. Rowley went back to feeding the pot. After an immeasurable time, there was a potful. 'We'll run out of fuel if this tries to boil. Warm water, anyone?'

'I had some earlier,' stated Tom.

Petra caught his eye. She thought, 'Who's into heroics now?'

Tom shrugged his shoulders. 'Split it three ways, then. Daz can have some of the next lot.'

They drank the horrid metallic stuff, made from snow that had lingered for uncounted years on that mountain top. Tom drank his cupful in one go, then spluttered a little as his taste-buds caught up. He shivered, and made a wry face.

'I recollect a man, name of Bentall, went mad up a mountain because he wouldn't drink. A stubborn old sod. Pre-war, as we used to say. He went out with Jock and Pat on one of their South American wild-goose chases. He knew someone in the embassy who could get them into wild Indian country.'

'Oh yeah?' muttered Daz's sleeping bag. But Tom went on.

'A peak called 'El Chiruco', or 'the Boot'. One of those granite domes. Pegs and bolts all the way up. Tropical sun bouncing off white granite. Not like Glencoe.' He paused for breath.

'You didn't want to go?' enquired Rowley, feeding the next potful.

'Not my style: bang and dangle up a 3,000-foot wall. It was bigger than El Cap, even though it wasn't as hard, and it was a long way from anywhere. Bentall spent three months in a Venezuelan hospital having his kidneys treated. He was having visions. Imagining cannibals coming to scalp him. Pat and Jock had to lower him from the face, in a cat's-cradle of ropes which he couldn't undo. And they didn't finish the ascent. That's what really hurt, not Bentall's hospital bills.'

'Did any of your lot go on to climb anything big?' As Rowley asked the question, Petra could hear the rumbling vibration of Daz beginning to snore.

Tom shook his head. 'Not Everest. No 26,000-foot peaks. South America, Norway, Canada. Adventure climbing, not stuff for the history books. I often thought — ' He stopped.

'What was that?' asked Rowley.

'Well. What will you do next?'

'Ask me after tomorrow.'

'You think you'll know?'

'I can't see beyond the summit. I doubt you can. Here's some more snow-water. Petra, wake that fat lump to make him drink.'

Petra took her own mouthful of nasty water, which stayed down rather than returning, so she was already feeling happier. She prodded Daz as instructed. He awoke with a grunt and a snort, and appeared to be still half-asleep as he drank.

He flopped down to sleep again. Petra rested her own head on the one small patch of groundsheet that was still clear. She pulled the sleeping bag over her head and pulled the string tight.

Rowley remarked loudly: 'I haven't had a piss since yesterday.' Petra puzzled at the apparent *non sequitur*. Then she was suddenly asleep.

CHAPTER 8

She awoke feeling very cold. The wind was howling around the tent; the fabric vibrated like a taut harpstring. The night was still dark. She shivered. The sounds were familiar ones but enormously exaggerated; the wind itself was so strong that it was lifting the tent upwards, simply by the aerofoil effect as it swept over the ridge. The fabric of the tent was tautened outwards, convexly, like the wall of a bubble. A conventional tent would already have been lifted up and sucked away; the dome-tent, with its integral groundsheet, was partly held down by the four bodies who resided in it.

This was suddenly very frightening. Because there was nothing they could do but sit tight.

Petra did not try to wake anyone, but gradually she became aware that everyone was already awake.

No one had spoken, however, perhaps for the same reason that Petra did not speak. She did not wish to let loose that cold primitive fear, which she could not help but show in her voice.

Up till now they had only been playing games with danger. The summit had begun to look easy. 'Ask me after tomorrow,' Rowley had said, as if success were certain on the next day.

But somewhere in the small hours between today and tomorrow, the storm wind had blown away certainty. Petra for sure, and probably all the others bar Tom, had never been trapped in this way before. It was a repeat of the situation beside the flooded river on the walk-in, which had so worried Ieuan, but magnified a thousand times over.

Petra said, 'God, poor Ieuan,' because he was away down the mountain and would have to imagine what was happening to the summit team. At that, the danger became less formless, because it could be shared. She wiggled herself into a sitting position. The tent lifted and flapped.

'Don't rock the boat,' muttered Daz beside her.

Rowley still had his bag over his head. 'I wish I believed in God. I sure do.'

'Eleven Hail Marys,' said Daz.

'Don't be funny,' said Petra. 'Tom, have you heard wind like this before?'

Tom stirred. 'This is nowt to what the wind'll be on the face. We're in a hollow. Hear it howling through the gap in the ridge?'

'Force ten?' asked Daz.

'At least.'

'Bugger. We've got the wrong sort of tent. Should have got one of those orange Scout jobs.' It was too dark to see Daz's face, but the forced smile was patent in his voice.

'How do we get out of here?' whispered Petra. She no longer felt the need to be laconic.

'Wait.' Tom was blunter than ever. 'We're safe while we stay put here. We can't retreat.'

'Yugh,' remarked Rowley from inside his bag.

'We've all had practice surviving. This is the real thing. That's all. As Pet says, pity the folks down the mountain.'

Petra had a sudden violent thought. 'I hope the others know to stay put.'

Tom, very still beside her, replied, 'Well, they've read the book.'

Harry Lennard's account
22 September 1953

I have been asked by the other members of the expedition to set down in writing the events of these few days while the events are still fresh in our memory. Disbelief and shock are fresh also. This cannot be a dispassionate account. However our general feeling is that we owe it to our dear friend, now lost to us, to put on record all that happened. If the account is confused, so too were events.

Every mountaineer understands the irresistible lure of the summit. Each one of us has trusted his luck beyond what it can very well stand, in the hope of seizing that goal.

We understand that Hannah was so much attracted by Himalchand that she actually feared the prospect of retreating with the peak unclimbed more than she feared the dangers.

On 31 August I was indisposed at Base Camp. Ormerod, Patterson, McKie, Hannah and Tai Singh were at the advance base, intending to strike camp on the following day. Hayter and Amory had made a trip round to the South Munshu glacier to reconnoitre an approach from that side. They intended it rather as a last outing before the retreat, rather than with any serious intention of attempting the route. During the night they spent at Base Camp before starting the reconnaissance, we three had talked about plans for next year.

After Hayter and Amory had departed I was alone at base for four days. The whole of the third and fourth days the weather was atrocious. I felt too weak to move out of my tent. I was not surprised that no one had come to join me in that terrible weather. Fortunately I was well supplied with food and water.

On the fifth day a solitary figure approached across the glacier. It was Jock McKie. I was shocked to see that strong, rough-hewn mountaineer so shaken with emotion. He did not know how to tell me, and so he burst out with 'Hannah's killed' as his first words. I did not believe him then, and I hardly can now. I asked him again and again. I believe I shook him to make him speak. 'How, why?' I asked, as if that would change what had happened.

He gave me the letter which she had left for me. He apologised for having read it, but they had been frantically searching for clues when they found her gone that morning. The letter said something of why. McKie's words were, 'The lassie's more of a man than the most of us.' Already we were thinking: 'If only'. A fatal mix of competent climbing skills and a treacherous sense of the romantic have brought Hannah down. None of us guessed, because she seemed a solid, capable, sensible girl with no nonsense about her at all.

On the morning of the second day, when I was already ensconced at Base Camp, the inhabitants of the advanced base had woken late. They were reluctant to rise because their only task was to dismantle and pack up the camp. Ormerod made breakfast, and it was he who went to Hannah's tent to call her to the meal. He found her gone. He was not at first alarmed, but when he found that Tai Singh had gone too, and all their personal gear, he roused Patterson and McKie. Together they searched Hannah's belongings and found the letter addressed to me.

Only then did they look up at the mountain. The early mist was parting, and high up, near Camp Two, they saw two tiny dark figures.

McKie and Patterson were weary from their recent exertions, and were disinclined to expend energy in pursuit. No one really believed that Hannah would attempt the summit.

But at evening, Tai Singh returned to the advanced base. He insisted that he had had no choice but to obey when Hannah sent him back. He too had wished to try for the summit. The boy is only seventeen.

The three climbers were left with the choice of waiting or following. In the event, Ormerod and Patterson set off at first light, in the hope of performing a rescue. McKie and Tai Singh waited.

The morning was clear, and the mountain looked all too climbable. I, in my weakened state at Base Camp, felt how unfair the gods had been in denying us such weather when there had been a real prospect of the summit. At about three o'clock in the afternoon, a bank of black cloud came pouring up the valley, and within less than an hour the day had turned to night. Even at Base Camp the wind was so strong that I could not stand upright. I crawled to the spring to replenish my water. Thereafter I was trapped in my tent until the storm abated.

Ormerod and Patterson weathered the storm in the tiny tent halfway up the face of Himalchand. They did not venture outside. When the wind dropped at last the tent was buried up to its ridgepole in new snow. The rock-band was invisible, buried under the new snowfall. The ridge was still out of sight in the cloud.

To their credit, and despite lack of food and sleep, Ormerod and Patterson reclimbed that formidable step in search of our lost comrade. They found the abandoned tent on the ridge, still standing, still with provisions inside. Blown snow had drifted through the seams so that everything inside was covered in a thin layer of white. No one could have been there for several days.

They are experienced mountaineers. They know that even barring accidents, the chance of survival on such a mountain in such weather is zero, without the protection of a tent and without provisions. The summit ridge had become unjustifiably precarious with the new heaping-up of snow. Therefore they made that decision which is the hardest any mountaineer can take. They turned back.

The news reached McKie by a pre-arranged signal from Camp Two. Ormerod and Patterson staggered into the glacier camp at three o'clock the next morning.

They have all made their statements to the authorities, as is proper. But I would like to set down here, on record, that their endeavours exceeded the call of duty, to the extent of taking unreasonable risks. I applaud them.

'I tell you what it reminded me of.' Rowley was sitting up now, but with his sleeping bag hood held closely round his head.

'What's that?' Daz was resolutely horizontal.

'It was like he was blaming Hannah for everything. All he

could do was show how he was solid behind his mates. Ain't that true, Tom?'

Tom, lying flat, staring at the roof of the tent, made a sort of grunted reply. Then: 'It's coming on to dawn.'

Rowley had his lamp on, but he turned it off. The tent roof was indeed a faintly pink canopy above their heads. Inside the tent, darkness persisted.

'Save your batteries,' said Tom.

Petra tried to sit up, and found that she was giddy and a little light-headed. Three days: that was how long the storm had lasted last time. They had provisions, sure. But simply to live through three days of chaos would take more than food.

'We should reckon up what we've got. How long it'll spin out.' Tom was still apparently talking to the ceiling. 'We should reckon on a week.'

Daz, muffled still: 'This is why I didn't go for the Antarctic Survey. Six months of winter with a load of prats with smelly feet all clapped up in a wooden hut. It'd be worse than prison.' He rolled over. 'This joint stinks of puke.'

Everything was visible now, dim and misty within the closed confines of the tent. The wind shrieked. Words were audible only because everyone was crammed up so close together. The tent had been designed for two or three inhabitants.

'Rules of this tent,' Daz continued. 'Stay in your bag. Respect discipline when pissing.'

'Sod off,' Rowley muttered.

Petra, detached, remarked, 'We're like a bunch of kittens, all fighting for the warmest place in the middle.'

'Aah.' Rowley played an imaginary violin.

'I remember,' said Daz. 'I remember when you two used to try and sleep the both of you in one sleeping bag. Not much sleeping either. Sound effects.'

'Sod off or I'll thump you,' declared Rowley.

'Just trying to take your mind off the present.'

Rowley directed a head-butt which caused the tent to quake on its moorings.

Petra sat up again, suddenly. 'Stop it! Stop it. That was all years ago and it's nothing to fight about now.'

'D'you hear that, Ben?' Daz had his bag over his head again. 'Petra admits to having been one of your collection of girlfriends.'

'I heard. If you want it spelt out that's one reason why me and the Rat went off to Sheffield. Apart from the climbing scene.'

'What?'

'Pet wanted to stop it getting into a habit. You do some damn silly things when you're seventeen.'

'That right, Petra?' Daz sounded curious and slightly puzzled.

'Right.' Petra's memories were even vaguer than usual. 'Yes. It wasn't getting anywhere and neither of us wanted it to anyway. We got a bit of an off feeling about it after a while.'

'Tim too?'

'No. Not Tim. Tim? Save me that.'

Rowley wriggled deep into his sack. 'Must you go on, you two?'

'It's absolutely fascinating,' said Daz, unperturbed.

There was a particularly morbid shriek, as the wind went critical, and a moment later the buffeting redoubled, until Petra was quite sure that the whole tent would take off, with the climbers in it. When, after a tense half-minute, the wind settled to its previous eerie howl, there was another minute or two of pure silence from the mountaineers.

'We'll get through it,' said Tom. He sounded oddly confident, given the extreme precariousness of their location.

'Oh?'

'That last blast was the strongest I've ever heard. Even when I was here before, in that long storm, it didn't get stronger. The tent's made of good stuff.'

Petra stretched out a hand and felt the taut, paper-thin fabric. She felt the inward bulge where snow had drifted against the wall. Soon the whole tent would be an igloo.

'We'll be buried by snow.'

'That'll protect us from the wind. Remember those climbers snow-holing at the top of Everest? Tents will soon go out of date for this sort of trip.'

'Um.' Petra put her hand back inside the bag.

'I wish we'd thought of snow-holing, me and Pat, when we were out in that tent on the face. We'd have been warmer. I remember the canvas of the roof sagged inwards till it nearly touched together under the ridge-pole. We were neck deep in snow when we dug our way out. Everything was frozen. If it hadn't been so cold we'd have been soaked through.'

'Yugh.'

'Yeah. What did you talk about?' asked Rowley.

'Me and Pat? Not much. He wasn't one for talking.'

'You just festered in the tent?'

'That's about it.'

'Maybe we'd be better off doing the same. Daz is usually the one who is good at festering. He's usually quite quiet, unlike now.'

Daz responded with a generalised convulsion, and let his head out of the aperture of the sleeping bag.

'Don't whinge, Rowley. There were just things I wanted to find out about our past before the Big One got me.'

'Anything else?'

'Nothing I can ask anyone here.'

'Anything you want to confess about, now you're in the mood?'

'Nope. Except I'm going to settle down and write articles for *Climber and Rambler* when this is all over.'

Petra shivered. The black void outside the tent walls seemed to her to be infinite and perpetual. She had no illusions about skipping about on a cloud, playing a harp. The end, when it came, would be an irreversible downward fall. What she had not been prepared for was the prospect of a slow sinking, as supplies and resources gave out. If the wind got stronger. If the temperature dropped. If the snow piled up too deep. For the first time she felt sympathy for those British heroes about whom she had been forced to learn at school. Captain Oates going out of the tent, saying, 'I may be some time.' He was the one who had not lingered on to the end. He had taken his own fate in his hands. How long? Petra thought. How long before one of us wants to be Captain Oates?

'That reminds me of a story.' Tom's words snapped Petra's attention back to the immediate present. Tom trying to make things safe by telling yet another tale. She wondered how she had ever thought him taciturn.

Thereafter, survival was a matter of sticking together and holding back the darkness.

Only on the surface did the experience resemble life at Allin's Hut last winter. The tales were of the same sort, the language similarly lavatorial; the obsession with food and drink, never far from a climber's mind, occupied a central part of existence. But food had to be eked out. Water had to be made. The utter limit of survival would be when no more fuel remained to melt snow.

And however close-knit the group now was, there were people missing.

'Old Patterson did some new-routing in Alaska in the sixties. He had a rich friend who hired an aeroplane.' Tom's stories were a means of filling the silence. The gale howled, but Tom's voice, low and even, kept the most elemental of fears tied down to earth.

'One of those biplanes. Range of hundreds of miles and could land on anything. Lakes, meadows, glaciers. Not trees. Pat ended up dangling from a spruce by his braces. I've been there since. Wide, lonely valley with just the one tree. They had to walk out.'

'How long?' Rowley asked.

'Three weeks. Vile country, with all the valleys running the wrong direction. The American moaned every step of the way. Pat had to persuade him along with Glaswegian blasphemies.'

Daz chortled. 'Like Billy Connolly stuff?'

'Nothing so tame. Pat calls Connolly a wee fairy.'

'Did Pat go back to climbing with Jock after that?'

Tom paused. The wind had acquired a whining note, ululating like a creature in distress.

'No. McKie had a bad time in '63. Got a coronary shovelling snow outside his croft. He was only about forty-five, but he has had to take things easy since. Not much climbing and nothing in winter. His sister looks after him. He'd say that's the worst of it.'

'Christ,' muttered Daz. 'Don't we know any stories with a happy ending?'

'I do.' Rowley, in between bouts of running the gas stove, lived with his head buried in the hood of his sleeping bag. 'I know a rude version of *Snow White and the Seven Dwarfs*.'

But by the second day, humour came less easily. Silences were longer. Petra felt glad that the singing in her head had got no worse, and she had not been sick again. At least the Rat's 'bug' had not crept up to the high camp. But Daz did not make any more jokes about puke.

There had been absolutely no change in the weather. The tent vibrated a little less because of the snow stacked up around it. The cold air in the tent made clouds out of exhaled breath, and the steam condensed and froze on the fabric. At least the packing of snow made things a little warmer. But if the snow muffled the impact of the wind, it did not drown out the sound. Every note in the scale was represented, in a complex cacophony. Sometimes it sounded almost like howls of pain. Sometimes it whistled. Sometimes an earsplitting shriek would startle a new increase in fear among those listening.

Petra found that she could almost ignore the wind in the daylight hours of that second day. The sound which enclosed them was like a wall – part of the structure of their environment. But night-time was different, and the night after the second day (which was the third night of the storm) she began to hear voices in the wind.

She heard the words 'for ever' and then, more mundanely, 'eat up'. Then a crying child, incessantly calling 'Mummee!' Petra thought, 'I have no children. Why is it crying?'

She froze still in her down coverings. This was it. This was the beginning of the hallucinations. She knew that the next stages were delirium and death.

'Tom,' she whispered.

He was not asleep. 'Mm?'

Irregular snorings came from the other two recumbent forms.

'I can hear voices.'

'How?'

'Noises in the wind. Like words.' She could not keep the trembling out of her voice, though she tried to speak calmly and slowly.

Tom shifted position a little. His elbow dug into her. 'And I can hear the "Hallelujah" chorus.'

'It's like seeing things. My brain's going off.'

'No, it's not.'

'It's the first sign.'

'No. You're perfectly rational. Just don't go all female on us now.'

'I'm not. I'm afraid. It's nothing to do with being female.'

'Then what am I to do about it?'

Petra took two or three gulps of air, and then tried to persuade herself to breathe slowly.

'I'm sorry.' She breathed again, in–two–three, out. 'Tom. You're not afraid too?'

'I am – who wouldn't be?'

The song of the wind, and the grunts and snorts of the sleepers were suddenly muffled. The atmosphere in the cold tent seemed very still.

'But you're never afraid.' It was almost as if the mountain itself had shaken upon its granite foundations. 'You take things as they come. You don't get upset.'

'You know that's nonsense. Remember the last time we were here?'

'When we found the tent? Yes. Were you scared then?'

'I was. That was your turn to be brave. It's not mountains and precipices that scare us, it's other people.'

Petra caught herself breathing fast again. The black night and the tempest were closing in once more. 'You mean Hannah?'

'Who else. I didn't tell you. No one else knows this. There was something else of Hannah's I found when I got here, just ahead of Patterson.'

'In that tent all full of snow?'

'It was like ice on a windowpane. Filigree crystals, each one tiny and perfect. Ice on the cover of the sleeping bag, and on the pressure stove, and on the spare socks and the bits of clutter which someone leaves behind in a tent when they just pop out for a moment.'

'There was a note?'

'Yes. She wrote a formal claim to having made the first ascent of Himalchand. No one has disputed that claim. The note is in the archives of her old climbing club. What I have told no one is that the note was just the first page of a notebook. She wrote more of her diary, listening to voices in the wind. I didn't think that part was for publication.'

Petra whispered, 'She was alone here. All through that storm.'

'The words peter out at the end. It's horrible. Not Hannah at all.'

'But why destroy it? You did destroy it?'

Tom did not answer.

'But why?'

'Because the world loves a hero. Heroes don't have regrets.'

'You'd say she was a hero?'

'More than that. Oh, much more. And none of us guessed at it until too late. I blame that fat hulk Lennard. He always acted as if he owned her.'

'He thought she was dull and ordinary.'

'Sensible, he called her. She had a wild streak all right, which I could have taken to. But I was just a mascot.'

'Tom?' Petra felt the keening of the wind go right through her. 'It's all over. It was over thirty years ago. You can't be sad about it now.'

'No.' His face was invisible in the darkness, but his voice was no longer muffled by duck down. 'No. But it's a really spectacular fool who makes the same mistake twice.'

'Tom.' Petra was urgent now. She had to be understood. 'Tom, don't regret it. None of us regret coming here. It's a great adventure. And we'll get out of it. We just have to keep on trying.'

Tom muttered, 'I didn't mean I was giving up. But you get to thinking.'

1 September 1953

> I was there. When you follow me you will know the summit by its three-cornered shape, a level, gently domed platform of formed snow, which falls away towards North Munshu, and South Munshu, and towards Tibet. Auraz and Tengdatta, on a level with my eyes, almost fuse into one peak from this angle. The Munshu valley is a tiny green nick in a pattern of black and white. Overhead the sky is deep clear blue, leading upwards into outer space. I have often wondered what colour the sky is, seen from the other side. Mountaineering on the moon? Now that's an idea.
>
> That would be fantasy. The reality, the truth which I set down here, is that I have stood on the summit of Himalchand, alone. I was satisfied. Turning back now seems natural: the return home of the weary traveller. I have left an empty sardine tin, stuffed with my red spotted handkerchief, in place of a flag. If anyone material-minded chooses to doubt me, let him come here to check for himself.

In the dark dome-tent, among the echoes of the wintry wind, a sleeper stirred and grumbled in his sleep. 'No more chips. Ate up all the chips. Bread and marge.' Petra, interrupted in her thoughts of the summit, listened while Daz turned over and resumed his irregular snores. She understood now.

'Is that why you didn't go on? Nothing to do with being noble, or "giving the mountain best". Would you have gone on if she hadn't climbed it and left a sardine-tin behind?'

'No, don't doubt me, we'd have gone on looking for her, if she hadn't made it quite clear that there was no point. How do you stand three days alone like this? She was cold, out of water, nearly out of food. She had lost count of the days. We thought she'd probably chosen a compass point at random. If she had any sense of direction left.'

Petra said, 'No,' loudly and clearly, so she could hear herself above the wind. 'No, not us.'

They could last a week. They had all agreed. They had plenty of supplies and a very good tent. Nowadays, surviving under these conditions was nothing remarkable.

But the night no longer permitted sleep. Day came, different only by a perceptible grey light, filtered pale pink by the nylon tent. The storm continued.

Talking became difficult. The high cold air was very dry, and left the throat raw. Besides, no one had much more to say. Daz had long since stopped trying to make jokes. Rowley, if he talked to anyone, spoke only about food or water. The old days back in London when they were all teenagers seemed impossibly remote, belonging to the lives of other people. To think about the past sent thoughts turning over and over about the chances and choices that had led inevitably to this epic on the mountain.

An epic was the term used by climbers to mean a moderate upset of planning: a forced bivouac, a failed rendezvous, a flooded tent. Some other word was needed for this. Something not yet a disaster but advancing hour by hour towards one. It did not help that the previous drama on Himalchand was so unforgettable. Petra spent nearly a whole hour thinking about the sardine tin. It was such a plain, commonplace object. It defied flights of the imagination.

Towards the end of the fourth day she found a stub of pencil among the debris in her duvet pocket. She used it to write on the empty paper wrapper of some high-altitude rations.

'I shall never sleep or dream again. It is as if we are joined to the sky, not the earth. Being alive is like a dream. We are not people. We are something that we ourselves imagined. We imagined coming here, once, when we were sitting in a bus-shelter in the rain, in Fort William, eating chips out of newspaper, waiting for the weather.'

There was ice on the outer covering of the sleeping bags. That night, Petra felt the warm breath of the sleepers, which was their only source of heat. They were four individual bodies, keeping warm together, but without society; each alone with their inward voices.

Too late, the storm ended. Waking in the darkness before dawn, Petra did not at first realise what had changed in her world. The tent was still. The outer walls curved inwards, beneath a circular red halo which was beginning to glow faintly. The sleeping bags were packed sardine-fashion, immobile. For the first time Petra could smell the stink of unwashed bodies. The tent, enclosed by snow, was almost airless.

Then realisation came, followed by a shuddering hammer of heartbeats. There was no wind. She was too excited for coherent thought. Here at last was the way out. They had survived.

'Tom, Tom.' She shook him. He grunted, and snored again.

'Rowley, Daz!' Her voice sounded high and piping, like the plaintive cry of the newborn. She could hardly hear herself, because her ears were still full of the roar of the wind.

She seized Rowley, and made him turn over. He muttered the single word 'sleep'.

Only Daz woke up properly, a pale, shaggy Daz, his face lit by the peculiar overhead light.

'We've got to get going, I suppose.'

He moved slowly, wearily, looking for the stove and the billycan which were the first essentials of the day. He swore undemonstratively under his breath.

'Effing gizmo. Get on with you. Light.'

The blue flame flickered. The gas pressure was perceptibly

low. 'Come on. Light you bugger. Then we can be off the sodding mountain.'

Petra stared, wide-eyed. She had not even considered that they might turn back at this point. She did not speak, however. She realised even as she framed the words that she would be alone in her protest.

Rowley blinked his eyes and woke up all of a sudden. 'We're alive.' He wriggled and sat up. 'Wham-o. We've got through it.'

'There's still the bad step on the way back.' Daz was gloomy and the snow on the stove still was not melting. 'All the ropes will be buried under feet of the stuff. We'll be climbing blind.'

'Shit, it's better than dying slowly up here.'

'I just want to go home. A pint of Robinsons in the Railway Inn. What I wouldn't give for that.'

Rowley grinned and scratched himself. 'No more snow. Mixed grill at the Hollies. What've we got on the menu now?'

'Raven Foods' Hi-energy bar.'

'Sod that. I'd rather eat snow.'

Petra tested each of her stiff muscles, one by one, in a surreptitious version of the stretching exercises she used to do while training to climb. She felt quite weak, as if she was just recovering from the flu. Nearly four days of immobility and poor rations would have taken their physical toll. But it was more than that. It was the effect of this talk of returning. It was the heart going out of the enterprise. She dared not think of how much energy had been wasted.

'Aren't you glad to be alive?' Tom, awake beside her, had not spoken until now.

'What?'

'We've got a break in the weather. It needn't have stopped till winter.'

'You didn't say that.'

'I didn't want to believe it myself.'

She did not look at him. 'So nearly?'

'We're alive. God knows— ' He stopped, as though he had been about to say something else.

'Let's just go.'

After that they were busy, sorting out gear, checking it through, unbending hanks of rope which had frozen into peculiar postures. The stove kept going, warming water, its heat barely perceptible from even a couple of inches away. Rowley tried to open up the snow tunnel at the entrance of the tent. The fabric was frozen solid.

'Jeez, we're going to have to burrow our way out.'

It was good hard work. Daz and Rowley took turns, mostly. It was a job for someone with a long reach. When enough light was visible at the end of the snow-tunnel, Rowley went out first. But before he went he was fully dressed in crampons, downgear and a rope.

His red bulk blocked the daylight out for a moment, then he shot forward with an exclamation. Petra's heart started racing again before she realised that it had been a cry of amazement, not fear.

'See this, lads!'

She emerged last, creeping out of the stuffy pink cavern into clear daylight. She too stopped in her tracks.

She had never seen anything like it. Possibly no one had ever seen anything like it, except Hannah. The foul furious weather had gone, evaporated like mist on a summer's day. The clear blue security of a high-pressure system had supervened. It was winter creeping over from Tibet, dry and clear and cold. The mountains all around were like a lesson in physical geography, with jagged ridges alternating with snow-clad faces; deep cirques and nascent glaciers; tumbled moraines and cones of avalanche debris. Even in the dawn light the air was so clear, so free of any taint of moisture, that the near mountains seemed almost to be within touching distance. The further peaks were stacked one behind the other, with no perceptible distance between, like the two-dimensional panorama of a theatrical set.

The summit of Himalchand was very near indeed.

'Six hundred feet,' said Daz.

'A quarter of a mile, maybe.' Rowley was still staring, rapt.

The source of temptation was apparent. Against all reason, the summit looked like something which could be snatched before lunch.

There were no shadows, no clouds, no mysteries. Before their feet lay a few hundred yards of contorted, serrated, upward-tending snow-capped ridge. The general angle was easy, although there were several steeper pinnacles. Some of the pinnacles were topped by preposterous white fur caps of new snow. What lay on the far side of each pinnacle was entirely unknown.

Petra shook the snow crystals off her hair. The image did not change.

'This is wild,' declared Rowley, waving his axe.

But Petra was still rooted to the spot by the twelve points of her crampons. She did not believe that she could step forward on to the ridge. She had seen that image so often in her mind's eye. This surely was another fantasy.

'What've we survived for, if not for this?' Rowley was insistent. Daz was still hesitating, but only just.

Tom remained silent. He closed his eyes, as if to shut out the white waves of snow. Surely he had not been defeated by four days of close imprisonment?

'Tom?'

Petra had to say his name again: 'Tom?' before he would look at her.

'Why not, Tom?'

'I was thinking about the folk in the valley.'

'Don't.'

'I know. The risk's enormous either way. They won't give up waiting. But I was remembering what it was like to have to wait.'

'The risk's worst if we split up,' insisted Petra.

'It may mean another night in that tent.' He glanced back. Only the very apex of the tent's dome stood visible above the snowdrift. The wind would never blow it away now.

Rowley did not spare the domed tent even a glance. 'Bollocks. It was just creepy in the dark. Eh, Daz?'

'I'm feeling grand.'

'What about you, Pet?'

She looked at him in surprise. His face, with its haze of blond beard and mirror-glass goggles, seemed suddenly alien.

'What do you mean?'

'Are you for staying or going?'

She realised that she had never actually expressed an opinion. She had been wishing, silently, but no one had read her mind. She had been like a little girl, staying good and quiet and wishing.

'The summit, of course.'

'Good girl!' Rowley smiled triumphantly.

'Don't. You sound like Gobert-Jones.'

The smile faded. 'What about you, Tom?'

'On condition.' Tom was not smiling at all. The air was so cold that the snow particles on his jacket had not melted at all.

'What's that?'

'I go first.'

'What?'

'This is my mountain. I go first. We go in two ropes of two, and we keep together. As Petra said, the danger gets worse if we don't climb as a team.'

Rowley's head went down, an involuntary gesture of denial.

'We need to be careful, with all this new snow. And I've been here before.'

The younger man looked up again. His chin went out. 'What?'

'As far as the second pinnacle. No, that's not in the legend either. I may be slow, but I've been here before, and I'm very, very careful.'

'Shit,' growled Rowley.

'If you're worried about priority, we can all arrange to step on to the summit together. But it's only a second ascent, after all.'

Rowley did not answer. Daz said nothing. Petra did her own

mind-reading. Had Hannah indeed reached the summit of Himalchand? This was the heart of the matter then. Chivalry, the conspiracy of friends thirty years before, the epic nature of the tale – all these factors had conspired to award Hannah Kemp the summit. There was in fact no means of knowing if her claim was true. She need not have lied; she need only have been mistaken. She could have created the claim out of her own visionary imagination. But no one had yet disputed that claim aloud, because loyalty to the legend was what raised this mountain peak above all the thousands of others within the circle of this Himalayan horizon.

'Well,' demanded Rowley. 'We don't know if she did get there, do we? There weren't footprints, were there?'

'It had snowed.'

'But even you aren't sure.'

Now it was Tom's turn to stick his chin out. The speckled beard bristled. 'I'm sure. And if there's any more of that, I'll back out. I won't climb with a team that's always arguing.'

Petra almost held her breath, except that the thin air made her gasp again almost immediately. They did not have very long. Already the time spent deciding was time taken away from the actual climb. But she was not going to be peacemaker.

For no more than a few seconds Rowley stood his ground. Then he gave up with a shrug of his shoulders, and, 'Well, if you like.'

'Thanks. There's no good arguing over something we haven't got yet. Me and the lass in the lead, then?'

Rowley bristled slightly again, but again shrugged his shoulders. 'You and Pet. Fine.' He did not look at her.

Daz made a joke. 'She'll be a light weight to test the cornice.'

They climbed. New snow lay upon old snow, which lay over centuries of ice. Where rock showed through it was brittle and shattered and more fragile even than the ice. And the new snow was particularly treacherous. It was fine and powdery, like confectioner's sugar, and it rested only lightly on the harder snow beneath. It was also very cold snow, so no amount of pressure would cause it to compact. It would have been very poor snow for snowballs.

Petra, excavating away with her ice-axe, trying to clear a furrow in the snow so that her feet would touch the bottom, thought furiously about the principles of avalanche prediction. New snow on old snow was bad. New powder snow on old snow-ice was worse. The first twenty-four hours after a new snowfall was a particularly unsafe time. But going down would have meant those same risks and without a summit to show for it. At least on the ridge no avalanche could come from above.

Tom, ahead of her, carrying a loose coil of rope in one hand, an axe in the other, had ploughed his way as far as the first tower.

'It'll go.' He spoke conversationally. The air was so still that there was no need to shout. And shouting was another thing which caused avalanches.

Tom crept around the tower, on the west side, away from the precipice. The snowslope at the foot of the tower was very steep, and had accumulated only about six inches of snow. Tom kicked away white flurries as he traversed.

Petra followed. The tower, about fifty feet high, was sheer black crystalline rock. Snow lay in crevices, and in a rounded, teetering mass on the top. Petra gritted her teeth and concentrated on treading the crampon-points of each foot one at a time, then the ice-axe, with the shaft held diagonal, so that the pickaxe head and the point of the ferrule both bit into the ice. Her short ice-hammer was at her belt. Moving together, carrying coils, meant that a second ice tool was a liability. She remembered how, on her first training course in winter climbing, she had wondered if successful mountaineers had to grow extra hands.

A little way behind her, Daz stamped and hacked, with an audible commentary of expletives. Rowley was bringing up the rear. Petra could not remember when she had seen Rowley bringing up the rear before. He had been subdued by more than Tom's insistence. It was as if he had caught a glimpse of himself, of his own bravado.

'The trouble with Rowley,' Petra thought, 'is that I know him too well.'

She concentrated on the matter in hand. Before long, the ridge flattened out again. At first glance, the going seemed easy. Tom had stopped at the angle between the nether side of the pinnacle and the wider, gently inclined ridge.

'Cornice.' He pointed with his ice-axe towards the next pinnacle, a couple of hundred yards distant. 'The ridge curves westwards. It's not straight. See the crevice in the snow there?'

Petra blinked and stared. The snow was pinkish, seen through her sun goggles. She raised the goggles for a moment, and stared into the snow ahead. A faint indentation, a furrow rather than a crack, ran for two or three yards and then disappeared. It was at least twenty feet from the right-hand edge of the ridge, running parallel with the edge.

'Step to the right of the crack and it'll be a one-bounce flier. Seven thousand feet sheer.'

Petra knew about cornices. She had met them in Scotland and in the Alps. Ben Nevis sometimes grew a forty-foot crest of snow, horizontally outwards from the leeward side of the ridge. She knew that a cornice always snaps off far further away from its edge than seems intuitive. She had once ended up in Glen Nevis, on the wrong side of the mountain, because her party had been trying so hard to stay away from the cornice above Coire Leis.

But this was something remarkably different.

'You know what to do?'

'In theory.' Petra fixed her goggles in place again. 'What do you weigh, Tom?'

'Eleven stone four.'

'I'm eight stone. A bit less. Shouldn't I go first?'

Tom shook his head. 'I've had to do it once. My partner was

fourteen stone of North American. He fell one way and I leapt the other. It held.'

'You're lying. It's one of your tall tales!'

'Maybe.' He smiled. 'You're ready?'

They trod that icy tightrope between air and earth, walking a judicious distance apart, carrying their axes and coiled ropes, staying as far down the windward slope as conditions permitted. There was no longer any point in being afraid. Petra felt as if she had stepped over some threshold.

Tom had been beyond that threshold a long time; that was why he had smiled. It was the point beyond which risk could no longer be measured and balanced. It was the moment for trusting to luck – more, it was a question of seizing luck with both hands, clasping it in your arms, hugging it as the only safe haven in a world which could disintegrate within a fraction of a second into a long, soundless fall.

And then the second pinnacle was before them, and it too had an escape route to the west. Daz and Rowley came safe across in their footprints, and they too turned the pinnacle. They had to lose a bit of height at this point, and the struggle back up to the ridge through deep snow was exhausting. Here the ridge narrowed, and was crowned with complex cornice formations and séracs. The séracs, towers of ice with cornices on all four sides, were larger than any Petra had seen.

'Is there a way round?'

'Not here.' Tom screwed up his eyes against the glare. The sun was very bright, even with snow goggles. 'I think this is as far as I came. We're going to have to pitch this bit. But unless there's a sting in the tail, I believe there's only a short step beyond to the summit.'

Now they were using the full armamentarium of modern gear – ice screws, belay plates, a tough, springy nylon rope nearly half an inch thick. Hannah had come this way alone, with ten-point crampons and a three-foot axe.

Petra stopped thinking about anything else. The route was quite complex ice-climbing, delicate and precarious. It required intense concentration. She could not even think about the yawning abyss beneath her feet (because here there was no chance of entirely avoiding the break-line of the cornice); she concentrated on each movement individually.

When she came up with Tom beyond the last of the séracs, she too smiled.

The summit was there, three-cornered and gently domed.

They waited until Rowley and Daz came up, and then they made a closely-formed procession up to the top. Petra looked down at her feet, right until the last moment. Then she looked up.

They were there.

Standing, fixed to the earth, she was on the summit of Himalchand.

Hannah had written more in that last letter, after her challenge to posterity to come and check. What she had written was well known. It was in all the mountaineering anthologies:

1 September 1953

> I am no hero. None of us are heroes. I have reached the summit and my conquest is of as much consequence as a leaf blown in the wind. I do not possess the mountain. I am the mountain, inasmuch as I am part of the earth, I shall never leave it behind. I have thought of Himalchand as a person, a personification of the unattainable. Well, I have attained the summit; the mountain is unchanged.
>
> He keeps his own peace, under the centuries of snow. He is not to be conquered by footprints. He can be discovered again, each year slightly different, but with new snow blown over the tracks and new danger among the rocks and séracs, and from the weather. The discovery is not of the mountain, which is old, but of ourselves, who are always scrambling after new things.

CHAPTER 9

Rowley gave a yelp of triumph. He hugged Petra and kissed her. They all hugged each other. Tom kissed her too. She was left with the taste on her lips: ice, salt and suncream, and the sense of exuberance, the sheer joy of being. The moment was timeless, as if the past thirty years had never been. Petra saw Tom as he had been when he was young, as he would have been if Hannah had not walked out into the snow alone.

She turned her face away. The taste was still on her lips, but the salt was from her own tears.

There was no sign, anywhere on that summit, that anyone had ever stood there. Petra, at least, had never expected that there would be.

They took photographs. They placed a tiny flag on a spike in the snow, and took some photographs of that. They photographed each other, huge close-up faces against the faint blue distance. It was not just a case of taking tourist snapshots: it was a methodical record of the summit.

Then, with the blue in the distant east already fading, being tainted dangerously with orange by an afternoon sun, the four climbers turned back.

This time Rowley went first. Daz had been particularly subdued by the ascent, and he did not attempt to take the lead. But Rowley was still smiling and still exuberant. Despite the length of the descent, and its repeated challenges, nothing could rob them of the summit now.

He was bubbling like champagne. At this altitude, downhill was always four times as easy as uphill. The technical problems were no less, but they were a known quantity.

He moved very quickly down the first part of the ridge, using the footprints that had been made on the ascent. He belayed where they had belayed before. Daz followed. When he had completed the pitch there was some discussion, and then Daz led straight on through.

Petra was leading the second rope. She had gone perhaps thirty feet along the contorted ridge when she heard a faint crack. Tom, still on the summit, shouted, 'Daz! Belay!'

There was a whispering of snow. Petra froze in her footprints. She saw little showers of powder slipping off the crown of one of the séracs ahead. It was at the highest point of the ridge between her and Rowley.

He was standing with his mouth open. His mirror-glass lenses reflected a bright point of light. Then, very slowly, he turned and unclipped from the ice peg to which he was belayed.

Petra had time for thought but no time to call out. The crack, widening beside Rowley's feet, snapped open entirely, and a huge section of cornice broke away and tumbled into the void. A red spider-like figure followed it, free on the end of the rope. He flew, swung, bounced, swung again, bounced gently on the end of the rope, forty feet down the 7,000-foot precipice. The sun glinted on the ice-axe as it spun away into infinity.

'Petra, come back.' Tom's voice seemed indistinct, but urgent.

She could not take her eyes away from Rowley, swinging there on the end of his rope. He was saying 'Jesus Jesus Jesus,' rapidly and pointlessly.

'Come back, or you'll be over too. Come now.'

She shivered. She looked down at her feet. There were cracks everywhere. Somehow she scrambled back to the summit, taking no precautions at all.

Daz, hidden beyond a sérac, shouted 'Ben! Are you there? Are you there?'

'Jesus Jesus Jesus,' reiterated Rowley.

'Fucking use your fucking jumar.' Daz sounded more desperate than Rowley. 'I can't hold on here long. The rope's cutting me.'

'Shit. Where is it? Where is it? Where's the jumar?'

'By your fucking belt. In the whatsit loop. I saw it. A jumar and a fucking prussik loop.' There was a deep breath and then a groan. 'Climb the rope, Ben. I can't pull you up.'

Rowley fumbled, shaking all over. The world circled beneath his feet as he turned this way and that. The perfectly straight rope ran to a notch in the ridge. It ran straight along the snow around the sérac. The sérac was acting like a bollard on a dockside, applying friction to the rope to mitigate what would otherwise have been a dead weight.

Petra and Tom could not come to the aid of their friends. A forty-foot cleft had opened in the ridge, with a tumbled mass of rock and broken snow at its base. The cleft was simply impassable. Rowley had been standing at the far end of the broken portion. By releasing his belay he had avoided being carried away by the tons of ice to which he had been secured. He was dangling over the cliff face from the nearest portion of sound ridge on the far side. He only had to climb the rope to get back to safety.

No one was shouting instructions any more. It was up to Rowley to concentrate on the task in hand. He had to do something for which he had rehearsed, often, playing about on tall trees and roadside outcrops. It was a technical problem to climb the rope, because no one could climb a slippery smooth nylon rope less than half an inch in diameter hand-over-hand. He had to clip in his jumar clamp, with its long sling, then loop on the prussik knot to make a second hold on the rope. Then he could move one at a time, the sling from the jumar clipped to his waistbelt and the prussik loop around his foot. Thus he had to inch his way up the twisting, turning rope, teeth gritted, while small pieces of frozen snow continued to bounce off him from above.

He found the jumar, and the prussik knot, and kept his head

enough not to drop anything. When he began to climb, the rope jerked about a good deal. Daz cried out, 'Ben, you're cutting me!'

Rowley continued to climb, each jerk taking him six inches up the rope. After a few moves he had to pause for breath, because it was an exhausting process.

Petra, watching from too far away, believed that she had stopped breathing. Rowley was in the shadow of the mountain now. He was enfolded in cold dark-blue shadow. The red jacket and gold hair were extinguished.

'Come, sit down.' Tom was beside her, making her bend her knees and lower her head. 'You mustn't keel over too.'

'Ben!' she gasped soundlessly.

She shut her eyes. Then she opened them again. She could not watch but she could not bear not to watch. An overwhelming sense of the foolishness of their whole endeavour threatened to overturn her entirely. Ben, whom she had dragged away from school as a truant, long ago; who had once been a temporary and inconstant lover; who had been present, or temporarily absent, but always part of life ever since – he was hers, even when she did not want him. A habit, perhaps, but like a member of the family, an essential part of her world. He thought of himself as Rowley the mountaineer, but to Petra he was a boy who would never turn down a dare.

'Go, go, go!' shouted Daz. The rope was biting deep into the snow, melting a groove by pressure alone.

'Nearly!' Rowley called out and then had to fight for breath before moving again. He edged upwards, more slowly now, but almost free of the vertical portion of the rope. Three more painful minutes got him within arm's reach of the ridge. He took his ice-hammer from the holster at his belt, and plunged the pick into the ancient ice above his head. A loop of line ran from the end of the hammer to a clip at his belt. In an unorthodox move he put his free foot into the loop of line and stood up.

'Don't let go!' he cried.

'Jesus no,' replied Daz, but he took a giant deep breath. Rowley's move had reduced the tension in the rope, in a temporary and precarious manner. Rowley moved the ascending devices, one at a time, as far up the freed rope as he could reach.

'Take me again.'

'OK.'

The rope went taut as he moved up, and stretched and twanged against the edge of the precipice.

This time he plunged the ice-hammer in high up. The crampon-points of his free foot found a grip in the ice.

'Tight rope!' He heaved hard on all points of contact and hauled himself belly-flat over the edge.

'Hooray!' cried Petra.

Rowley just lay there gasping for breath.

'You up?' asked Daz, who could not see him.

'Yeah.' More frantic breathing. 'Let's get the fuck out of here.'

He stood up, moving like a robot, as if stiff in every joint. For a moment he hung his head, as if overwhelmed by weakness. Petra sighed, enormously. The miracle had happened.

Then Rowley looked up. He looked across the yawning chasm to the summit of the mountain. He had lost his sunglasses. He met Petra's gaze, eye to eye.

Everything turned to silence, as if the noise of the emergency had been turned off by a switch.

'Pet!'

'I'm OK. Are you OK?'

'Jesus, how are you going to get down?'

Tom gripped her shoulder. She did not look at him.

'Well done, Rowley,' said the veteran.

'Bloody right. But how are we going to get you over all that choss?' He moved as if to peer over the windward side of the ridge.

'That's our problem. You've got to get on down. Go on. Go.'

'But what about you and Pet?'

This time Petra answered: 'We'll look for a way. But there's no point your risking more than you need.'

'But Pet.' He sounded very young indeed, not at all like a cool and competent mountaineer who had just evaded death by inches.

Petra was forced to keep staring at the problem. Great jagged lumps of ice lay in a crumbled heap in the huge V-shaped defect in the ridge. The wall on the far side was formed of multiple strata of old ice, each representing a winter's snowfall. Many years of nature's work had been undone in an instant. The last straw had probably been Rowley screwing in the ice screw for his belay.

Even if there had not been forty feet of steep ice-climbing at either end of the gap, the snow and ice was altogether too precarious even to consider trusting one's weight to it. There was in fact no means of returning by the way they had come.

'What's the problem?' asked Daz.

'Pet and Tom are stranded. Bloody chunk out of the ridge. Oh Jesus, Daz, Petra's trapped on the summit.'

'Shit,' remarked Daz, almost conversationally. 'They'll have to go down the other way.'

The four of them wasted several more precious minutes in discussion, but there was really nothing more to discuss. The snow-ridge had gone, irrevocably. There was another ridge, somewhere beyond the summit, which led down to a col above the South Munshu glacier. The lower slopes on that side of the mountain had been surveyed, in conditions of poor visibility, by Hayter and Amory in 1953. That part of the mountain was made of shale, loose, fragile and slippery. It was not an easy way down. But they had no choice but to try it. Tom was already re-coiling the rope.

It was up to Petra to make the obvious request, 'When you get down, can you send people to look for us on the South Munshu?'

Rowley stared at Petra and Tom as if he could not believe what was happening. It was one matter to snatch yourself from the jaws of death. It was quite another to calmly leave your friends behind in a fix from which they were unlikely to escape.

'Can you do it?' he asked.

'It'll be one for the record books. Goodbye, Rowley.'

'Goodbye Pet, Tom.' He turned away without looking at Petra again, though she watched him until he was out of sight beyond the last tower.

The mountain silence flowed in. Tibet was blue. India was green and brown. Himalchand was white, luminous and isolated. Petra sat hunched on the summit.

Tom knelt down beside her. He was silent too, for a long while.

'What can we do?' Petra heard her own voice shaking.

Tom started to reply. 'I—' Then he bent his head and buried his face in his hands. The big mittens covered his face, but Petra could hear the rasp of his breathing as he struggled for composure.

She could not bear it. 'Tom, don't despair.' It was horrible, almost as horrible as the sight of that great cleft in the mountain, as if something seemingly secure had fallen away from beneath her feet.

She tugged at his arm, but he still would not show his face.

'Stop, Tom, stop it.'

The rising tide of panic caught at her throat. She wanted to yell and weep, too, out of anger at the sheer stupidity of their plight. But Tom was still sobbing, and not out of anger. Petra could feel the shaking of his whole body through the six layers of clothing, as if the earth itself were shaking.

She reached out and grasped his hands in her own, tearing them away by force from his face. She saw the look in his eyes. Something terrible. A soul at the Last Trump.

'Tom!'

'What have I done? Pet, Pet.' He turned his face away and tried to shake free.

'I won't let you go.' Already he seemed to be drifting away, so Petra gripped harder. She was abruptly aware of an uncanny calm, as if she had been floating on the sea and had at last touched dry land.

'We need each other, Tom.' The certainty was overwhelming. 'We're not alone. We'll find the way down.'

Then he did look at her, staring as if he were afraid that she might disappear at any moment. 'Hannah didn't.'

She blinked. The angry tears had crept up on her unawares. 'Don't be stupid. People are always coming down on the wrong side of mountains by accident.'

He shook his head. 'Only in stories.'

'But they're true. Don't give up. I can't bear it.' Tears began to obscure her eyes.

He was still now. Very quiet and still. The shaking had ceased. 'We would be sensible if we were to give up now. It would be less pain.'

The mountain-top was surrounded by silence. A circle of low cloud had risen, obscuring the horizon, so that all that could be seen was the clear circle of blue sky above, and a few square yards of domed, untrodden snow upon which two people crouched. Petra took off her gloves. The cold air felt sharp on the exposed skin. She pulled off her hat and stuffed it in her pocket. Her head was bared to the skies. A few limp strands of brown hair straggled across her face.

'We're life, Tom. We're alive. Can't you feel it?'

He was watching her. She waited. She did not see him remove his own gloves, but it was a dry, warm, weatherbeaten hand which stretched across and gently swept the hair out of her eyes.

One touch.

'Don't speak.'

Blue eyes, with the promise of infinite distance; the sadness of wisdom.

Petra felt the sudden cessation of all breath. She could not have spoken, even had Tom desired it. Precious, necessary, beloved Tom.

'You?'

'Pet, Pet.'

Their embrace had the impact of a desperate, long-prevented need. Too late, too hastily, they clung together, as if by holding on to one another they could save themselves.

It was hardly a physical pleasure, with cracked lips tainted with glacier cream, and the bulk of unwashed clothing and ironmongery. But it was the promise of what might have been: love, anger, pity, fear; the hope of redemption.

Petra tasted blood and did not know if it was her own or Tom's. His arms were ferociously strong, and entirely without tenderness.

They had to draw breath at last, giddy from the thin air. 'So now we know,' said Tom.

'Does it make any difference?'

'Not here.'

But even in that wilderness the voices of civilisation could be heard mocking. Tom was in fact a year or two older than Petra's own father, even if the latter did spend his life on a sofa in front of the television. And there was that huge area of doubtful ground between the idea of the hero and the lover.

Petra fought against it. 'I do love you. I couldn't imagine anything else.'

'Nor I. Not till now.' It was there in every line of his brown face, and in those wild blue eyes: that vulnerability of the spirit which is the key to passion.

'I can't bear it, Tom.' She turned her face away. There was in fact no means of escape, no means of returning to earth again so that passion could find its natural end.

She shivered. The sun, a degree or two lower, had allowed the air to cool still further. The atmosphere was still perfectly calm, and the blue sky contained no threatening clouds. The day was running out.

Tom's voice was clear and concise. 'We have to go down a bit of a way. Dig a snow-hole.'

Petra nodded. Somehow things had not been made easier at

all. She and Tom were completely dependent on each other in every way now. They could no longer pretend to be cool in an emergency. There was no place for a stiff upper lip. One word spoken in the wrong sort of voice would tell everything. And added to fears of personal danger was that fear for the safety of the other which had no place in the rational contract between climbing partners.

'Let's decide which way to head. There's one ridge which is too steep.'

'That's the south-east ridge. We need south-west.'

Petra looked around at the way they had come. 'Isn't Tengdatta on about a north-east bearing from here?'

'If you believe the map. We just have to go and look. Have you got everything?'

Petra clutched her axe and checked the knotted rope on her harness. She pulled her snow goggles on again, like a mask. She reverted to the familiar words of the cragger: 'Climb when you're ready.'

The way down was a new and hidden landscape. Seen from above, the ridge was peculiarly foreshortened, as if each step forward lay towards the brink of a precipice. To find the way off the summit would be hard enough: the southern ridges were steeper and more broken than the north-eastern one, and the covering of new snow obscured all perspective. Tom, going first, had to spend a long time inspecting the integrity of the uneven snow on the far side of the summit triangle, while bearing in mind that his general direction had to tend towards the northern precipice. Petra watched him, casting this way and that, and from time to time glancing back over his shoulder. He looked sightless behind the dark glasses, a blind man looking for the way through a maze.

He found a belay. Petra followed. She moved slowly, always aware of the need for haste, always knowing that no false step was now permissible. The mountain, so far playing with the climbers like a cat teasing a mouse, might choose to end the game ruthlessly, at any moment.

When she came to the belay, a peg on an ice cone, she had to stand still to sort out the ropes. She could feel the tension in Tom, even though they were separated by a definite space of clear air. She found that her own hands were not steady.

'I'll lead through,' she said.

'It takes experience, working out this kind of descent.'

'You'll have to trust me.'

Tom shook his head. 'I'm not losing my nerve.'

'I know. But we need to protect each other. It'll take too long, otherwise.'

He shivered. 'Go on, then.'

She looked away. Below the high place where they stood, the ridge swooped away. It was a jumble of snowy pinnacles, perched between the steep drop to the north and the graduated snowslope which fell away into the glacier cwm at the head of the South Munshu. At some point, but not yet, they would be able to descend the snow-face that formed the left-hand side of the ridge. But the headwall of the cwm, where it met the ridge, was nearly as vertical as the precipice to the north. Only as the ridge levelled out, in its lower section, did the snow come right up to the base of the pinnacles. Beyond, the ridge swept upwards again towards the first of the three peaks of Gopalkand.

For once, Petra looked not towards the summit of the mountain, but towards the beckoning valley. There was snow on the glacier, but at its further end the surface was broken up with holes, and rocks protruded through. Petra found herself looking ahead, seeing which way would be best for crossing the glacier.

'Go on,' Tom said again.

She turned around, because the angle of the ridge was sufficient to require her to go down backwards. For a moment she looked at Tom, then quickly she looked at her feet again.

She stepped down. First one foot. Then the other foot. Then the ice-axe, held crossways in the classic style. She repeated the move, trying for a rhythm, but always having to glance between her feet at the next patch of snow. Remarkably, there was no cornice at this section of ridge. It faced directly into the full blast of the wind. The snow had been scoured off the more exposed parts, leaving firm, hard ice. The going was difficult, and would have been impossible without front-point crampons, but the hazard was visible, not hidden under the round white outline of the new snow.

Petra got out her ice-hammer. Forty feet out on the rope she paused and placed an ice screw. Her hands seemed clumsy, crippled by fear and exhaustion. But the screw went in. She used it as a running belay, moving on, downwards, where the ridge took a turn to the north and then dissolved into a wider, flatter area of snow-covered boulders. She found a possible belay. She signalled for Tom to follow.

He came downwards steadily, moving by instinct. He was like an insect crawling on the white wall of the mountain. When he came up to her he paused only to take the rack of gear from her, and snapped in the ice screws which he had removed on the descent.

They had six ice screws between them, six karabiners, one pair of jumars and a descender each. A hundred and sixty-five feet of rope. It was less gear than a weekending team would require on a gully on Ben Nevis. There was no need for either climber to remind the other not to drop things.

'I'll go on now.' He seemed insubstantial, as if he were smaller and lighter than Petra. As he moved on, he walked slowly, with the peculiar gait that is necessary while wearing crampons. Each leg had to swing outwards, away from the other, so that crampon points did not snag in the snow gaiters. The crampons themselves, in giving grip on hard snow, had to be carefully lifted and placed. There was no chance of putting a swing in the step, even on easy ground.

Tom wandered onwards, with this half-crippled gait, threading a way through snow-encrusted blocks, glancing back now and again to check that the rope was not going to jam. At the edge of the small plateau he paused, looked down, and then looked back towards Petra, shading his eyes.

'Seventy feet at least. I can't see the bottom.'
'I'll come up to you.'
'No time.'
'I'm coming.'

Petra unbelayed, and stamped her own tracks across the maze. She too looked over the edge.

'We'll have to try it. I wish my head would stop buzzing.' She shook her head, as if to get rid of a troublesome fly. 'This is no place for a night out.'

Tom smiled slightly. He had made a kind of belay around a block, but it was not a good one. 'Stay lucky, Pet.'

She went over the edge, down a steepening, crumbling slope, held together only by ice. The waning day, which made the threat of darkness so imminent, had taken away the heat from the sun. Nothing was melting. Everything that had melted was freezing again. The snow-ice, white and pure, was the perfect medium for crampon points.

It would have been a superb pitch, had there been any question of enjoying the climb. But the mountain had become an enemy. Perhaps it had already decided to put an end to things. Perhaps this lonely struggle was in vain. Only the habit of survival remained: the careful placement of each metal spike, the permanent watchfulness, despite the compulsion of tiredness.

The game had changed. This was no longer a team of climbers laying down a challenge to the mountain, the artificial game played by Westerners with no danger in their lives. Petra and Tom had become fugitives from a known and fearsome beast.

She climbed all the way down the steep section, perhaps fifty feet, to a step. She made a flimsy running belay and went on down. The lower section was out of sight of Tom. It was a little less steep, but longer. Petra had to belay on quite steep ground. The ridge was perhaps twelve feet wide at this point.

She tugged on the rope and shouted. An age later the rope began to snake slowly downwards, indicating that Tom had begun to descend.

A very long time later he reappeared, coming backwards over the edge of the step. He moved awkwardly, as if uncertain of where his limbs were. In the evening light the snow was no longer white, but faintly peach-coloured, as in an interior designer's catalogue.

Petra watched as Tom picked his way down the steep ground. His unrhythmical movements made him look as if he were climbing by numbers, each muscle subject to a separate command. Petra drew in the rope. She knew that there was little that either of them could do if Tom fell, but it was still important to stay roped.

A continuous stream of snow-particles came rustling down the slope, dislodged by his crampons and axe. They whispered past Petra, and out into the void.

Then he was with her, sharing the precarious ledge. It seemed as if he could barely stand.

'We're too tired, Pet.'

'I'll do.'

'You won't. You're moving like a snail. We'll have to stop.'

'Where?' The question was entirely rhetorical. The ledge they stood on was narrow and sloping. The snow-ice was as solid as concrete, and slippery.

'You know what I mean. We must start looking for somewhere to snow-hole.'

One more pitch perhaps. Or two or three. Still at 21,000 feet, at nightfall, at the beginning of winter.

'Give me the gear, Pet.'

She let him go, because neither of them had a choice. He crept on down, balanced between the two precipices, barely able to place one foot in front of the other. He reached a pinnacle, and traversed it on the southern side. Then he came back, even more slowly, and crouched under the uphill side of the pinnacle to belay.

This was bad news. What lay beyond the pinnacle? Petra tried not to think about it as she placed each careful footstep in the snow. At least here she could descend facing outwards.

Tom sat hunched under the snow-capped pinnacle. Petra had to come right up to him before he looked up. He had been concentrating his whole mind on taking in the rope.

'What's up?'

Tom's face was blank and grey. The fading light was hardly enough to pick out his features.

'Worse lower down. It's all broken. Blocks tipped this way and that. If we were fit.'

Petra swallowed on a dry throat. She did not doubt his judgement. 'Tom. Oh my dear.'

'I can't think straight. Petra, what'd you do?'

'Dig, if we can. Sleep.'

'I wish.'

'Don't wish. We're in it together. Don't wish you were on your own.'

'Mind-reading.'

'Don't you do it too?'

The place was too narrow for them to stand close to one another, but she grasped his hand. 'Don't mind-read. Get your breath. Think about snow-holing. Those guys did it on the summit of Everest, years ago.'

'We'll be worse in the morning.'

'Not if we sleep.'

'Maybe not.'

They had nothing to dig with except their axes and their mitten-covered hands. It was a far cry from Petra's previous experience, on snow-climbing courses in Scotland, where there was always a spade and lots of keen novices to take turns. But Tom had found the one place where a snow-hole might be dug. The pinnacle had collected a wedge of snow between itself and the main ridge, perhaps by wind-drift or by avalanche. Careful excavation on the southern side of the pinnacle might create a chamber large enough for two people, with room for a protective wall of snow on the outside.

The work of digging kept them warm as the last of the light went out of the sky and even the distant pink peaks were swallowed up in haze. The work became harder in the darkness, with the erratic beams of headlamps serving only to confuse the perception of surface and depth. Petra got inside the hole and scraped stuff out. Tom made snowballs for the wall. Before they had started they had been dangerously exhausted. The job of digging the snow-hole took three hours.

When it was finished, they were almost too weary for sleep. They crept inside, covered from head to toe in encrusted snow. They filled in the entrance hole, to leave just a small aperture for ventilation. They breathed warm air in clouds, and the vapour was not snatched away by the wind. This was shelter.

'What down-gear have you got?' Petra heard herself speak but hardly knew that this was her own voice.

'Sleeping bag.'

'I've got my duvet too. All over sick.' She giggled.

'Space blanket?'

'I've got mine, I think.'

They reviewed the contents of their rucksacks. There was no water. No food except for some squashed dates which had plastered themselves all over the base of Tom's sack. There was no cooking stove or matches, and the batteries of the two headlamps were failing fast. There was just enough warm clothing but only by accident. Petra had stuffed her duvet away in the bottom of her sack, because of the smell it made in the tent. She had omitted to take it out when she was packing for the summit bid.

'Feet in the rucksack,' said Tom. 'Take crampons off first, mind.'

They sat on their waterproofs and wrapped the space blanket around them. It was sixteen square feet of silver-coloured plastic, designed to keep heat in under conditions of extreme cold. Petra had kept it, unopened for years, in the pocket of her cagoule. It had an incongruously glamorous appearance in that dark, cold bivouac, like a night-club singer entertaining frontline troops. It crackled like a giant sweet-wrapper.

Petra was going to say something, but she saw that Tom had

fallen suddenly asleep. She turned out her light. The space blanket still crackled in the darkness. She thought, 'I wonder if we'll wake up from this sleep?' Then the darkness overtook her also.

Tom's voice woke her from dreamless sleep. She could feel his warm breath on her cheek. All her body was stiff and cold; her feet were numb. The solid snow was wrapped around her body as if she had been buried in a cold tomb.

'Pet, Pet, wake up.'

The warm breath, and a fainter perception of solid warmth where his body touched hers, were the only signs of continuing life.

'Wake up. Open your eyes.' His voice held the very slightest note of panic, as if despair were only a little way beneath the surface. Petra felt an answering ripple of fear within herself. She was still alive. They were both still alive, and they still had to fight their way free.

'Mmm.' She tried to speak, but found that her dry lips were stuck together. She opened her eyes wide as the new fear kicked her sluggish heart into beating. The cavern was full of an even, greyish light, filtered by the translucent enclosing wall. The ventilation hole was a ragged circle of paler grey.

Then Tom's face filled her view. His eyes too were wide open and staring. His face looked gaunt. Ice had melted and frozen like glass on his beard and moustache. More ice rimmed the edge of his woolly hat.

'Pet, can you move?'

With a conscious effort she persuaded her tongue to move, to prise her lips apart. Tom held up a handful of snow-powder.

'Lick the snow. There's no water. Even the place we're sitting on has frozen.'

She blinked. The grey light showed up the smooth, glistening sheen of the cave walls. But this was not water. Anything that had melted from the warmth of their bodies had promptly frozen in the deep cold of the night. She tasted the snow. It was cold, but seemed no colder than her own lips.

'I'm tired, Tom.'

'Come on. Take some more snow. We must climb on down.'

He did not even try to smile. He seemed gently determined. Petra wondered what would happen when they both lost heart simultaneously.

Slowly, creaking at all joints, she moved. The fabric of her duvet jacket had frozen to the wall of the snow-hole and had to be ripped away. Even when she had got her feet to move, her toes remained numb. She got her feet out of the rucksack, then struggled to replace her crampons. Tom was already destroying the front wall of the cave.

'No new snow. Not much wind.'

'That's lucky.'

'Is it?' Tom subsided back on to his heels, panting for breath from the exertion. 'I should have told you before, shouldn't I?'

Petra tugged at her crampon strap with cold fingers. The black rubber strap was slippery and stringy, like a giant stick of liquorice.

'What's that, Tom?'

'I didn't forget what Hannah wrote. I didn't destroy the notebook, though I should have done. I couldn't be part of the conspiracy to that extent.'

He used his ice-axe to aim another blow at the imprisoning wall.

'She said she wished there were a God who could lead her home.'

3 September 1953

If I could believe in a god like that. The Girl Guide God who rewards patience and virtue. But I've done wrong, haven't I? I'm a limbless fish struggling at the edge of the water because I have strayed into a place where that God never intended me to be.

No one will come to help me now. I have told the men that I have no need of them. The mountain hates me. I have been to the top of the mountain and there is no way back.

My choice is plain. I die here, slow and cold, with starvation stalking around me like the Devil's hunting dog. Or else I trust myself to the wind.

I cannot go home now, even in my imagination. There is no England any more, no quiet garden where Hannah Lennard could have lived a bored and restless life. I did not know what I was choosing when I made the choice to go out alone. I never could have known that a lifetime of seeming choices would lead to this.

I do not want to die. I would give anything to the future if I could be allowed to live. But I cannot make promises to that non-existent God.

My friends, please come and find me. Please. Please.

Petra shut her eyes. 'Oh Christ.'

'It was terrible.'

She felt wasteful tears gathering around her eyes. She shook her head angrily. 'Why? Why tell me now, Tom?'

'If I don't get another chance.'

'But why?'

'I couldn't say it better, nor could you. We want to get home.'

'Let's climb then.'

She wrenched the strap of her crampon on to its last buckle, and tucked away the end. She was ready to move. Tom hesitated in the entrance of the cave.

'Go on.'

He held out his hand to her, reaching backwards for comfort. His grip was hard, as if he did not want to let go. Petra thought how flimsy was this clinging-on to life, as if anything mattered at all now. There would be no one to tell her story, or Tom's. There was just this vestige of life to be got through in whatever way. But the two of them would continue to behave as if there were still a purpose, as if there were still some means of finding the way back.

But who would come to find them? Rowley and Daz still

had a dangerous descent to make. Ieuan, that professional saver of lives, was a man who did not understand mountains. The Rat was ill. Diane was not a mountaineer, however much she cared for her friends. And down in the valley were an assortment of men and women who honoured and feared the mountain as a god. No one would be in a position to challenge the judgement of Himalchand. All this was said, but not spoken, in that farewell clasping of hands.

Petra watched the slow coils of rope unwinding as Tom went ahead, and when the rope had all run out, she followed.

The sky was white, like the snow. The sun was a hard-edged disc of thin light. Petra could stare straight into the sun without hurting her eyes. There were no shadows. The mist, which hid the sun, masked the distant peaks. Gopalkand, with its three-pointed summit, was half-visible in drifting cloud. Tom, standing at the very edge of the precipice, was a blurred and fading figure.

Petra came up to him, taking in coils of rope. She looked down. The sight was no less horrid in daylight than it had been at dusk. The ridge, so sharp and definite in its upper part, seemed to have slumped into anarchy.

Long flat slabs of rock lay balanced across one another, teetering like sticks in a game of spillikins. Some bristled skywards, others stood out frankly over the precipice, as if contemplating suicide. The whole lot looked as if it would slide away at the touch of a single foot. That great mass of rock would start creaking and rumbling; begin to slither; then fall, stone over stone, down the untrodden snowslope to the bergschrund of the south Munshu glacier.

Petra shut her eyes, but that did not shut out the sight. She made herself look again. Tom was silent beside her.

There had to be a way. There had to be a way of thinking out the problem. Otherwise there was no point in their having slept out the night. That rest, however uncomfortable, had resulted in a short period of lucidity, before exhaustion, hunger and thirst would take over again.

'Coil the rope,' said Tom. He was already untying the knot at his waist.

She obeyed without thinking. Then: 'We're climbing unroped?'

'It'll pull things off on top of us. Better chance without.'

She still did not argue. She could think of summer days in Snowdonia when a carelessly trailed rope on a clifftop had flicked lethal fragments of rock on to climbers at the foot of the crag. That was why people wore climbing-helmets.

On the flanks of Himalchand, a climbing-helmet would not be much protection against those giant boulders.

'Now what, Tom?'

'See how it goes.'

'We might be able to get on to the snow, beyond.'

'Aye.'

He set off first. That was something Petra was coming to recognise. She would be out ahead only if Tom let her, or if he were to give up hope entirely.

She watched him go, in just a few moves, testing each hand and foothold for hidden insecurity. Tom had learned to climb in the days when the first rule of the sport was: 'The leader never falls.' He was putting every scrap of experience from forty-odd years of climbing into the job of staying secure.

Petra followed, using the same footprints. The snow helped, from that point of view. But under the covering of snow were hidden cavities into which a foot, or a leg, or a whole climber might be lost.

The jumble of rocks was a maze, through which it was difficult to be sure of keeping in the right direction. From time to time, the peaks of Gopalkand would come out of the mist, and allow the climbers to get their bearings. But there was no question of proceeding in a straight line.

Tom crept across a flat-topped boulder, and then made a precarious step across to the tip of a snub-nosed rock like a whale. The whale rocked slightly and shed some of its snow. As Petra attempted the step, it rocked a little more. Tom seized her by the collar and heaved her up – an unorthodox move which preceded an alarming grinding noise as the whale-rock settled in a new position. Minor boulders rattled into the crevices between the rocks.

'Move!'

They scrambled off the other side. This time Petra went first. She crossed a field of small pointed rocks and hauled herself up on to the next slab. As she did so she heard the whale-rock begin to slide.

Tom was up beside her, gasping. They watched the rockfall grow and develop. Whole chunks of the ridge slid away, leaving gaping black scars.

'On, on.'

They could not be careful any more. Safety now lay only in the instinct for flight. They leapt from rock to rock, over and sometimes under the balanced blocks, their crampons screeching as they scrabbled for footholds. Bits of ridge kept giving way, but always at a short delay behind the climbers, and the rocks so far had always fallen sideways, towards the glacier. It was as if the mountain were still in pursuit, but not yet ready for its prey.

Petra kept going, with Tom close behind. They had breath enough for haste only because they continued to go generally downhill, but there was no breath for talking.

They slipped and slid across 500 feet of precarious ground, as the mountain slope disintegrated behind them. Petra never looked further than the next foothold, so the end of the passage arrived suddenly. She found firm ground under her feet: firm crisp snow, on a white slope of ridge which shallowed out towards the col.

She ploughed forwards through untouched snow – five yards, ten yards, thirty yards. Then she stopped, gasping for air.

She crouched down and put her head between her knees. The small segment of her brain that was not wholly taken up with the fight for breath was considering her remarkable luck.

The technical problems were over. In the Everest year, Hayter and Amory had come up to this col on their reconnaissance. They had said that the mountain ridge was 'as slippery as soap', but they had called the glacier approach a dull snow-pod.

She felt as if her lungs were too small to take in all the air that she needed. There were bright lights dancing in patterns before her eyes. She could hear a sound like the ringing of bells. All she could do was breathe and breathe and breathe.

When at last she looked up again at Himalchand, the mountain stood as it always had, impassive and distant. She heard a rushing sound which was not inside her head, and the great ten-foot wingspan of the Lammergeier, the wild Himalayan eagle, swept past, just above the crest of the ridge. She could almost have touched its feathers.

She gasped, and looked back towards Tom. He was sitting, hunched up, a good twenty feet away, staring after the bird as it swept down into the valley. It seemed to be leading the way.

Petra waved her arm, languidly. Tom, who had been carrying the rope, unhooked it from around his shoulders and began to peel off the coils. He still did not stand up. It was as if his legs would not hold him.

'You OK?' Petra started back towards him, slightly uphill.

He flashed her a grin. He had to pause in his uncoiling of the rope, as if he did not have enough breath to do both.

Petra took another step. Something shook. There was a cracking sound which she had heard before.

She was unroped. There was nowhere she could jump to for safety. She felt the ground beneath her feet beginning to subside, slowly at first but gathering pace with each instant. Her last view, before the avalanche took her, was of Tom, whirling away down the mountainside in a tangle of bright green rope.

My friends, please come and find me. Please. Please.
I would promise anything.
I cannot go home now.

CHAPTER 10

The darkness went on and on, tumbling and roaring. The solid earth had come unstuck from its roots. Earth, air and sky were returned to the primeval chaos from which they had been separated at the Creation.

Only Petra's mind remained, crying for help. She was encased in a rushing fluid which was also solid and opaque. Someone said: 'Swim'. Somewhere, in the years of her education, she had been told that the way to survive an avalanche was to swim as if in water. That way you could float near the top and would not be buried deep when the avalanche came to a halt. She had never known upon what experience this advice had been based. But, as if drowning in a storm at sea, she clutched at the idea.

She waved her arms and legs, helplessly, like a stranded beetle, and still she kept on falling, over and over and over.

Then, abruptly, she came to a halt. The shock knocked the breath out of her. Her mind went blank, but her arms and legs kept waving until the load of snow from above pinned her down.

She was still conscious. There was no pain. She had no sensation, in fact, that she was still attached to her body. She felt her own heart beating: the thudding noise of a drum which was being played a long way away.

The world was still in darkness. After a while, she realised that her eyes were shut, so she opened them. There was light. It was all around: a pale diffuse white light which filled up the whole of her field of view.

Then she did feel pain, as if the sudden return of hope was burning into her. She tried to breathe, and her chest was all pain. She could get no obedience from her limbs.

She remembered, horribly, that people buried in avalanches sometimes try to dig themselves out in the wrong direction. Disorientated by the fall, they dig downwards rather than upwards, until they finally collapse. Rescuers find the evidence of their hopeless efforts. Petra did not know anyone who had survived being buried by an avalanche. She had always tried to think of it as a sudden way of dying.

But there was that light. Surely that could only mean that the sky was not far away; that Petra herself was facing towards the surface; and that a short period of digging would return her to the air?

She opened her mouth. Snow crystals fell into it, sharp and sweet. That was good news too. The avalanche was made of powder snow, less dangerous sort of snow. The fallen snow would not be compacted completely solid. If she could get her limbs to move, they would not be struggling against an irresistible casing.

She took another burning breath. Snow powder entered her lungs and made her cough. She made one desperate, convulsive movement, an instinctive struggling effort which did not involve her having to tell each individual limb what to do. She could not bear the thought of suffocating in the snow.

More snow fell on her face. Somehow she had her hands in front of her face, sweeping the snow away. Then she could see the white sky, and the sun.

She worked hard, chipping away at her snowy covering, freeing first her arms and then her chest, and finally her leaden, disobedient legs. She crept out of the engulfing carapace of snow like a butterfly emerging from a chrysalis. She could not stand up for weakness. She crawled on to the surface and stayed there, four-footed like an animal.

Her ice-axe had gone, together with her ruckack, both crampons, her hat and snow goggles. She had been stripped bare of all the man-made gear upon which she had depended. She was alone and empty-handed.

She raised her head and stared out over the emptiness: the utter desolation of the mountainside.

It was a place that she did not recognise. Around her was the tumbled debris of the avalanche cone. She was crouched upon its very apex. More debris spread out below her, for a couple of hundred feet, and beyond was the smooth snow of the glacier. Behind her was the headwall of the cwm, with a great scooped bite out of it where the avalanche had broken away.

Before, she and Tom had reckoned that the headwall was 800 or 1,000 feet tall. The avalanche had taken her down nearly that entire distance. Petra's survival was among those legendary tales such as Tom used to tell, of a thousand-foot fall, cushioned by snow, from which a climber had walked away scatheless.

Tom and his stories. Tom. He was not there. The ruined glacier was empty of human life. There was no clue as to where he might be buried in that limitless expanse.

The pain of loss was appalling. She did not know how she could stand it. Tom was gone and she was alone with the pain. Pain gripped at her throat and sapped her strength in a way that no mere physical injury had ever done. She curled up into a tight ball, clutching herself with her arms as if to stop the pain bursting out and destroying her.

She could not contain the agony, but shouted aloud, 'No!' The mountains echoed. Something rumbled on the peak of Gopalkand, then ceased. Petra looked up as the eagle swept across again. It was free, as separate from the raw ugliness of humanity as the spirits of the dead.

There were no gods to pray to. The mountain which had been the be-all and end-all had betrayed her and her love.

But even misery was a luxury. She heard Tom say, quite clearly, 'This is no place to linger.'

She uncoiled herself, like a hatching chick. She blinked, because the sun had become bright. The mist was breaking up into ephemeral streamers, and the snow itself was beginning to sparkle. Petra felt no warmth. The sun's heat mocked her. Too late. Too late.

Slowly, painfully, she got to her feet. She made a tentative step, testing the solidity of the snow. Her foot stayed where she had put it. She took another step, like a child learning to walk. The snow was slippery. She balanced by stretching her arms out sideways, and by leaning back a little so that her weight went on her heels. That was habit reasserting itself, as if she were simply coming down off an easy gully in north Wales.

The surface of the avalanche cone was rough where lumps of fallen snow lay jumbled one on top of another. Petra had to watch her feet as she picked her way down. She had to think only about the next step. Tired as she was, that effort left very little room for other thoughts.

Then she tripped. A large block of snow crumbled under her foot, and she was flung sideways. She tried to save herself, but the other foot was caught, sending her tumbling. She did not fall far. She sat up, covered all over in snow again, and felt for the ankle that had been wrenched.

Then her heart did stop. She was tugging at a loop of rope which had got caught around her foot. Bright green rope. She had bought 800 feet of that ghastly rope for the expedition because it was cheap.

She tried to remember, but could not. Had Tom been tied on to that rope when he fell? She tried to work out how much time had passed since the accident, how long he must have been buried.

And even as the thoughts raced through her mind, she was pulling at the loop of rope, yanking it out of the snow, looking to see which way it ran. The rope was 165 feet long, and the only mark on it was an ink mark to show the mid-point. She knew that people who venture out under avalanche conditions, such as rescue workers in the Alps, sometimes trail a length of line with marks every nine feet, so that their rescuers know how far to dig. By that logic, Tom could be 165 feet down in the centre of that mass of snow. But the place was marked. Petra did not have to dig up the whole mountainside.

She grubbed away at the loose snow. She found another, unconnected loop. That was good news, since it meant that the rope was not stretched out straight. She remembered now how Tom had seemed to be tangled up in the rope as he fell.

She found a third loop, and then had to decide which line to follow. All the time she dug away with her hands. Soon she discarded her gloves because she could dig faster bare-handed. The sun was hot on the back of her head, and the blood was beating in her ears. 'Hurry. Hurry.'

She had to pause for breath, great painful gulps of cold air. She coughed. Breathed again. Pitched forward and dug some more. Until that moment she had believed that she had already been making the maximum possible human effort towards survival.

The snow was soft, white and pure. After a while Petra could feel no sensation in her hands at all. The white snow became streaked with blood. She found the free end of the rope and flung it away. The other strand of rope was snaking about this way and that, but it was no longer leading inexorably towards the interior of the snowfall. Then it was joined by several other strands. Petra found an ice screw. She tugged at it and it did not move free. She dug more furiously and encountered a fold of cloth.

Then she stopped. Swallowed hard. There was a vile taste in her mouth.

She found one blue hand, gloveless. She could not feel it because her own hands were so cold. She followed the hand and arm, then found a mat of grey hair and pulled.

Tom's eyes were shut. His face was still. The skin was blue, like his hand. Petra cleared away the snow from his face with her clumsy, nerveless fingers. Then she carried on digging out the snow from around him.

She had seen death before. That was one of the incidental hazards of being a mountain leader. She had been scooped into search-and-rescue operations in the British hills, where ill-equipped visitors could get into serious trouble a few miles from a road. She had helped carry a fallen climber from the base of a crag, when it was not worth getting out a helicopter just for a body. Once, she had helped to dig people out of the snow. She had been twenty years old at the time, contemptuous of the possibility that anyone could come so seriously adrift as to perish in a snowdrift in Scotland. It had been one of those episodes that had led to massive changes in the bureaucracy of mountain leadership. She remembered the pale faces and crumpled limbs of the dead as they had emerged from the snow. She remembered the awkward shapes distorting the black plastic bags in which the bodies had to be carried away.

She had seen death before, but not like this. Tom looked as if he were asleep. His face was relaxed in the deep peace of a sleeping child. The craggy lines were gone. The eyelashes, sand-coloured and thick, lay lightly on his cheeks. His lips were moist and slightly parted, and perfect six-pointed snowflakes peppered his beard.

On his moustache, the snow had melted into fine droplets. Petra tried to pull him out of the hole, but had to give up. He was too heavy. She bent her head, panting for breath, with her arms still around his shoulders. There were tears starting in her eyes, not from sorrow but from anger at her helplessness.

Her face was very close to his; she could feel the roughness of his beard. Then she heard a sound like a sigh, and felt warm breath on her cheek.

'Tom?' She shook him.

'Tom! Tom!'

His limbs were as lax as those of a puppet. She could not feel for his pulse because her own hands were so cold. But there had been something. Perhaps he was not out of reach after all.

She put her lips to his and breathed, in the approved Red Cross fashion. The air returned, passively. Again she breathed, and again the breath returned. She altered her position to make things easier. Then she set to breathing for him, in and out, in and out, while the sun crept up and melted all the clinging snow on their bodies.

Petra did not in fact know when she ought to give up trying. She knew quite simply that she could not leave Tom now.

She was no longer afraid. From time to time she straightened up and looked about her. The mountains were still. The eagle had departed. There were no rumblings from the gullies on Gopalkand or on the western face of Himalchand. It was as if time itself had become suspended.

Then she heard something which sounded like a whistle. It was a peculiar noise for a bird to have made. She looked about again for the eagle, but did not see him. Far away, at the rim of the glacier basin, she saw a glint of light.

It was there for an instant, then was gone. She blinked and stared and saw nothing, but the glimpse had distracted her from her task of resuscitation for longer than before. She heard what she had been praying to hear for so long, the long deep sigh of Tom taking a breath of his own.

She breathed her own sigh, then waited for the next sign from Tom. Obediently, he breathed again. His lips were purple now, not blue. There was the faintest fluttering beneath his eyelids.

Petra looked around again, peering down the valley, hoping for another spark of light. Nothing she could do herself would be any good unless her friends were coming to find her. That in itself was a ridiculous hope, because Rowley and Daz could hardly have got down the mountain yet with the news.

But it was there again, the transient spark of sunlight reflected on glass. And someone whistled again. The two facts together could only mean the presence of other people on the glacier.

She stood up, waved her arms. Then she realised that this was stupid. If she could not see them, they would not be able to see her at all.

She could feel the blood coming back into her hands. All that exertion had warmed her up. The sensation was familiar, a dull painful ache of returning life.

In the pocket of her anorak was the neatly folded package of the space blanket, which she had put away again after the bivouac. Her fingers struggled to undo the zip on the pocket. The square of silver fabric opened out like a flower. It reflected the sun from a thousand folds and facets. Petra took two corners and flapped the blanket, like a housewife shaking out a rug. It crackled and snapped and glittered in the sun. She hoisted the flag high above her head, waving and calling out, so that her voice echoed from mountain to mountain.

She was in the perfect centre of that curved valley. The sound of her voice leapt from Himalchand to Gopalkand, to the lesser peak of Kandar above the valley, and came back to her, a second or two later, hardly diminished by its journey.

Close upon the crest of that returning tide of sound came three fierce blasts of a whistle, followed by a whole incoherent chorus of toots.

Petra counted a line of little black figures creeping over the rim of the basin. The figures in the lead stopped for a moment, and there was that flash of reflected sunlight again.

She counted five figures. All of them. Someone else had got out their own space blanket and was waving it in response to her signal. She leapt up and down, then had to flop back on to the snow because the exertion had taken her breath away.

Tom was still breathing quietly in his private hollow in the snow. She touched his lips again with hers, feeling the warmth.

'We're back on earth again,' she whispered.

She remained there a long time, holding him close, in the last moments of solitude.

Then, looking down on to the world again, she saw that something truly extraordinary had occurred.

The ranks of the rescuers had been multiplied. The leader was seen in colour, in his lime-green coat. The second figure was wrapped all about in silver. The third, bowed down by his pack, wore a sensible khaki jersey, like a birdwatcher. Everyone else was in shades of brown or grey.

Petra counted them. Twenty people, most of whom

appeared to be Indian hillmen, were climbing up the South Munshu glacier, at least a day before any rescue party could have been expected to arrive.

The leaders halted. Everyone else came together in a huddle. Faces were upturned. The party was now only a couple of hundred feet below where Petra sat. There seemed to be some discussion. The three brightly dressed mountaineers came on – Diane, Ieuan and the Rat.

They were moving roped together, ice-axes in hand, testing each step carefully. Seen from below, Petra's eyrie would have seemed a dangerous place.

She did not call out or wave again. She sat, holding Tom's hand in hers, until the Rat came to a halt below her.

He had to let his breathing catch up before he could speak. He looked infinitely older than the bumptious youth who had set out from England, a few weeks before. His face was thinner, half-covered by tangled hair and unshaven beard, but that was not why he looked different.

He just spoke her name. 'Pet?'

'I'm all right. It's Tom.'

'Gone?'

'I dug him out. He's in this hole.'

The Rat looked at Petra, then at the great mound of snow on which she sat. He bent his head and came on up. A dozen steps and he was kneeling down at Petra's side, staring at Tom.

He shouted over his shoulder: 'Ieuan!' The doctor was not more than ten yards behind. There was no need to shout. Ieuan moved up deliberately, and carefully unshouldered his pack.

He did not spare even one glance for Petra. He was already looking Tom over as if he were some technical climbing problem. He took a little torch out of his pocket.

Petra looked away, as another wave of unthinkable thoughts swept over her. Diane, panting hard and wearing the space blanket like a silver cloak, came up the last few feet on hands and knees. Her ice-axe was swinging by its loop from her wrist. Petra was caught in a whirl of embracing arms and loosened hair. Diane was sobbing with relief and breathlessness. She could not speak, and neither could Petra. They were crying and clinging together like children. That touch of humanity had banished the wilderness as if it were an invention of the mind.

Of the seventeen villagers who had come to help, two were familiar faces. One was the young man, the son of Tai Singh, who had come to help them on their way from Munshu. The other was Tai Singh himself.

Petra came down on to the glacier first. The rest of them were going to lower Tom down the steep bit with ropes. She hardly recognised Tai Singh as the grand old man of Kala. Gone were the embroidered cap and waistcoat. Instead he wore two layers of ragged homespun knitwear. He still carried a long wooden stave, upon which he was leaning, watching the activity going on up the mountainside. He was shod rather better than the rest, in brown canvas army boots.

'Sister!' he called out. 'What is news?'

'I'm here. I got out of the avalanche.'

'And Mr Tom, he fell also?'

'He's alive.'

'Thank God, thank God.'

He spread his arms wide, raising his stick, as if to embrace the heavens. The sun, in its clear blue sky, shone benignly. But Petra noticed that Tai Singh was not smiling in reply: his face was deeply solemn.

She looked back. A tangle of ropes and a lot of argument seemed at last to have resulted in a co-ordinated effort. Tom had been made into a long parcel in a sleeping bag, and tied about with a cat's cradle of rope loops. The Rat had put in a snow anchor above the dip where Tom lay, and a system of pulleys had been constructed. The Rat was having to give a lot of instructions.

Petra turned to Tai Singh. 'Where are the other two? My friends. What happened to them?'

'They are tired. Oh, very tired. Doctor gave them whisky.'

'But they'd come off the mountain?'

'Yesterday they came. Yesterday in the night.'

'But how?' Petra did not finish her sentence because there was a yell from above.

'Lower away! 'Ware below!'

All the men, who had got into a huddle to smoke cigarettes, looked up at the avalanche cone.

'Pet, make them stand back.'

She did what she could, but everyone had their own advice to give. There was much argument and waving of arms.

Inch by inch, the long blue bundle slid down the steep snow. Diane, on an abseil rope, had the job of preventing Tom from bumping too hard as he slid. She had one hand for her belay plate and one hand for the guide rope around Tom. Everyone seemed to think that they would have done better than she, including the Rat and Ieuan, who were operating the pulley system. Diane kept her cool remarkably well. Petra was fairly sure that her friend had never done anything of the sort before.

The procedure took quite a long time, but by now Petra had ceased to reckon time. She had surrendered responsibility to this eager band of rescuers.

At last Tom came to a halt on the shallower ground. He was still unconscious, an unwieldy piece of luggage. Rope loops sprouted all along the parcel. A nose and a pair of closed eyes were visible within the hood of the sleeping bag.

Diane, very much in charge, arranged for eight of the men to carry the burden for a short way down the glacier. Each of the rope loops could be slung over one man's shoulder. It was a makeshift stretcher, and very difficult to carry.

'Keep his head from wobbling! Tai Singh, can someone hold his head?'

There were more instructions. After one or two pauses for rest, the parcel was set to rest on a nearly level area.

'Has someone got the poles? Those sticks.' Diane made an illustrative gesture.

Tai Singh was shaking his head. 'We were leaving them a short way back. Very heavy.'

'Could you ask, please? Could you ask some men to go back for them?'

'They will go.'

Tai Singh was the only one who had remained calm. Except for Petra. She looked on as if she were watching a show, as if this whole business did not affect her at all.

The Rat and Ieuan came on down, carrying the spare rope. By the time everything had been sorted out, the hillmen were back with the carrying poles. These were the trunks of young conifers, stripped of their branches.

The stretcher was completed with a length of groundsheet, suitably sewn.

'I was stitching all night,' remarked Diane. She sat down next to Petra while the men told each other what to do.

'What?'

'The second base camp tent. The old one. We snipped it up to make a stretcher.'

'It's all very well planned.'

'We thought it all out during the storm. What we'd do if there was an emergency.' Diane stabbed her ice-axe in the snow and leant on the head. 'We didn't know what to think when the weather broke. We thought you might have blown away.'

'We nearly did. I'm sorry.'

'Luckily Tim seems to be able to imagine the impossible. Who'd have thought you'd go on for the summit after that storm?'

'Rowley told you?'

'What an epic! I hope Tom'll be all right.'

'I must see how he is.' Petra tried to stand up, but felt dizzy and had to sit down again. Diane, intensely concerned, made her put her head between her knees. 'Are you better now? Will you be able to walk down?'

The porters had hoisted the stretcher shoulder high. It took eight men to carry the burden. Another eight would be needed for relays.

'I think so,' Petra replied. 'I just realised I haven't eaten or drunk since yesterday. Have you got any food?'

The Rat's contingency plans had included making a new campsite at the junction of the main glacier and the South Munshu. A ridge of side-moraine ran down from the South Munshu and out across the surface of the convergent glacier. It provided a route to get up from the valley to the cwm of the South Munshu without venturing across any glacial crevasses. Its improbable existence was referred to in one throwaway line in the book: 'Hayter and Amory took the clinker ridge up to S. Munshu. Four hours from river.'

However, the campsite was a new discovery. A patch of level ground was enclosed by the side-moraines of the two glaciers, beneath the steep south-west ridge. A tiny blue pool, fed by a spring, lay at the base of this depression. There were lichens and alpine flowers growing among the rocks, and big pale-green cushions of moss.

Petra was led to the place like a blind person. She could not work out where to put her feet, so one or other of her friends had to be constantly at her side.

Tents had already been pitched. Petra was bodily levered inside one of them. Two warm sleeping bundles were already present, which Petra vaguely identified as belonging to Daz and Rowley. She burrowed into the middle of the heap and went to sleep too.

When she awoke, from a sleep disturbed by an unnatural timetable of sleeping and waking which had blurred the difference between night and day, she found that darkness had fallen. She lay there in the dark, tryng to guess where she was, because her memories did not seem to lead to a place like this.

She was alone in the tent. The groundsheet was bumpy from the rocks beneath. The entrance was zipped tight against the outside air.

Then, like the sudden switching on of a light, she remembered every horrible detail of the retreat. She could see Tom.

She sat up, called out his name, but nobody answered. Out of the darkness came a murmuring of voices. Listening, she could pick out the fluent, song-like speech of Tai Singh and his friends. Nearer, deeper, and more intermittently she could hear her own friends in discussion.

Diane's voice carried more clearly than the others. 'What do you mean?'

'Just that.' Ieuan, carefully spoken, reverberant in the darkness. 'I can't know if we've done the right thing.'

'You mean he may still die?'

'I'd say it was likely. Several ribs are broken. He'll get pneumonia if nothing else. And he's shown no sign of wakening.'

'Don't tell Petra.'

'It's not her fault. You could call it *folie à deux*, I suppose.'

Rowley, rather high-pitched but rasping: 'What the hell's that?'

'Oh, sit down.' This was the Rat. 'Nothing is anybody's fault. If I'd been up there when the weather cleared, I'd have gone for the top – no question.'

Ieuan again: 'Actually, I think everyone has done extraordinarily well. It wasn't just a matter of luck that we got off the mountain in one piece. Everyone went on for twice as long as was humanly possible, and then some more.'

'Good of you,' said Rowley.

Daz, in a lazy, remarkably relaxed drawl: 'I'm surprised too. Amazing what you can do when you pull out the big one. But who magicked Tai Singh here? I'm still not clear about that.'

'The Rat left a message.' Diane again. 'Didn't you, Tim?'

'Well.' The Rat paused. In the silence the bubbling of conversation from the porters' encampment could be heard.

'It's bloody odd. I left word that seven men should come up on 3 September to carry our kit back down. There must have been a misunderstanding. And I can't work out why Tai Singh came, unless it was just for the jaunt.'

'What's today?' Diane counted audibly on her fingers. 'Thirty-first of August. Four, no, three days early.'

'God, I hope the message the lad took will get through without scrambling. What d'you reckon, Ieuan? Do you believe the helicopter will come?'

There was another pause for reflection. Petra heard a stick explode in the camp fire.

Ieuan, when he spoke, sounded very tired indeed. 'I believe it. There's a walkie-talkie at the army post at Munshu. If Tai Singh's lad gets there without breaking a leg in the dark, we should see the chopper sometime tomorrow. I don't think there'll be a misunderstanding.'

'Oh yeah?' Rowley sounded almost hysterical, as if his recent experience had left a raw, sensitive place. He sounded mortally afraid that something else was going to go wrong.

'It'll be all right. OK, if the chopper doesn't come tomorrow we'll have to send one of us down. We'll lose the day, but none of us was fit for the journey tonight. Whatever happens, we can't carry Tom out by hand.'

They were all quiet for a moment. Petra, emerging into full wakefulness, shuffled to the entrance of the tent and undid the zip. She could see the sky, black, cold and full of stars.

Someone got up from the campfire and scrunched towards her on the stony ground.

'How is he?'

'Fine.' Ieuan squatted down by the tent. 'How are you? Do you want to see him?'

'What time is it?'

'Five. Nearly dawn.'

She crept on leaden limbs out of her sleeping bag. Even twelve hours' sleep had not restored her energy. Her boots were difficult to put on. But Ieuan did not try to make her stay in bed.

Tom's tent was beyond the campfire, on the most level area of ground. Ieuan opened the tent door and ducked his head inside, flashing a torch.

'Isn't anyone sitting with him?'

'I look in every so often,' replied the doctor. 'If I sat by him I'd just be fretting, and do the wrong thing.'

Tom's breathing sounded far more gentle and controlled than anything they had been used to hearing in the high-altitude camps. There was none of the uneven, stop-start breathing, or the horrible rasping snores which reflected poor adaptation to the thin air. It sounded settled and safe.

Petra crept into the tent after Ieuan and saw the beam of the torch playing on Tom's face. He was asleep. Not even his eyelids were flickering.

'You'll tell me the truth, won't you?'

'He's sick. He needs to get out of here. Proper doctoring.' Ieuan had taken off his glove and was feeling for a pulse at the side of Tom's neck. 'Still, heart seems to be holding out.'

Petra clutched at his hand. 'You must save him. You have to.'

'I'll do my best. But it doesn't help getting emotionally involved. I'm sorry, Petra.'

'Ieuan, you know it matters.'

The torch had been switched off. They were only shadows in the half-darkness.

'I know, Pet.' Ieuan's was a good voice for tenderness. He too had been fond of Tom. He understood that there was more to most things than met the eye. That was some comfort. But Ieuan, whatever his virtues, was not Tom.

'You do know, don't you?'

'That Tom would have found a reason to go with you, wherever your spirit led? Oh yes. But that was his secret. I didn't suppose you'd be of the same mind.'

'It's not just romance.'

'No. It wouldn't be. Not with you two. But everyone except you is going to find it odd.'

'You as well?'

'Extremely odd.'

'I can't explain.'

Ieuan's only reply was a quick squeeze of the hand; then he was out of the tent, striding across the loose stones of the campsite towards the fire.

'Pile on that wood! I said there'd be a beacon from dawn onwards.'

There was more clumping of feet, and then the fierce crackling of new flames. There was another sort of fizzling and crackling, and a signal rocket went up into the sky with a whoosh of pink sparks. It sped up in a clear arc overhead, before disintegrating in a small explosion and more pink sparks.

Petra was still sitting beside Tom, holding his hand, when she saw a lightening in the sky behind Tengdatta, and the reflected light of dawn on the truncated peak of Munshu. Bright daylight followed, and still Petra sat there, watching.

Out of the valley, clattering and whirling in a cluster of navigation lights, came the helicopter.

Another signal flare went up. There was general cheering. Petra got up and came to join the party. People were leaping about hugging each other, as if the successful ascent of Himalchand had not been touched by tragedy.

'That youth must have run the whole way,' remarked Daz.

The Rat was trying to watch the helicopter through his binoculars. 'It'll be with us in ten minutes.'

The sunshine was now achingly bright. The Rat directed a spare tent, bright orange in colour, to be spread out on the ground near the pool. The big fire was damped down to make it smoke. Everyone moved away to the edges of the site.

At the end of a very short ten minutes, the helicopter was overhead. It was quite a small one, painted in camouflage colours, with Indian Air Force insignia. But the noise it made was tremendous. The rattling and clattering echoed off every facet of the mountainside and prevented any human speech from being heard.

The pilot was leaning out of the door, jabbing his finger downwards, as if to indicate that he was about to land. They all ducked their heads, as the wind from the rotor blades threatened to flatten them. Dust whirled upwards.

As the motor slowed and stopped, other sounds came back: the surge of the river in the distance, and the sound of Tai Singh and his men praying aloud.

Out of the helicopter climbed a large man with a handlebar moustache, clad in full tropical uniform. He had very large feet. A lady in a white trouser suit hopped out after him. They came across the stony ground bent double, instinctively ducking to avoid the now stationary rotor blades.

'Flight-Lieutenant Davinder Singh.' The large man saluted: a very correct military salute. 'Who is your leader?'

The Rat stepped forward. 'Tim Radinsky.' He offered a laconic handshake.

The pilot returned it vigorously. 'How can I be of assistance? I have with me Dr Mehta of the University Hospital.'

'Good-o,' replied the Rat.

'I was told there had been an accident to a lady mountaineer,' said Dr Mehta.

'Oh, Pet's all right. It's the old guy, Tom Ormerod. He's still out cold.' The Rat turned to Ieuan. 'You explain.'

The Welshman, coming solemnly forward, offered Dr Mehta his hand. 'I'm Dr Price, madam. I have the casualty here.'

They walked off together to Tom's tent. Dr Mehta could be heard asking, 'From which medical school do you come, Dr Price?' She was about a foot shorter than Ieuan, but suddenly very much in charge.

The rest of them sat down in a ring on the stony ground, Tai Singh and his men as well as the mountaineers. The pilot asked a number of official questions regarding identities, times and dates. When he talked to Tai Singh he used Hindi, but there was a good deal of cross purposes, requiring expressive gestures on the part of the hillman, because Tai Singh's own language was a substantially distinct dialect.

Finally Davinder Singh folded his arms and expressed his

opinion. 'You have been reckless but very lucky. The police will require a full report. You must go to the police HQ in Udinath when you return. You will receive a bill in due course.'

There was a short pause, as if no one knew quite what to say.

Petra found her voice. 'Thank you for coming, Mr Singh.'

Her friends echoed in chorus, though Daz and Rowley were still unusually subdued.

'That is my pleasure,' replied Mr Singh. He gave Petra a broad smile, full of very white teeth. 'It is my pleasure to fly among these mountains.'

She realised only then that he was not very much older than she was; the fact had been heavily disguised by the official manner.

'Now, I can take two back with me. That will be the serious casualty and also yourself, ma'am?'

The Rat interrupted. 'Better get yours and Tom's papers together, Pet.'

'No.' Petra found herself rejecting the offer. 'Send Ieuan in the chopper, he'll be more use.'

'You'll walk out?'

'I'm fit. Just bruises.'

She had said goodbye to Tom once already. She did not want to watch the slow lingering. 'Where are you going back to, Mr Singh?'

'Refuelling may be necessary at Bhaipur air base, but we will proceed to Delhi.'

'The University Hospital?'

'Three hours' flying from here.'

CHAPTER 11

The rest of them took a day and a half to reach Munshu, carrying with them as much gear as could reasonably be salvaged, and camping for the night beside the river. No one wanted to remain beneath Himalchand for a moment longer than necessary.

Petra, still very tired, and aching all over from the battering she had taken in the avalanche, kept going on some last shred of determination. She did not want to be left behind. She slept exhaustedly at the night camp, and barely felt rested in the morning. She was carrying nothing; nevertheless she crept along so slowly that it was almost sunset when at last they came over the pass and began the rapid descent down to Munshu.

Ahead in the woods, the porters were calling to one another in glee, running downhill despite their loads.

On the last shoulder of high ground, Petra looked backward to the mountain for the last time. She found that she was beginning to forget why she had wanted to go there. Himalchand, in the softening light of the evening, seemed as beautiful and inaccessible as ever, but the sight no longer had the power to inspire. The mountain was inanimate, cold, passionless.

Round the bend in the path, Petra came upon a ramshackle construction: a cross between a hut and a tent, like something which had escaped from a refugee camp. Rowley and Daz, also making slow progress, had stopped by the hut and were talking to its occupant, who was sitting outside.

'Hi.' Petra stopped and sat down too.

'It's Mr Karia,' said Rowley.

Petra vaguely remembered the round, talkative man who had helped them during the bus journey to Munshu. She would not have recognised him again, however. He had discarded his dapper urban clothes for a voluminous orange robe, and his beard had grown substantially. Smears of white ash coloured his forehead and cheeks. He looked like one of those devotees whom Petra had seen walking down streets in London, ringing little bells and chanting 'Hare Krishna'.

He made the traditional salute, hands together as if praying. '*Namaste.*' That, however, was the end of formality. The disguise was no more than skin deep. Mr Karia wanted to know everything that had happened.

'How tremendous that you have conquered the summit. I am most envious. I only have watched every day through field glasses. Except on days of bad weather. Then I have been occupied in preserving my hermitage from the leaking of rain.'

'You stayed here through that storm?' asked Daz, with something like surprise.

'Most certainly. Also on the second day I had many companions in my humble abode and they have eaten nearly all my provisions. But these hillmen are so convivial, one does not grudge hospitality. Sri Kotai Singh had some excellent arrack as a remedy against the cold.'

'Seventeen men in here?' asked Rowley.

'It was a squash.'

Daz looked in through the doorway. 'Yeah. Like sardines.'

'Will you take tea?' enquired the hermit.

They did not refuse. All haste was over. Diane and the Rat were already running ahead down the path, and could be relied upon to do any organising.

The remaining trio from the summit party sat in the dark, odorous interior of the hermitage and drank sweet, spiced tea. They gave their account of the ascent and the retreat from the mountain, an opportunity to hear each other's version of the tale, and to put their ideas in order before they had to explain it to anyone official.

Mr Karia poured the tea and made admiring interjections.

'And what are your plans now, my young friends?'

'Dunno.' Rowley looked into his tea. 'The Rat wants to start a trekking company.'

'Yeah. Diane's going to be business manager,' said Daz. 'They've both got lots of ideas.'

'They weren't there.'

Rowley did not need to say more. The shared experience was enough to distance them from their other friends; that much did not need explanation.

But Daz asked the questions which the Rat and Diane had been in too much of a hurry to ask when they passed by.

'Why did Kotai Singh and his men come? Why did they come so early? Did they tell you, Mr Karia?'

'Ah. Now that is fantastical. These simple pahari men are closer to God than we are. They have very strong beliefs. You must not think them ignorant.'

'I don't,' replied the Manchester man bluntly.

The hermit had a string of beads hanging from his belt. He clicked them between his fingers, as if counting them. Then he reached up and rang a small bell which was hanging from one of the roof beams. '*Hare Ram.*' Then he folded his arms.

'Let me tell you. Sri Kotai Singh was the recipient of a vision. He has for many years devoted himself to the goddess, having been a witness to her assumption. He was the last living man to see the lady alive. He has made *puja* on the appointed days, and has maintained a private shrine. This is not uncommon. All of us have our favourite gods.

'On the night upon which the great storm began, he awoke to the sound of a voice. He could hear the voice of the goddess in the storm. He saw her also, among the branches of his apricot tree. She was instructing him to take seventeen men, including his favourite son, and before the end of the third day to bring them to Himalchand. He knew this vision to be a portent of disaster. And thus he was able to avert disaster and save the life of his friend. This he believes.'

Mr Karia rang his bell again, several times. Outside the door of the hermitage, the daylight was quickly fading.

Rowley got to his feet, crouching to avoid hitting his head on the roof. 'We've got to go. Thanks for the tea, Mr Karia.'

He backed out of the hut, picked up his pack and was away down the path.

'That is a boy with too much imagination.' The hermit gave his bell another shake.

'Come on, Pet.' Daz stood up.

They said their goodbyes and received a complicated blessing from the amateur hermit. They had to walk slowly to avoid tripping up in the gathering darkness.

'He was talking about Hannah,' Petra said at last.

'Aye. Better get on, lass, if we're to reach the village.'

Nearly two hours later, the pair of them entered Munshu, whence they could continue their journey by bus, train and aeroplane. The village was bright with torches. A great crowd of people were holding flaming branches of resinous wood, from which an aromatic scent arose like incense. There was a band, made up of drums and cymbals and a monotonous flute. Beneath the general hubbub, someone was intoning a chant.

The place was crowded. The populations of several villages must have been there, children included. Petra recognised a small girl who had brought them drinks the night they stayed at Kala.

'Tai Singh's village have all come.' Petra stopped at the edge of the blaze.

'You reckon?' Daz too had paused and was looking about him. 'I wonder if there's owt to drink?'

The other three mountaineers could be seen at the centre of the teeming crowd. The male climbers stood a head taller than most of the people and Diane's auburn hair was bright in the torchlight. All three of them were wearing garlands of white flowers about their necks.

Daz stepped forward. 'This is weird.' He was spotted by a

troop of boys, who rushed forward with another garland. One tiny boy was sitting on his friend's shoulders, balancing a small brass pot in one hand. Daz was made to bow down, and some red paint was applied to his face by the small boy. The tooting of the flute became frantic.

Petra saw that this was a welcome. Here were the people who had helped her to safety, but who took pleasure in that act of rescue. She had none of the sense of the alien that had afflicted her at that long-ago *tamasha* at Kala. These were her fellows, the rest of humankind from whom she had been separated for so long. She hurried forward to the bright lights and warmth.

She stopped. All the people had fallen back before her. The lights receded even as she advanced. She remembered that Hannah, for whom she had sought in vain, had remained with these people: a vision in an apricot tree; an incarnation of Parvati, the daughter of the mountains. She stood in confusion, with the darkness behind her, until the crowd parted to let her pass.

Daz, Rowley, Diane and the Rat were standing in the middle of a poor muddy village street, festooned with limp garlands.

Tai Singh, small and old and shabby, was holding up a garland for Petra. The flowers smelt of soap. She bent her head. As she felt the weight of the flowers on her neck, someone gave a great shout, and the music started again.

'My sister!' declared Tai Singh. For a worried moment Petra thought he was going to hug her, but that was not part of the ceremony. He dabbed the same red paint on her face, and then made his bow, hands held palm to palm. 'We welcome you back.'

Petra found herself being nudged by Diane. 'Your speech, Pet. Then we can sit down.'

Tai Singh held up his hand, and the music gradually subsided. She had no idea of what she was going to say, until she spoke.

'Thank you, friends. Without you we would still be trapped

there in the snow. We're glad to be home. We're glad to leave the mountain behind. But we will be sorry to leave you.'

To Petra it sounded like an address to an assembly of Rotarian wives. There were simply no suitable words to be spoken at such a time. She and her friends had hardly talked at all, all the way back from the mountain.

But the people, who could understand the feeling if not the words, responded with applause. Then the party began again.

The five climbers sat down in a row on a log, where they were supplied with drink. Rowley emptied his mug and asked for more. Daz and the Rat echoed him.

'Here we are again,' remarked Diane cheerfully. 'A round of pints in the pub.'

'People don't change.' Petra was holding on to her tin mug with both hands.

Diane glanced at her sharply. 'You believe that – you of all people?'

Petra stared down into her cup. 'This isn't real. It'll be different in England.'

She waited. Diane said nothing. The dancers were getting into full, wild swing, and the torches flared still higher. Someone was waving a sword, whirling it about his head with flashes of silver light.

Petra took a wry sip of the grey fluid in her cup. 'It'd be easier if I could forget.'

'Why? Why, after all this?' Diane's arm made a great encompassing gesture, to include the people, and their gods, and the great mountains which lay hidden beyond the darkness.

'It's Tom. I can't think of anything else. I wish he would come back. I wish I could forget him dying.'

'But he's alive, dear heart.' Diane put her arm around Petra's shoulders and hugged her close. 'We saved him. We, and all these people, and the wonderful helicopter.'

Petra sniffed. 'I'll never be able to forget it. He smiled at me, and the earth fell away. We'd been there on the summit together, and then it was all gone. It'll never come back.'

Tears came – not easily, because Petra had never had much use for tears. Diane held on to her and did not say anything more. Somewhere, a long way away in the Plains of India, Tom Ormerod's fate would be decided by others.

Tom's friends would not know the answer for a few days yet. If the news was bad, they might receive it at Udinath, at the police post. Or else they might have to wait until they could reach the University Hospital in Delhi. Or they might try to find out something on the telephone, if they could find one that was reliable.

Petra found that she did not want to know. Not yet. She wanted to live in hope, even though it was a painful, fearful hope. Knowledge would be another kind of death.

It had happened so often before: the triumphs and disasters, the furious endeavour that makes up a climber's life. Tom used to tell stories; he had known that the tale, however full of noise and action, must end in silence.

Petra was still travelling. Once beyond Udinath she would pass by Kala, without stopping at the apricot tree. She would follow that winding road through the crumbling spurs of the greater mountains. In a day or two's time she would come to the Plains themselves, and would be able to look back at the solid wall of the Himalaya, but she would not be able to make out the peak of Himalchand among the thousands of others.